BROKEN ARROW

END DAYS BOOK 2

E.E. ISHERWOOD
CRAIG MARTELLE

CONNECT WITH CRAIG MARTELLE

Website & Newsletter:
www.craigmartelle.com

Bookbub:
www.bookbub.com/authors/craig-martelle

Facebook:
www.facebook.com/AuthorCraigMartelle/

CONNECT WITH E.E. ISHERWOOD

Website & Newsletter:
www.sincethesirens.com

Facebook:
www.facebook.com/SinceTheSirens/

Cover Illustration by Heather Hamilton-Senter
Editing services provided by Lynne Stiegler
Formatting by James Osiris Baldwin – jamesosiris.com

We couldn't do what we do without the support of great people around us.
We thank our spouses and our families for giving us time alone to think,
write, and review. We thank our editor (Lynne), cover artist (Heather), and
insider team of beta readers (Micky Cocker, Kelly O'Donnell, Dr. James
Caplan, and John Ashmore). It's not who we are as authors, but who we are
surrounded by that makes this all happen. Enjoy the story.

 Created with Vellum

ONE

Pole Line Motel, Mono Lake, CA

Buck woke to big brown eyes and a lolling tongue. The handsome young Golden Retriever gently pawed at him, anxious for his human to open his eyes.

"You're up early," he said through a yawn. "Let me guess; you need to go outside?"

Big Mac's ears perked up.

"I know you too well," Buck added. "Okay, let me get dressed, and we'll go mess up Fred's lawn." He snickered at the immature notion of sticking it to the motel proprietor, but it was how he felt after the previous day's hassle for supposedly passing counterfeit money.

The dog hopped off the bed and scratched at the door as if Buck was going to forget.

He grabbed his phone and peeked through the drapes. Last night he had woken up several times when loud vehicles pulled into the motel. He wondered who the new neighbors were.

"Wow, the place is popular." The motel lot was almost full. "I can't imagine Fred's dumpy motel does a lot of business, but maybe there's more to do around here than I can see." Mono Lake was beautiful in the midst of the stark desert surrounding it, but there wasn't much in the way of towns, parks, or anything remotely recreational. The motel, gas station, and a few wind-blown mobile homes were the only civilization for as far as he could see.

Buck attached his brand-new black leash to Mac's collar. He trusted him not to run away under normal circumstances, as a hundred stops over the past two weeks attested, but any number of dogs could be lurking in other rooms, and he didn't trust those owners.

"Let's go, buddy. We'll get you to the side yard."

The L-shaped motel had a back lot big enough for him to park his tractor-trailer. He often walked around his truck and inspected it while Mac did his thing, so that was where he went first.

Once at the back of the motel and clear of other guests, he took off the leash. "Go make!" Buck said excitedly.

Mac found a scrubby little bush in the dry terrain and got right to it.

"Good pup!"

He stood at the back of his trailer and admired the early morning scenery. The air was fresh and cool, which was a godsend after a night in the stuffy motel room. Mono Lake reflected the brightness of the sun as it peeked over the distant hills of Nevada—a new day to appreciate waking up on the right side of the dirt.

"Let's see how Garth is doing, shall we?"

He found his son in the frequently-dialed numbers, but the phone didn't make any sound to indicate it had gone through. Cell service had been unreliable ever since the blue burst of light in the sky yesterday, so he had expected the failure. After hitting redial a number of times, he decided to try texting.

'Morning. You OK?' It was nine o'clock on the East Coast. He was sure his boy was awake, and if he wasn't, then he was willing to wake him.

He looked up to check on Mac while waiting for the reply. The dog sniffed some more of the green scraps of the arid land, intent on finding previous canine calling cards. The flat, dry terrain was perfect for throwing the tennis ball for exercise, but it was in the cab. He was going to go get it, but Garth's reply stopped him.

'Hey, dad. Yes. Good. Waking up. Going to your locker next.'

Buck's locker was his gun safe. During their previous phone call, he'd given Garth instructions to protect himself. Part of him hated to dump all that on his son; he was only fifteen, but no one was too young to get attacked if the civilized world collapsed. After the near-riot he had seen yesterday in Walmart, he was willing to bet things were going to keep getting worse. Modern society wasn't built to endure simultaneous problems, and the news yesterday had listed more than a few. All of them had been bad.

He typed back, 'Sounds good. Be careful.'

I'm sure he wouldn't if I didn't say it.

At least he couldn't be accused of being a helicopter parent. His son was twenty-seven hundred miles away.

It was hard to sound nonchalant in a text, but he did his best. 'So, are you going out with Sam today?'

Buck had lost sleep thinking about Garth going into the city with his friend Sam. It helped to know the boys had made it home safely from the airport yesterday, but there was no need to tempt fate and go back out. He figured Sam's parents would be fine if they took a cab home by themselves. They didn't require their son to meet them at the gate.

But Buck tried not to press the issue too hard, for fear Garth would do it just to piss him off. Their last meeting before he had gone on the road wasn't going to win him any parent-of-the-year t-shirts, although a lot of that had been smoothed over last night when they chatted. However, it was always best to play it safe when dealing with a moody teenager.

'I'm staying home, but I haven't told him. Need to get organized. Be ready for trouble.'

"*Yes!*" Buck said to himself. His son was doing the right thing.

Engine noises in the main parking lot of the motel caught Buck's attention, so he walked to the front of his black Peterbilt sleeper cab. A new-ish yellow Volkswagen Beetle had been parked right in front of his bumper, like the owner wanted to be first off the lot. He continued alongside the German car to get a look at the action in front of the place.

He texted. 'Got to go son. All good. Be home soon. Bye.'

'Bye Dad. Can't wait.'

Buck closed his phone and shoved it in his pocket.

"Come on, pup. We're going back to the room." It seemed prudent to brush his teeth and be on his way.

When he walked to the front of the motel, several cars sat at the gas station, but they were just the beginning of the procession. The T junction at the base of the road from Yosemite was already clogged with cars, but many more lined up behind them as if someone had led a parade over the pass.

Buck reached down and re-attached Mac's leash.

"We've got to get out of here.

. . .

Staten Island, NY

'Bye dad. Can't wait.' Garth's final message was heart-felt. He turned off his phone and laid in bed for a minute to think about what to do next. After telling Dad he wasn't going with Sam, he had to figure out how he was going to break the news to his best bud.

Garth had spent the night at Sam's house, as he normally did when his dad was on the road, although now he was anxious to get home. When he was ready, he rolled out of bed and got dressed in a hurry, but when he made it downstairs to the kitchen, he found Sam sitting in front of a big pile of pancakes like it was just any other day.'

Sam smiled mischievously when he saw him. "Eat up. You can microwave a ton more if you want some."

"Can I have some of yours? You've got at least ten there."

"No way, dude. I made them for me. Get your own." Sam pointed to the mudroom, which contained the giant freezer. The appliance was a treasure trove of frozen junk food and bad breakfasts, including frozen waffles and pancakes, as well as several gallons of ice cream.

"Asshole," Garth said without malice.

"Good morning to you, too," Sam replied.

Garth got out the pancakes and had just put them in the microwave when someone banged on the front door. Sam dropped his fork on the table. They looked at each other through several seconds of startled silence, but then the person hammered on the door a few more times.

"Open up!" the man shouted from outside.

Sam sprang from the table to a pile of junk on a countertop next to the refrigerator. He shoved aside some papers and pulled out a tablet.

"We have a doorbell camera," Sam said as it turned on.

"Really? You never told me about it."

Sam laughed quietly. "Yeah, I like to watch you pick your nose before I open the door for you."

"Bullshit!" Garth hissed. "I don't pick my nose."

"Sure, you don't," Sam said distractedly. He pointed at the screen. The image was a little distorted—it was almost like looking through a fish-eye lens—but the man was easily identified. He was middle-aged and wore a loose-fitting business suit with his top button undone and no tie.

"What do you think he wants?" Garth asked.

"No idea," Sam replied. "But I think I better answer."

Garth wanted to argue, but the guy's banging hadn't let up, and it now bordered on violent.

They both ran to the front door and looked out the small glass window centered on the heavy wooden entry. The man stopped knocking the second he saw them.

"I need a ride!" the guy shouted.

"What the fuck?" Sam replied to Garth. "A ride?"

The man's patience lasted about five seconds, then he leaned in and cupped his hands over the window so he could see the boys. "Come on, get the cabbie! I need a ride."

"Oh, shit," Garth replied quietly. "You have a cab parked in your backyard."

Sam's garage sat behind the house, and Garth had parked the cab on the driveway leading up to the outbuilding. It never occurred to him to put it inside.

Sam's eyes were wide with indecision.

Garth faced the door. "The cab is out of service. Our dad is a driver, but he got sick last night. Puking. Diarrhea. All of it."

The man jumped away from the door. "He's sick? Does he have Ebola? Fuck me!" He backed up, then tumbled down the front steps of the porch. The man got back to his feet and ran out to the street like he was being chased.

"Release the hounds," Sam said happily. "Welp, back to pancakes."

The man's question had left Garth confused. "Why would he think someone had Ebola? We don't look sick, do we?"

"Me? No. I have that suave Italian skin."

"Dude, your family is from Poland." Garth chuckled.

Sam shuffled into his seat and pointed at Garth. "Don't ruin it. You look like an Icelander."

Sam was right, to a degree. Neither of them spent much time out in the sunshine, despite Sam's mom's best efforts at keeping them out of the house on nice summer days. Thus, they both looked like they spent all their time playing video games in someone's basement.

"Yeah, whatever," Garth replied. Then, forgetting all his carefully laid plans to ease into the topic, he added: "I've got to get over to my house."

Sam looked up, his mouth stuffed with pancakes. "Are you coming back?"

Garth shook his head.

"You aren't going with me?" Sam asked. "The airlines aren't flying, but they put them on a bus overnight. They'll be at Grand Central Station in a couple of hours."

It was the moment he'd been dreading. He really wanted to go with his buddy, but his dad had warned him in a not-so-subtle way things were getting more dangerous outside. Dad brought up the fight in Walmart and end-of-the-world predictions, but it was Garth's own encounters with strange events yesterday that made him believe Dad knew what he was talking about.

"I'm going to stay here and load up on guns and ammo, so I can be ready for anything. It's what my dad recommended we *both* do."

"Dude, I don't have any guns. My parents don't believe in them. You know that."

Garth nodded. "You can come over to my house. My dad said I could share a gun with you, although he did say to give you the one with training wheels." He smiled.

Sam laughed. "I'd probably need them, at least until the sick people come over. I'm a great shot against the undead. I'm an expert at *World of Zombies*, as you know better than anyone."

He was hopeful his friend was going to see it his way, but then Sam dug back into the pancakes. "I'll get my parents without you, dude, then I'll be over later to play with your guns."

"You shouldn't go out," Garth replied seriously.

"Bah. I'll be fine. Yesterday was a fluke. I'll take the ferry and be back with the parental units in two hours."

It felt unnatural to not go with Sam, but he had a point. It wouldn't take long to use the ferry and subway to get to the airport, and it wouldn't be nearly as complicated as the day before if he only went there and back. Maybe not going with Sam would keep him focused on his parents rather than cheap cologne gags.

"I'm going over to my house. I'll be there when you get back." Garth choked down his pancakes, gave Sam the finger, and dashed out the front door, stopping to pick his nose in front of the door's camera. He smiled and waved one last time before jogging away from Sam's house. Garth didn't have far to go, but the unease from yesterday's trials and the man banging on the door wanting a cab made him leery.

He didn't care. He needed to get home and break out the guns and ammunition.

Better to not need them and have them than need them and not have them.

TWO

Search for Nuclear, Astrophysical, and Krono-metric Extremes (SNAKE). Red Mesa, Colorado

"Thank you for seeing me, General Smith." Faith stood outside her own office, which had been taken from her.

"Come in," the general replied.

After her press conference the previous evening, the military sent the reporters away with lightning speed but kept her people locked inside SNAKE "for their own protection." She'd spent an uncomfortable night in the auditorium with everyone else, but this morning she was hot to get some answers.

Faith went in firing both barrels. "There are tanks in my parking lot, general. Tanks!"

"Dr. Sinclair, thank you for coming. Please sit down. Relax."

Her office was the largest and carried the most authority, so it had naturally been the one he commandeered. She stood in front of her own messy desk. "I can't sit down, not while this injustice continues."

The general leaned back in the swivel chair as if to decide if she was serious, then got up, walked around her, and shut the door.

"Please, I need to talk to you. Things on the outside have gotten worse overnight, and I need to know how the hell your supercollider did all of it."

The fact that she thought he could be right took all the wind out of her sails. She sighed, hung her head, and sat in the plastic seat in front of her own desk as if the Inquisition had started and she was the only one on trial.

General Smith didn't go to the desk again, but instead grabbed the other plastic chair and sat close to her.

He chuckled then spoke quietly. "Those aren't tanks, Dr. Sinclair. They are unarmed Humvees. It's how we drove here."

"Fine—it's all semantics. It doesn't change the fact that you locked my people inside this vault, took away our phones, and shut off all other forms of communication with the outside. Our families are going to wonder..."

"I have a whole nation to protect, but as of this moment, I have no idea how to do that. Changes are happening in military equipment that leaves us vulnerable to attack. You don't have sufficient clearance for me to explain about those issues, but turn on any news channel, and you'll get a pretty big clue what's wrong with the rest of the world."

"There's a time distortion," she said in a businesslike voice. She had slept for about fifteen minutes overnight and used the rest of the time to have her team work through the math and science of what they saw on cable news. Skylab had returned from 1979. The lost Malaysian Airlines flight 370 had arrived safely from 2014. Flight 586 had crashed in New York City; a ticket found in the debris said the flight had taken off two weeks ago. The only answer that made any sense was that they'd somehow broken time.

We do study chronometric extremes.

"I'll take your word for it. I'm just a four-star general." He laughed hesitantly, as if he were waiting to see if she'd laugh with him. When she kept her sour look, he went on. "But overnight I brought in more scientists on military transports. More will be here later today."

"Someone to check my work?" she snapped.

"It was a risk to fly them in," he added like it was important, "but they all made it."

"I'm glad no one was hurt," she allowed. "I'm sorry, sir. I don't mean to sound ungrateful, but we could work a lot faster without your interference."

"There are very few scientists in the world who can truly check your work. I tried to find them. Some of the top names are already here, and others were lost when CERN Switzerland went offline."

An awkward pause settled over them both. She had no idea what had made him shut up, but her silence was for the American science team who died at CERN.

He continued reflectively, "Do you know what keeps me up at night?"

She looked away while rolling her eyes. "Nuclear attacks?"

"Ha! I never stop thinking about those during the day, but I'm not afraid of them. We can detect missiles launching, we can track them flying, and we know where they go. They are horrible, terrible weapons, but very easy to identify. No, my nightmares are made up of things that hit America like a knife in the small of her back. Things that don't show up on radar or seismic equipment. Things that destroy us from the inside."

"That sounds farfetched," she said, drawn into his scenario despite herself. "Nothing can destroy America."

"Farfetched? Last night I received communiques from all over the country that suggest to me the collapse has already begun. A giant storm left a path of destruction in the Central Valley of California. Looting has been extreme, as have evacuations. The governor declared an emergency from his car because Sacramento was flattened. That's a nightmare."

He looked into her eyes.

"Also last night, I heard about a prison in Idaho. The guards walked off the job. They left all the cages open and ran for it. Why would they do that?"

She shook her head because there was no logic to it.

"And this morning, five thousand Cubans showed up in boats in the Florida Keys. They all think it is 1980." He sighed. "Where do you think they'll go?"

He didn't wait for her to answer.

"There are hundreds of these stories all across America. In the last twenty-four hours, the nation has come unglued. Three Mile Island went into meltdown yesterday, and if their containment efforts fail, it threatens God knows how many people on the East Coast. Worse, all the other nuke plants shut down for safety reasons. Whole states are now experiencing rolling blackouts like it's the Third World. Do you know what all this adds up to?"

"Lots of people who need help?"

"Bingo," he said. "And do you know where that help is going to come from?"

"You guys. The government."

"Nice try. I told you—we have our own problems. Every plane in the world is grounded for reasons I can't divulge. No, security now falls on local authorities, and they are already overloaded. My nightmare is going to come true unless you and I and both of our scientific groups can figure out how to fix it. That was why I kept your people locked up last night. I need them here, not out in the streets looting."

"You think it is that bad already? It's only been one day."

"The old saying is that polite civilization has about three days before chaos takes over, but that was from a different era. Our fast-paced world depends on a lot more moving pieces to hold together. Most people don't keep real food in their pantries, nor have they experienced actual hunger in their whole lives. You take away food for half a day and you'll see some fireworks. You take away food, the internet, and their power at the same time for twenty-four hours with no hope of restoration, and you'll have—"

"Chaos." She nodded in agreement.

He nodded back grimly. "We can't keep the role of this facility a secret for long, Dr. Sinclair. It was a calculated risk, but we let the reporters clear out of here so they wouldn't become the story. They'll be back today, I'm sure. Almost certainly, some of the staff warned family on the outside before we confiscated all the phones."

She held his gaze while trying not to think of her text to Dez, explaining SNAKE's role in the weirdness of the world. Her sister was in Australia, so she couldn't possibly be a threat. Faith wasn't even certain the warning message had gone through since there had been no reply before her phone was taken.

He continued, "There are thousands of potential vectors for the plague to get out into the wild."

"Plague?" she asked. "You don't mean that literally?"

"No, of course not." He scooted farther into her

personal space, almost to the point of discomfort. "But truth can spread in dangerous ways. We both have things we're trying to hide."

Not Dez, she thought.

"SNAKE blasted the world with the blue light and is responsible for all the crazy things that have resulted from it. That's what you have to hope doesn't get out. As for me, I've learned from multiple sources that the time dilation is getting worse by the hour. If anyone knew that, they might assume the world was on the brink of ending."

He whispered, "If either of those things became common knowledge, my nightmare would become real. The plague of truth would infect everyone. America would unravel, and SNAKE would be the first body on the burn pile."

Pole Line Motel, Mono Lake, CA

Buck and Mac headed for their room, but he stopped when Fred spotted them. The motel owner stood up against Buck's door as if intending to prevent him from getting his stuff.

I slept for too long.

He had gotten up at six o'clock intending to clear out before Fred could give him any grief about the money, but now he figured he should have made it five.

"Come on," he said to Mac. "Let's go see what he wants."

Cars and trucks swarmed the intersection where the road came down from Yosemite. Vehicles went both north and south, but a few came across the highway to the already-crowded motel parking area.

"Hello, Fred," Buck said as he neared his door.

"I called my brother in Reno, and he confirmed there have been no changes to hundred-dollar bills that would make Ben Franklin look so huge. Plus—"

"Sir, I told you last night, this is a bill fresh from my bank. I don't appreciate the implication." Buck stood in front of the window of the adjacent motel room since he didn't want to get too close to the owner. The guy didn't look like he was capable of physically restraining Buck, but there was no sense giving him a shot at it.

I left the gun in the room.

Buck shook his head, realizing he'd made another clumsy mistake. Even walking the dog was a dangerous adventure.

"But this is from 2019!" Fred shouted.

That caught Buck off guard. The man had complained about the date being twenty-some-odd years off last night, too, but he hadn't picked up on it at the time.

"What year should it say?" Buck asked.

"Anything up to and including 1990."

Buck cracked up. "That's like thirty years ago. There's been plenty of bills since then."

The deadbolt spun on the door next to Buck. He stepped away from it, thinking he was talking too loudly.

Fred looked to the intersection and the numerous cars pulling into his lot. "Don't joke around about this, sir. I can't tell what game you're playing, but if your money doesn't say 1990, you tried to rip me off. That's a crime."

Mac tugged at his leash as if he wanted to go sniff Fred, but Buck held him back.

"All I can tell you is that it isn't 1990. I wasn't old enough to drive back then."

Fred huffed. "If you don't explain your con, I'm going to call the police. I can't stand around all day and watch you, but I did write down your license plate number. If you run, I'll have something to identify you with."

Buck rolled his eyes.

The door next to him opened about six inches. He saw a woman's face in the crack, but nothing below her neck. She handed out a ten-dollar bill. "This is from 1999. It's the oldest one I have."

Fred's eyes grew wide when he saw the date, and he looked at the lady. "You're trying to rip me off too!"

"Sir, I don't know this woman. What are the odds that two random strangers would come to your place with counterfeit bills? And who would counterfeit a ten?"

Fred scrunched his face like it took a lot of energy to think, but he pointed down at Mac before he could answer the question. "That piss puddle is your fault!"

The Retriever pup had watered on the sidewalk near Fred's cowboy boots.

"I should make you hose that off," Fred lashed out. "People are so impolite these days. I'm sure you two are working together about this money. That much is clear."

Buck wanted to laugh in the guy's face, but it wasn't worth the risk to further anger the furious man. He pointed to the influx of cars. "I bet if you go ask any of those people what year their money was printed, they'll say it was after 1990. Take a look at some of those cars. Have you ever seen any like them before? Hell, if they don't back me up, I'll call the cops myself."

He laughed politely to suggest he was being jovial, but he didn't feel that way inside. The cars had come out of the mountains because something had happened. The longer he spent dealing with fake money problems, the more danger he was in.

Fred took a couple of steps back. "Don't either of you go

anywhere. I'm going to check out some of these other people like you said. Should be easy to confirm that you are a liar."

"Agreed," Buck said without hesitation. He'd already planned to escape the guy, no matter what the outcome. He only needed to get his stuff out of the room, and he'd be on his way.

Fred scampered off to the gas station and motel lobby.

"Good dog, Mac. That was perfect timing." He scratched under the dog's chin.

"Did you train him to do that?" the woman in the doorway asked.

Buck turned to her, but she remained inside her dark room. A few locks of red hair hung like twisted vines over her ear and chin, but she made no effort to reveal herself. He assumed she'd been sleeping when he and Fred had woken her up.

"No, but I guess he's a good judge of people. Thanks, by the way. I needed the backup on that one. The owner has been giving me grief about my money since last night. Now he says it's 1990."

"No problem," she replied.

A long pause followed, so he kept on. "I'm sorry for the loud voices, ma'am. Feel free to go back to sleep." More quietly, he added, "As for me, I'm getting out of here before he calls the police. I don't have time for delays."

"It's no problem," she replied softly. "If you'll excuse me, I have to make a call."

She shut the door without further explanation.

"Well, we're on the clock, Wonder Dog. Let's get our stuff and cruise. Garth is counting on us to make some distance today."

He opened the door to his room, hurried inside, and started packing the few things he'd brought in.

Outside, cars kept piling into the lot like it was the last place on Earth.

THREE

Sydney, Australia

Destiny watched the sleepy city of Sydney go by in a blur as she went south. Her taxi driver had a fifty-pound note on the line if he could get her to the Central railway station before 7:35 this morning.

The drive over the Sydney Harbor Bridge was surreal because its companion, the Sydney Opera House, wasn't there.

"Did you see it disappear?" she asked the driver.

"No, not me. I heard from a guy who knows a driver who saw it disappear, though. He said it faded slowly, like someone brushed it out of the picture. Swears it was some kind of Department of Defence experiment, like advanced camouflage."

"He thinks the opera house is still there?" she asked.

The cab cruised along the single lane on the left side of the bridge, giving her a perfect view of the missing landmark. It was now a small point of land jutting out into Sydney Harbor filled with trees and rocks rather than a cultural icon.

Ahead, the tall skyscrapers of downtown Sydney remained as she remembered them, providing comfort that most things were still the same.

As fast as the driver sped over the bridge, still others passed them, including a pair of sports cars that looked like they had come right off the race track. The two blue-and-yellow vehicles zipped by with high-pitched engine noises that rattled the glass windows of the taxi.

"Whoa!" she exclaimed as they went into the downtown. "What's the rush?"

"Everyone's leaving town, miss. I figured that was what you're doing, being in a hurry and all."

"Leaving?" she said with surprise. "I'm not leaving. I'm only going to meet a friend at his game lodge. I won't be gone permanently."

The cab driver was an older man with gray hair. He half-turned to her in the back seat. "You haven't heard the news? People are freaked."

"About the opera house disappearing? Surely there has to be some logical explanation for that. Maybe it was the military like your friend said. Who knows? They just need some time to get scientists there or something."

"It isn't just that. News says it's all over the world. Planes falling from the sky yesterday. Ships lost at sea. Some are calling it a secret doomsday weapon. Personally, I think it's all overblown, but I've never made as much money as I have the last twenty hours."

"This has been going on that long?"

"Oh, yeah. Ever since that blue light yesterday, the whole city has lost its soup."

She'd spent yesterday fighting to survive a raging forest fire, and then she had passed out on her bed when she finally made it home. Except for one brief call to her friends at the Sydney Harbor Foundation to let them know she was alive and one brief text from her sister in America, she'd barely had contact with anyone in the world.

Faith said SNAKE caused all the wacky news, she recalled from her sister's cryptic text message. It had also mentioned things coming back from the past. Faith told her to stay home and be safe, but sitting in a room wasn't Dez's style.

That was why she was trying to catch a train to Canberra.

Zandre Ford called her last night claiming he'd spotted a *dromornis stirtoni*, also known as a Demon Duck of Doom. It was one of the largest birds ever to walk the Earth, but it had gone extinct over thirty thousand years ago. She had run out the door first thing this morning because she had to see it.

As an animal lover, she didn't like that Zandre ran a game preserve and hunting lodge. He was a big donor to the foundation she worked for, though, so she had learned to get along with him. He wouldn't have bothered her if he hadn't been telling the truth, and after seeing her Tasmanian Tiger, she was open to finding other rare creatures.

The cab driver weaved through traffic at over a hundred and twenty kilometers per hour as they went through a tunnel.

"Almost there, miss. Be ready to jump." He laughed a little as if it had been a joke, but she sensed it wouldn't be far from the truth.

She didn't think he should do too much chuckling until she paid the fare. "I'll get my bag out of the boot and run for it." Dez looked at her watch. "I think I'm going to make it."

The driver took a sharp turn, and the tires complained by squealing.

The old stone building appeared after one final curve. Dozens of cabs dumped people on the street next to the train station, so the driver had little choice of where to go. "Looks like I'm going to have to triple-park."

He slid into an opening near the entrance and jammed on the brake.

"And...go!" He jumped out to open the trunk.

She was overwhelmed by the petrol fumes and a sea of car horns. Everywhere she looked, people hopped out of cabs and ran for the train terminal. The cabbies sped off, but a few other drivers pulled their passenger cars into the grass and ran away as if they were abandoning their rides.

Destiny walked toward the back of her cab, feeling overwhelmed. "Why are people ditching their cars?"

"I don't know," the driver responded. He hefted her small suitcase out of the back, then held out his hand. "But I'd like to go."

A white car honked a few feet behind them.

She handed him the fare plus the bonus note.

"Thanks for the lift," she said.

"Good luck to ya!" the driver replied as he slid into the front seat. He slammed the door, then chirped the tires as he got out of the stopped traffic. She ducked behind another parked vehicle as the white car tore off after her cab.

It felt like she was seeing the fire climb the hillside behind her again. The rush of humanity intensified as if everyone in Sydney had decided to catch the 7:35.

When people started to run, she joined them.

Staten Island, NY

It was a short walk home for Garth because he lived almost next door to his best friend. Both of the homes were very nice, but Sam's parents weren't renting theirs like his dad was.

Once inside, he felt compelled to go to his dad's study, which was a fancy word for the third bedroom where his old man sat at his desk, played on the computer, and watched movies on his flat-screen television.

Garth stood at the door as if waiting for his dad to invite him in. That was how things worked when they were both home at the same time.

He went into the room and fell into the black high-backed desk chair. Garth expected the computer to be on since his dad left it on all the time, but it sat in silence. The DVD player under the television blinked on and off, signifying that there had been a power outage recently. Probably yesterday.

Dad, I hope you're wrong about it being bad outside, but I know you're not. You're right. I saw it for myself, but I don't want to believe it.

It tore him up to not go with Sam, but he'd wanted to see Dad's gun collection for a long time, and this was as good a reason as any. As he sat in the big chair, he couldn't stop thinking about what was in the basement. He felt as if he were trying to capture some of Dad's mindset by sitting in his space.

What would Dad do? WWDD.

Thanks to his father, he had an ingrained fear of opening the gun safe and shooting his foot off. Dad was happy to let him fire the weapons when they went to the Pine Barrens, but he always got the guns out and put them away without Garth's help. His reason was always some variation of, "I'll handle them inside the house, so you don't shoot your foot off."

Even sitting there in his desk, he couldn't say for sure whether his dad had been serious all those times.

"I'm going to get them, Dad," Garth told the room.

Don't shoot your foot off, his dad's voice replied in his mind.

"I won't."

Ten minutes later, he stood in front of the ugly green safe. It was as tall as he was and about as wide as a refrigerator, with one door. The combination lock reminded him of the kind found on his high school lockers, but it was a lot beefier.

He'd memorized the combination Dad had given him over the phone, and after he entered the last number, the safe's lock clicked and the door was free to swing open.

"*Dude*," he said when he saw what was inside. "Insane!"

His dad wasn't a simple hunter, as he often claimed. Nor was he "just" a gun enthusiast with a few extras, as he sometimes declared when they went shooting with shotguns or plinking with the .22 caliber.

Firearms filled the safe.

There were numerous pistols on a high shelf and dozens of ammo boxes of many types next to them. He'd have to pull things out to see how much was behind the first row.

In the bottom section, he recognized his dad's shotgun, a .22 rifle, and the synthetic-stock hunting rifle with the big scope. His dad had brought all those out in the past.

He'd never seen the rest of the guns on the bottom.

Ten black rifles sat side by side on their buttstocks. He recognized the AR-15 pattern, but as far as he knew, Dad only had one. In the neat row, they looked like they might be identical, which evoked memories of his dad once talking about how to best swap parts between guns. Garth had had no clue what the man had been talking about until that moment.

"Dad, you are a total gun nut!" He wasn't sure if he should be proud or embarrassed. The teachers at school sometimes made him feel like a loser for knowingly associating with a father who took him deer hunting. However, his dad was also ex-military, which made him proud. His father obviously took defending his home to a high level.

"Holy shit-monkeys, dude!"

Garth jumped in fright at the voice and bumped into the safe's door.

Sam had let himself in and come down into the basement.

Garth grabbed the door and caught his breath for a second, then looked at his buddy. "Damn, you scared the crap out of me."

"Yeah, well, I came to tell you I was leaving, but now I'm not sure I should leave you alone with all those guns. I thought you were going to start kissing them."

"Screw you," Garth replied with a laugh.

"I guess I don't have to worry about any bad guys getting you," Sam joked, "but you should try not to blow your foot off."

Sam laughed with his usual too-loud cackle because he knew all about Dad's joke. Garth always found it slightly insulting his dad would suggest he'd harm himself, even if he *was* trying to be funny. However, being with his goofy friend made him realize that Sam was the type of person who could easily do that very thing. He was always looking for the next bit of entertainment or diversion at the expense of what was taking place at that moment.

Dad is rubbing off on me.

Facing all the guns made him feel realize the enormous

amount of trust his father had placed in him. He saw everything in a new light, including his best friend.

"Are you going to take the cab?" Garth asked. "I can give you the key."

"Nah," Sam replied as he got close to the open safe. "I can't drive."

"You mean you don't want to drive."

Sam slapped him on the shoulder. "If you had parents who chauffeured you everywhere, you wouldn't bother, either."

Garth ignored the implication that he didn't have a mother, although it was true. Sam never meant to take digs at him in an unfriendly way. It was simply how they talked to each other.

"So, I came over to tell you I'm outta here. My parents texted me from their fourth different bus. They had all kinds of transfers on the way, but they said they'll be at Grand Central in an hour. I'll be back before your afternoon nap, I'm sure."

They stared at the long line of guns until Sam broke the silence. "Take care of things until I get back. If you come over, don't hog all the Mountain Dew, okay? We're down to one bottle, and that's for tonight."

"Gaming until midnight?" Garth asked.

"No. We're going to celebrate my parents being home. I'm going to game all night long, dude!"

Garth got tired just thinking about it. "Hurry back," he replied.

Sam wound up to punch his shoulder but instead gave him a firm pat.

"Don't worry, Rambo," Sam declared before saying like a robot, "I'll be back."

. . .

Pole Line Motel, Mono Lake, CA

Buck gathered his things into his travel bag and shuffled out the front door. His eyes were pegged on the two-pump station, but there were ten cars and a couple of motorcycles parked in line. He sighed out relief that Fred would likely be far too busy to worry about him.

He also was happy to have his pistol in the hip holster again. After giving it a secretive pat to make sure it was secure, he spun around to leave, but bumped into someone.

"Oh, excuse me," he said as he backed away from a slender woman in a shape-hugging tank-top dress

"No problem. I heard what you said about clearing out. That was smart. I'd like to avoid prison, too." The thirty-something redhead finished closing her door and grabbed the handle of her roller suitcase.

Her crystal blue eyes paralyzed him and stole his voice.

"Hello? Prison? You want to get out of here?" she said, badgering him. "I gave you a hand earlier, but now you have to save yourself." She cocked her head and smiled. "Are you okay?"

Buck blinked as if he'd stared into a bright light. After the gloomy room, it was a legitimate excuse, but not the truth. Buck couldn't tell if he was caught off-guard because someone agreed with him about the state of the nation, or if it was the beautiful woman before him. He wanted to believe that is was the madness in the world, but he knew the truth. It had been too long since he'd had the opportunity to spend any time with anyone else, quality or otherwise.

He did his best to reply. "Sorry, uh, yeah. You surprised me, is all."

"Well? Go, escape!" She motioned for him to walk.

He followed her instructions and took a few steps. Mac

resisted for a moment while nosing the woman's black cowgirl boots, but Buck yanked firmly on the leash to get both of them out of there.

"Come on, boy, we have to get on the road."

He looked back once, to see the pretty woman breeze toward the motel lobby and gas station. He assumed she was going to turn in her room key like a good citizen.

Mac hesitated as if he wanted to go back and check out the lady, but Buck figured that was his imagination trying to think up a reason to talk to her. Even if he had the time to go back, it was a lost cause after his introduction.

"Buck, you've still got it." He chuckled as he headed for his rig. "No one can put their foot in their mouth like you can."

FOUR

Search for Nuclear, Astrophysical, and Kronometric Extremes (SNAKE). Red Mesa, Colorado

Faith understood what the general meant by a plague of truth, but she was curious about his other revelation. "What do you mean, the time dilation is getting worse? What does that have to do with plane crashes and junk from space? Or," she continued with sarcasm, "do I not have the security clearance to know that?"

The general stood up and went back to the desk but didn't sit down. "You have a point. I think we're past clearance issues, doctor. I won't be handing out launch codes, but this is stuff you need to know since you're the one who is going to fix it."

He motioned for her to scoot closer to the desk. "We tracked you down by reverse-engineering a flaw we found in the global positioning satellites. The blue wave affected our birds at different times, corresponding to their distance from this location. Each lost a fraction of a second of time relative to control points on the ground. At first, the flaw was minor, but it is growing. As of right now, the discrepancy is a few minutes of error."

"That explains the plane crashes," she interjected. "Don't they need GPS to fly?"

"Fly? No. But it does help with landings, navigation, and avoiding other planes while in the air." His tone was friendly. "It sounds like you know something about GPS systems?"

"I use one when I go for bike rides, yes, but I do understand the principle. My GPS tracker talks to satellites in the sky and they tell me where I am."

"Right," he replied, "but those satellites are aging slower than those of us on the ground. If you tried to find your location right now, your bike GPS might say you are in Kansas. I'm told we can't adjust the calibration, either. Something is interfering with anything we broadcast up to the satellites."

She stared at him slack-jawed, her mind racing.

"You grasp the implications." The general shook his head at the seemingly insurmountable challenge before him. "As best we can tell, the effects are most pronounced in the upper atmosphere, which is probably why aircraft were affected first. But there are unexplained phenomena at ground locations, too. It doesn't seem to be uniform."

Faith stood and started to pace. "And it came from SNAKE's supercollider." She spoke as if to herself. "Which explains how you used concentric rings to zero in on our particle accelerator loop. A staff member reported *not* seeing the blue light when they were on the surface around noon yesterday, but he was inside the ring. That was another reason we didn't make the connection sooner. It means the blue light was broadcast from the ring, but it only went outward, like a ripple on a pond."

"That jibes with our data, doctor. Do you know what caused it?"

"That's the billion-dollar mystery." She looked out her window at the Dakota Hogback. "I've been studying physics all my adult life. One amazing theory is that it would take a supercollider as big as the solar system to learn all of nature's mysteries. Did you know such a thing was even possible?"

"Doctor, I knew SNAKE was here, but that's the limit of my physics expertise. What aren't you telling me?"

She detected mistrust in his statement.

"As I was saying, the power requirements of a cosmic-sized collider would be off the scale. There might not be enough mass in the solar system to build something that large, but that's the size engine you would need in order to answer the truly important questions about the nature of the universe. What is dark matter? Is time travel possible? What happened at the moment of the Big Bang? Those are what excite me, general. Wrecking the world, or hiding it from you, is the opposite of what I do."

"Did something happen to magnify SNAKE's power?" The general's question sounded sincere.

"Yesterday, I would have said no, but we touched upon at least one of those with our latest experiment. We've somehow disrupted time, but I'll be damned if I know how." She thought back to the Izanagi Project. She'd read the proposal, supervised the week-long setup, and overseen the experiment up until the final seconds. There was nothing time-related in any of it.

"Please sit down," he said as if they were in the school principal's office.

Her cheery mood went away. "General, I said I don't know."

"It isn't that. I believe you when you say you don't know how your supercollider was responsible. You haven't tried to hide the fact it is a mystery to you, and I appreciate that you are so open about it. Most people in charge would try to blame someone else."

"Thanks, I think."

"But if we are going to fix this, we have to know what happened. I need you to tell me the truth about this place. Whatever you were doing yesterday wasn't as innocent as you let on, was it?"

"Sir, I promise you I have no idea—yet—what could have unleashed this. I can make a lot more progress if you let my team do more than work on laptops in the auditorium."

He didn't let up. "Doctor, are you telling me you have no idea what's going on in your particle accelerator at this very moment? I find that hard to believe, even for you."

Her cheeks burned as she went into defensive mode. "We're not even running at full power right now. I was afraid to restart everything because I didn't want to damage the components if the power went off again. There's no freaking way anything is happening at SNAKE, at least in the loop."

The general seemed disappointed. "Then it pains me to tell you this, but my team—the people you said didn't need to be involved—reported almost immediately that there is a beam of energy connected to a section of your infrastructure."

"No, that's impossible. What are you saying?"

"I don't know for sure. I'm not a physicist, as I said, but the report suggests that your supercollider is still active. It's still broadcasting the blue wave of energy out into the world."

"Bullshit," she said, forgetting which side of the desk she was on.

Pole Line Motel, Mono Lake, CA

Buck fast-walked across the front lot of the motel but resisted the urge to run because he didn't want to be noticed, similar to a bank robber blending into the crowd while making good his escape. In his case, he didn't want to be falsely accused of a crime. Fred had turned out to be more tenacious than he had given him credit for.

"Awe, shit," he said when he rounded the corner to the rear parking lot. A rowdy bunch of motorcyclists had parked their hogs a couple of feet behind his trailer. He tugged on Mac's leash as he made for the sleeper cab. "We need them to move if we're going to get out of here."

The yellow VW bug remained in front of his Peterbilt as well. There wasn't enough room for him to get around it, short of pushing it into the busy two-lane road.

He helped Mac into the cab and left him inside. This time he shut the door and didn't look back to the scratching on the window, but instead walked with purpose toward the rear of his trailer.

Buck smelled the pot before he made it past the fifth wheel, and the odor almost burned his nostrils by the time he passed the tandems. His danger meter hammered the red zone as he came to the rear corner of the trailer. There were six burly men, and they looked rough. Unshaven. Tanned. Wind-blown. They probably lived on their bikes.

The confrontation made him nervous, but he projected confidence.

"Hey, guys, I hate to bother you, but I have to back up about ten feet." The land next to the parking area was flat and open, so the guys could park their bikes anywhere in the nearest square mile of land, even if the lot was full.

The closest guy leaned against the back of Buck's truck with a beer in one hand and a fat joint in the other. After taking a huge puff, he blew the fumes toward Buck. It gave him a chance to notice the devil-horned raccoon head stitched on the front of his black leather vest.

"We'll move when our brothers are done at the pump. Cool?"

The other five guys looked as tough as the first. They all wore matching vests, like they were part of a gang, and had the wiry-but-strong builds of construction workers, slaughterhouse operators, or cage fighters. One guy still wore his helmet; the words "fuck you" were plastered all over it.

Step away from the cliff, Buck.

He looked around the lot. Cars kept coming in, mostly from the gas station side of the motel, and soon there wouldn't be any room to maneuver.

The urge to turn around and leave almost overpowered him, but it was such a minor thing to ask. He'd move his tractor-trailer if someone needed to get out, so he hoped they'd see it his way if he kept at it. Many bikers liked to dress tough and look mean but were decent guys underneath. He'd met a lot of them on the road.

"It's just that me and my dog really need to get out of here. The motel guy thinks it's 1990. It's kind of crazy, you know?" He forced out a laugh and hoped it was contagious.

"Go fuck your dog!" one of the men shouted. The others broke out in laughter.

Buck retreated. These weren't the decent breed of bikers he'd imagined.

"It's 1982, you dumbshit!" another biker taunted.

"You wish," he replied quietly.

When he got to the front bumper, he confirmed again that there was no possible way to turn the wheels and get out. Even if he had a few feet to work with, the jagoffs in the back had made it so he couldn't back up a single foot.

It's my fault.

Buck knew better than to get boxed in on a parking lot. He had intentionally put the truck close to the roadway, but he'd never anticipated that someone would park in the wedge of space he'd left in the front. His options were to wait for the assholes to leave or push the VW out into traffic. He'd do it if there was no other choice, but it would mark up his bumper for sure, and probably put the VW at risk of being t-boned.

He stood on the gravel parking lot enveloped by swirls of dust kicked up from car tires and exhaust. Mac pawed at the window to get his human to come aboard, and he was about to grant the dog's wish and wait out the bikers, but someone yelped.

The biker men laughed uproariously, so he turned around.

"You've got to be kidding me," Buck said in growing frustration. Fred was on the gravel in front of another motorcycle that was part of the gang behind his truck. The biker had either hit Fred with his front tire or knocked him on his ass with his hand. Fred was shaking and had turned pasty white.

"Stop asking me that!" the biker seethed, rolling away from Fred. As he approached his gang friends, the guy gunned his engine like a lion's victory roar.

Buck ran over to help the motel owner despite his misgivings about their ongoing dispute. He held out a hand. "You okay?"

Fred looked up with dusty tears on his cheeks but didn't respond.

Buck shouted over the continued grumble of engine sounds, "Come on, man, you look fine."

Fred shook his head but grabbed a hand. "I'm not. Not at all. I've asked everyone. Everyone!" Once on his feet, he pulled Buck closer. "It isn't 1990."

"I know. That's what I've been trying to say. It's 2020."

Fred recoiled. "No. No, it isn't. It is 1982. It is 2015. It is 2001. Everyone tells me a different date." He shook with fright as he pointed around the parking lot, settling on the bikers. "All these people think they are from different times."

"Hey!" a biker shouted. "You got a problem with us?"

Buck ignored the biker, although his heart rate quickened as his sense of dread increased. How could every car be from some other time? What if that were true? He attempted to look at things with a new perspective.

An old Volvo drove between him and the bikers, on its way to a parking space. It stood out because the young couple inside were dressed in coats, and they had several pairs of skis secured on a roof rack.

Different times.

When the Volvo passed, two of the bikers strode away from their bunch and made for Buck and Fred. Buck immediately recognized the danger because the pair had no fear of the law. They didn't even bother to hide their joints.

"I don't suppose you have a gun?" he quietly asked the motel proprietor.

FIVE

Staten Island, NY

For the next half-hour, Garth was in heaven. He had full access to his dad's gun stash and all the camping and outdoor equipment he could ever use. He picked up each of the guns and carefully inspected them, as his dad had instructed. It was tempting to take them apart and clean and oil them, but he'd only learned how to do that with his .22 caliber rifle.

If the internet had been working he could have watched videos on how to clean them, but he decided they already looked ready for battle.

Oddly, Dad's biggest warning hadn't been to be on the lookout for criminals. He wanted him to watch out for the police. New York frowned on gun owners, and they wouldn't be pleased to see his stash, nor would they be happy to see how many thirty-round mags he kept hidden in the basement. Those were illegal in the state.

A text from Sam came in while he loaded cartridges into the first mag.

'Made it to the bus station fine. Only saw one weird thing. A free elephant walking down the street. I shit you not!'

'Free? Did you buy it?' he texted back.

'I should have!'

Garth laughed. Sam found excitement everywhere he went. 'All good here. I have things ready for your glorious return.'

He looked at the pile, which contained at least thirty mags. It made an impressive stack, but Dad had instructed him to load every single one in an emergency. If he didn't need them, it would be a snap to pull the cartridges back out of the magazines and put them away. However, if trouble *did* find him, Dad said, you would never complain about being too prepared.

"Dad, you crazy old dude! We'll never run out of ammo." His dad had many 500-round boxes of the stuff jammed behind retired holiday decorations and bags of musty old clothes that had never made it to the donation pile. Garth excitedly placed the unopened boxes together, expecting it to make an awesome pyramid, but he was disappointed to see twenty of them only took up about as much space as a small trunk.

"Were you expecting a war, Dad? 'Cause it looks like you were."

He was back to loading the magazines when the floor rattled under his feet.

Earthquake?

His heart rate jumped past full speed, and he stood absolutely still. For ten or fifteen seconds he leaned toward the stairs, intending to get clear of the basement, but there was no more shaking.

"Maybe I should take care of the upstairs," he suggested to himself in a reasonable voice.

He grabbed one rifle and a loaded magazine and shut the rest in the safe.

"I guess I'm now on guard duty," he said aloud to bolster his spirits as he returned to the main floor. It felt better to be out of the basement so he couldn't be buried in an earthquake, but it felt weird to carry a rifle indoors.

If you are going to shoot, then shoot to kill, his dad had told him. That rule applied anywhere, but especially inside your own home. If anyone broke into the house, he couldn't hesitate for a second.

Garth's body shook involuntarily as he considered the gravity of what he was doing. Being the man of the house was more responsibility than he had expected it would be. Defending the house wasn't as simple as calling 9-1-1 anymore, nor could he call out for Dad.

There was more to home defense than guns, however.

The other part of Dad's instructions was to board the windows with plywood. His dad had explained that he'd cut all the wood for the ground floor windows when he'd wanted to be prepared for Hurricane Sandy back in the day. All Garth had to do was get the planks out of the garage, screw them into the frames, and cut narrow slats for peepholes. The only difference from a hurricane, he'd said, was that he should place them on the inside of the house rather than the outside. That would keep intruders from taking them off and keep the average passerby from seeing that the home was boarded up.

He wrestled with how to get to the garage with his rifle. Dad hadn't given him instructions on that. If a cop drove by and saw him walking around with a gun, it could get him into trouble. On the flip side, if a bad guy came up to him and saw he was unarmed, it could lead to other kinds of trouble. It really came down to which threat was more likely.

The backyard looked normal. No criminals lurking around, at least. He cracked up at his own paranoia.

Does having this gun make me more paranoid?

The semi-automatic rifle hung on a sling over his shoulder, and he patted the leather strap as if to comfort it. "We're not paranoid, are we? It's called being security-minded."

What would dad do?

He had no idea.

To counter both threats, he placed the gun inside the back door of the house where he could easily get to it. It remained hidden from anyone who happened to walk around the house to where he'd be carrying the wood.

Garth was quite proud of himself, and was just about to walk outside to start his project when the hallway phone rang.

Dad?

Their old agreement was to call the hallway landline if they ever got in trouble and the cell phones were down. However, he'd already talked to Dad earlier in the morning. Everything had been fine then.

He ran to the phone and checked the caller ID to confirm it wasn't his dad's cell number. The safe play was to screen the call, so he let it go to voicemail.

"Hello," a computer voice began. "This is the New York City Emergency Alert System. Your area, the borough of Staten Island, is under a voluntary evacuation notice. Summer Storm Audrey is now Hurricane Audrey, with sustained winds in excess of seventy-five miles per hour. Projections show your area is within the expected path of the hurricane. All residents are advised to travel outside the path—"

The machine beeped and turned off.

Garth leaned over the answering system to confirm the screen showed full. Someone had called and filled up the voicemail.

"Damn! Now what?"

He walked to the back door, passing the gun. He ran into the yard, somehow expecting to see a hurricane on the horizon, but all he saw were fluffy white clouds high in the sky to the south. He didn't see anything alarming.

For a moment, he considered ignoring the message, but the drone of a distant tornado siren caught his attention. Once he made out what it was, a second siren started up closer to home.

What would Dad do?

It occurred to him that even with every advantage in guns, ammo, food, and a place to stay, he had very little idea what to do if natural disasters threatened the house. If he ran, where would he go? Sam wasn't home. He could take the car and join the flood of people trying to get off the island. He could stay and ride it out, but what if a tidal wave washed ashore? He'd seen too many movies.

Think, dude.

The siren on the next block kicked on. Its wail rose and fell like air raid sirens.

He had to make a decision.

Pole Line Motel, Mono Lake, CA

Buck sized up the situation and concluded his only chance was to talk his way out of the encounter. The two men walking his way might be assholes, but they hadn't yet broken any major laws. His personal rule was to only reveal his pistol if he intended to use it. The 9mm Beretta Storm remained under the hem of his Hawaiian shirt, ready for duty.

"You got something to say to me?" The biker pointed at Fred, who had somehow shrunk.

"N-no, sir. I'm—"

"You point to one Trash Panda, you point to all of us."

The two guys were a few feet away and Buck still hadn't done anything, so he held up his hands as if to request them to halt. "Hey, guys, this has all been a misunderstanding."

Both bikers sized him up like he was their dinner, and the leader stole a glance around to see who might be watching. Buck's heartrate broke into a gallop, and he took a deep breath. He wasn't one to back down from a good brawl—he *was* a Marine, after all—but the pair had blood in their eyes and five allies backing them up. Buck's partner was a skinny motel operator on the verge of running away.

I'm going to have to shoot him.

Using his weapon was the last thing in the world he wanted to do. Each of the bikers was likely packing, and a gunfight would get someone killed.

Time seemed to slow down as the confrontation escalated. Buck had moved his hand to the holster but froze in place when the first biker grabbed his partner and stopped him. The two men looked to the front of the lot at the yellow VW.

Buck figured the police had arrived, but that notion was

quickly scuttled when he saw what had caught their attention.

His neighbor, the redheaded cowgirl, stood at the yellow car's trunk. Since the car was parked so close to his front bumper, she had to lean over from the side to get her bag into the back. Her long dress and tall boots didn't expose much of the back of her legs, but she was shapely enough to get noticed. The pair of bikers saw her do that and changed their game plan.

The lead guy smacked his pal on the chest and pushed him away from Buck and Fred.

Buck eased off his holster as the men walked the length of his tractor-trailer toward the woman.

"Well, I'm glad we didn't tangle with those guys, but that woman may need our help, don't you—"

Fred was gone. Buck spun around to find the man talking to a yuppy-looking couple standing by the gray ski-carrying Volvo. He shot a quick look over his shoulder at the woman but hastened to Fred because he needed the owner to do something.

"This is 1999," the yuppy woman said to Fred. "What are you talking about?" Her chirpy voice was instantly grating, but Buck had to hear more.

"Everyone is telling me something different," Fred replied in exasperation.

"Excuse me," Buck interrupted, "but why are you saying it is 1999? It's June of 2020."

"No," the yuppy guy replied as he shed his coat. "This is December of 1999. We're on our way to Squaw Valley up at Lake Tahoe. We pulled in here because I got dizzy behind the wheel. I think I've had too much coffee."

Fred leaned over to Buck but made no effort to speak

quietly. "See, I told you. Everyone is mad. It isn't me. You are, too, with your hundred-dollar bill trick."

Buck didn't know what to make of things, but the woman at the yellow VW was now in real trouble. The two bikers were there, and her body language was a cry for help.

"Fred, this is great and all, but you have to deal with the bikers." Buck pulled at Fred's arm, so he was turned toward the redhead in distress. "See? They are going to hurt her if we don't do something."

There was no question in his mind that the bikers hadn't gone over to the redhead for a friendly chat. She looked furtively in all directions until she caught Buck's eye.

I have to help her.

He gave the cowgirl the sign for okay and gave Fred one last try.

"Fred, go call the police. There's going to be trouble if you don't help that woman." Buck pointed her way, so Fred had no excuse not to see her. She leaned against the door of her car, but the guys didn't give her enough room to open it.

"I'll give her a hand," Buck added with determination. "You can either stand there lost in a time that's past or do something in this one. Come on, man, there's a woman in need on your fucking parking lot!"

He left Fred and walked with purpose to his cab.

Once he climbed up and opened his door, he halted and hung there. "Hey, guys, I'm going to need you to move. I'm leaving."

The two guys wheeled around, and the leader recognized Buck. "You again? Can't you see we're busy?"

He locked eyes with the pretty redhead and gave her a small nod. She was terrified.

He climbed inside and got into his captain's chair.

Buck fired up the motor, then let loose with his air horns.

"And the crowd goes wild!" He gritted his teeth and prepared for battle. Enemy in front of him and enemy behind, but the law of gross tonnage was on his side. Motorcycles or human bodies never fared well against an eighteen-wheeler driven by an angry Marine father desperate to get home to his son.

SIX

Sydney to Canberra train, New South Wales, Australia

Destiny ran inside with all the other people who had been let off at the entrance to Central Station. Whatever had spooked the crowd, it reminded her of a herd of herbivores catching the scent of predators. She was almost crushed going through the doors, and the growing mass of humanity practically carried her to the ticket counters.

Central Station was a giant rectangular building with the ticket area on the long front side and platforms on the long back wall. A giant skylight ran along the top of the rounded, vaulted ceiling from one end to the other.

However, she scrambled away from the crowd because she had bought her ticket with her phone. Destiny knew exactly where to go. She moved through the people to where the trains loaded and unloaded, but she shrieked a little because hers was already in motion.

"Shit!"

She shoved aside a few lost-looking travelers and broke into a sprint.

There were about eight platforms, although only four had trains boarding. Hers, the short three-car one to Canberra, was the only one moving.

Destiny didn't bother calling out because that never worked. Instead, she pulled her duffel off her shoulder and held it with both hands so she could run faster.

"Excuse me!" she shouted at a group of elderly hogging the entire platform. "Sorry!" she added after nearly bowling a woman over.

Two people ahead of her jumped onto the train, giving her an example of how she'd need to do it.

Run, girl!

The train horn sounded ahead.

Her lungs were mostly back to normal after the fire, but they weren't quite one hundred percent. Running at top speed for a hundred meters sapped her, but she closed the distance to the rear car.

A woman in a navy-blue uniform stood in the side door of the last car, waving her on. "You can do it!"

She began to doubt it. Her lungs burned, and her legs were sore from climbing yesterday. Still, she didn't want to miss her big opportunity to find a new animal, so she spent all she had left.

It might have been easier if she'd worn proper trainers rather than her heavy hiking boots, but she finally got close.

First, she tossed the bag to the woman, who caught it easily.

Unencumbered by luggage, she gained a few steps on the rolling train. The end of the platform was ten meters away when she tossed herself toward the moving steps.

"Bloody hell!"

The conductor grabbed her arm in support, and they

cleared the platform a second later. She was in an awkward position in the doorway, but she was safe.

"Welcome aboard," the woman said to her like it was an everyday occurrence.

"Thanks. You left a little early." Destiny straightened and looked behind her. A dozen people had been following her to catch the train, but they stopped running once it left the station. She felt sorry for them, but there would be other trains later in the day.

"Yeah," the conductor said in a reflective voice, "but TrainLink must have had a pretty good reason. Come on, let's get inside. I have to secure this door."

"My name is Kristie," the rail worker said once they were inside. "If you need anything, just let me know."

"How long until Canberra?"

"On a normal schedule, it would be four hours and eight minutes, but we're skipping most stations today. VIPs are on board. It will only take about three."

Finally, some good luck.

The conductor continued, "If the train holds together."

Search for Nuclear, Astrophysical, and Kronometric Extremes (SNAKE). Red Mesa, Colorado

Faith was a woman of action. The second the general insisted SNAKE was still running an experiment in the collider ring, she invited him to accompany her on a tour. She figured there was no better way to prove to him that everything was offline than by giving him a walk through the equipment.

The general, for his part, was amenable to being shown around. That had probably been his plan all along. She led him and an aide down a long wood-paneled central corridor until they reached a set of double doors.

"We are on the admin level; the science department is below us. The best way to think of the administration level is by gluing the letters E and O together. The upright part of the E is the front offices and the exterior windows facing east. The topmost branch is the library, computer lab, and café. The bottom branch is the dorm wing. We're standing in the central corridor of the E as it meets the O at these doors." She pushed through them like a tour guide.

"And this is the race track." They came out in a well-lit corridor which curved in each direction. Doors lined the outside wall, while windows overlooking a giant workspace were on the inside of the curve.

"This can't go around the loop for sixty miles, can it?"

"No. Who would want to walk it?" She laughed. "There are many parts to a supercollider, including several smaller rings designed to help with particle acceleration. There are also several detectors spaced around the loop, but this is the largest." She pointed through the windows.

"There really isn't much to see when the experiment is taking place since all the action happens inside of a vacuum, but it does allow us to ensure that operations are going as they should."

She caught her admission.

"And no, there was nothing unusual down there yesterday. The power went off at precisely the time the blue wave beamed out of here."

The general nodded as they walked to the observation windows. They overlooked a five-story room that was almost as big around as the playing surface of a typical baseball stadium. Heavy equipment sat on either side of what would have been second base.

"This is where the collisions are recorded."

"It's massive," he remarked.

"It is the biggest machine on Planet Earth." She beamed.

The general whistled. "I am impressed."

"The proton bunches race around the sixty-two-mile loop about twenty-five hundred times a second—close to the speed of light—gathering energy the whole way. One beam goes clockwise, the other counter. When we have them at the speeds we want, we lock the two halves of the detector and crash them into each other inside." She pointed to the two bulky machines that appeared to fit together. They made the giant room look small.

"And this isn't big enough to discover the nature of the universe, like you said before?"

She could tell by his tone of voice he was excited by the equipment. It was difficult for anyone to see it and not get enthused. There were probably few places on Earth where science was done on such a grand scale. Cape Canaveral would be the closest comparison.

"Nope. Can you believe it?" She pointed but walked away from the windows.

"That's the collision chamber. When the halves are separated, no collisions can take place. The power to them is off. I'd like to take you into the tunnel." She went into a nearby stairwell on the opposite side of the hallway.

The general paused at the door and talked to his aide. "Get me the coordinates of the power spike, would you?"

Good luck finding one when the power is off.

"Yes, sir." The aide flipped open his phone and made a call.

"After you, doctor," the general insisted.

They walked down five flights of steps in total silence,

but when they got to the bottom and came out next to an elevator, the general gestured to it. "Why didn't we take that down?"

"I'm terrified of getting trapped in an elevator that is also trapped in a cave. If we lost power while we were inside that little box, I'd lose my lunch."

"You've never used the elevators?" he said in surprise.

Faith chuckled. "I've used them loads of times, but not since noon yesterday."

They stood on the main experimental floor. Most of Faith's life was spent looking at spreadsheets of data and computer models of what was happening inside the equipment, so being close to the machinery made it seem real.

"You can see the techs working in there." She pointed through the window to the giant mechanical devices. There should have been men and women in white gowns taking care of maintenance, but everyone was being held prisoner by the general's people, so the room was clear. "Oh, my bad. You have them locked up."

"Take me to the tunnel, please." He avoided her implication.

"Dammit, general. This place will fall apart if people don't take care of it. If you are going to keep us here, at least let us do our jobs. If cryo fails, it will take us weeks to re-cool the loop."

The general did briefly peer through the windows but was intent on moving on.

"General!" she snapped to his backside. "These people have families. They are going to wonder why they didn't call or come home last night."

He spun around but wasn't upset. "Doctor, I need you to show me the tunnel. I can't risk something happening to this equipment until I know what I'm dealing with or who

I can trust. My people say the power for your experiment is on. You say the power is off. What am I supposed to do?"

"Believe me," she suggested.

He motioned her away from the windows.

"Fine." She exhaled.

They walked a short way to a place that looked like a small underground subway stop. She slid a keycard to open the doors of a futuristic-looking tram car about thirty feet long. The aerodynamic silver vehicle was angled on both ends like a double-tipped needle.

The general waited outside the door as if there were a problem.

"Don't tell me you're worried?" she scoffed. "This tram is perfectly safe."

"You won't go into an elevator near the exit of your underground fortress, but you will get into an iron lung and go deeper into it without a problem? Doctor, you have a strange sense of fear."

She stuck with the facts. "The sixty-mile loop is divided into sections. Each one has emergency supplies, a phone, tools, and a little food and water. The tram has food and water, as well as oxygen tanks. If we stop, we won't have to walk more than about four miles."

The general held up his finger to pause the conversation. He picked up his phone and spoke for a few seconds, then hung up.

"Okay, take me to mile 7.8."

"The first insertion point? What's there? Who was on the phone?"

General Smith's blue eyes peered deep into her soul as if he were conducting a human lie detector test. She withstood his withering gaze without flinching because she had nothing to hide. However, when he spoke, she imagined she'd failed his test.

"Let's go look."

Pole Line Motel, Mono Lake, CA

Buck's ploy worked to perfection. The two bikers left the woman alone and ran toward the back of his truck to move their threatened motorcycles. They gave him glares straight from the pits of damnation, which raised the hair on the back of his neck, but he consoled himself that he was doing the right thing. Even assholes didn't deserve to be shot for no good reason.

He revved the motor, put it in reverse so the lights shown on the soon-to-be-leveled bikes, and waited for the rats to scurry from behind him.

"Come on, lady, get in your car." The woman was free of the men, but she wasn't getting into her VW. She just leaned against her door like a wilted flower.

Mac began to whine, probably sensing Buck's impatience and anxiety.

"It's fine, boy. We're leaving. I promise."

He wanted to believe it was the obnoxiously loud air horn that scared his pup, but things kept spiraling into madness, and the dog knew Buck too well. Once he had threatened the bikers, their own lives were in danger.

He checked his side mirror and discovered the biker with the "Fuck you" helmet coming up the driver's side of the truck. He held something metal in his hand, which Buck instantly identified as a gun.

"Son of a bitch!" he said to himself.

Ahead, the woman still hadn't moved.

The bikers approached along both sides of the trailer

like a pack of hyenas looking for easy prey. Buck knew that the negotiation had ended. He experienced a grim calm that came with the certainty of battle.

He had about three seconds to decide how to end it.

The Marine in him took over.

SEVEN

Staten Island, NY

Garth ran inside and turned on the television. His dad was too cheap to pay for cable service, so all he had were the local channels. Strangely, one of them was off the air, but the other two big networks were still broadcasting.

The first was in a commercial break, but the second showed what looked like a weather map. A large area of red had been drawn over New York City and lots of the cities around it.

"This has to be for the storm." He turned up the volume.

"...if you are anywhere from the tip of New Jersey in the south to the northern border of Connecticut, you will want to find a hardened shelter or evacuate. Do not remain outside during the next twelve to twenty-four hours."

He changed channels. The first station had their own take on it.

"Welcome back. If you are just joining us, we have new information on Hurricane Audrey. The slow-moving system built up in the overnight hours and is now a Category Four hurricane in terms of wind speed and precipitation. However, it is about half the size of a typical hurricane."

A second newscaster asked a question. "Trey, what will that mean for our viewers? How can they prepare?"

"This is a hurricane based on size and sustained wind speeds, but its organization is quite different. There are pockets of high winds and torrential, almost Biblical-sized rain cells. It has no eye like a typical hurricane. We recommend evacuating if you can. If not, try to harden your house and go to a central room or basement until the storm passes. As you can see, it has come up the coast and is now over the Washington D.C. and Baltimore metro areas. It should reach our viewers in the New York City region in about three hours."

Three?

The other channel advised people to shelter for twenty-four hours. That didn't seem right for a storm, even a big one. He changed back to the first channel.

"...the reactor core was taken offline, but it continued into meltdown. Radiation leakage has been confirmed, but malfunctioning sensors have made it difficult to say how much has gotten into the atmosphere. Pennsylvania Power advises its residents to plan for the worst. The governor of Pennsylvania has ordered the evacuation of Philadelphia. Yes, folks, this is bad. Get out if you can."

What the hell?

He flicked to the other channel, where they were still talking about the storm. Another flick and he was back on the broadcast talking about nuclear meltdown.

"Dad was right! The world is going to shit." It was starting to make sense. "Which of the two are the sirens for?" The horns had turned off after a few minutes, but that didn't stop the fear from messing up his stomach.

He flipped back and forth on the TV to ensure he didn't miss anything.

"State scientists have determined a cloud of radiation has escaped and is flowing on the prevailing winds toward the east. At this point, we are unable to predict what will happen when this cloud meets Audrey coming up from the south, but it could compound the disaster. The next three hours should be crucial for New York City. Avoid both, if at all possible."

The weather department put two projection paths on the map, a red one coming in from a nuclear power symbol near Philadelphia, and a blue one coming in from the Washington, D.C. area. They met and grew in size right over his house.

"No freakin' way, man," he said to the television screen.

He tried to text Sam, but that was mostly out of habit, not because he expected his friend to have answers. It concerned him greatly when the network symbol had a line through it, meaning it was down.

Garth tried to call Dad next, but that didn't go through, either.

He sat watching the TV for another few minutes as he tried to figure out what to do to protect the house and himself. Did it make sense to try to put the boards on the window and seal the place up? Could a house be sealed completely from radiation? He remembered lots of movies where nothing could stop radiation except getting far from it.

And what if the storm came through and blew his house down? Then he'd be in his basement with no roof over his head to protect him from the radiation-filled rain. That would suck.

"Stay or go?" he whispered.

Garth looked at his phone again. There was now one bar of service, so he cut and pasted a new text from his last message.

'Dad, nuclear fallout is headed this way. Should I shelter in the basement or get out?" He hit Send, then stared at the phone for several minutes until he accepted that an answer wasn't coming right back. Plus, the more he thought it over, the more he realized how incredible it was going to sound when his dad saw it.

'Will explain when we talk,' he texted as a clarification.

He's probably driving.

Dad hated to text when he was behind the wheel because he never wanted to risk his life looking at useless messages. Garth couldn't fault him for that since almost every text he'd ever sent over his lifetime had been non-essential, but this time was different.

"Come on, Dad, *answer!*"

The TV station changed to a series of colored bars, like it had gone off the air, then flickered back into a shot of the newsroom.

Garth understood that he'd already made up his mind about a course of action, almost from the first moment his dad said had something was seriously wrong with America. If he was in charge of things here at the house, he gave himself the okay to make an important decision about his own safety.

The tornado sirens started up another round of warnings.

Garth peeked out the back window.

"Dad, I hope this will make you proud."

. . .

Pole Line Motel, Mono Lake, CA

Buck set his Beretta on his lap, then pressed the button to lock both the doors. It was part of a step by step approach to the coming fight.

He let off the brake, making the reverse lights on the back of the trailer stand out that much more.

"He's doing it!" one of the bikers shouted. Some of the jackals on the sides of the trailer turned around like they were going to move their choppers, but at least two continued toward the cab.

Buck gave it a little gas and the truck lurched in reverse. He wanted to run over the guys like a steamroller, but if he went too fast, he risked damaging his trailer. He immediately felt resistance back there and imagined the first bike lodged up against the crash guard, which ironically was designed to stop vehicles from going underneath the trailer.

The men screamed—a howl of anguish he heard over his motor.

"Get him!"

"Fuck it," he hissed as he gave it more gas.

The nearest biker took a shot through his open window from below. The bullet tore into the fabric of his roof. After the fact, Buck crouched lower behind the wheel.

Outside, bystanders jumped in their cars or cowered behind them.

The Peterbilt bounced with the torque of the rapid reverse, and he felt more impacts through the kingpin and fifth wheel. He let the trailer roll backward about ten feet, which was what he had told them he needed. It should have leveled most of the bikes that were in the way. He put the truck into first gear.

He fought the tunnel vision and took a deep breath.

"Here we go!" He spun the wheel to the left and gave the engine some gas.

The man down below took another shot, but it went through the fiberglass frame of the sleeper. He figured the jerky motion of the powerful tractor made him a more difficult target.

A man's arm appeared on the passenger side. Buck clenched his teeth because he'd been expecting it. He picked up his Beretta as the big biker appeared outside the far window. The man clearly didn't expect to see Buck with his own weapon. The shock on his face led to a spastic effort to bring his pistol to bear.

Buck fired once through the lower part of the door frame, which was also center mass of the attacker. He quickly followed with a second shot. A double tap. In close quarters combat, it was standard practice. His Marine training kicked in fully in the fight for his life.

"Fuck you!" he yelled in anger at being forced to shoot the man.

Mac whined from his crate, but Buck heard it only distantly. It wasn't the ringing from the concussion of the gun, but blood pounded in his ears like a thousand beating drums.

Gun in hand, he checked his left mirror for the guy who'd already shot at him twice. That man tried to climb on the side step as his friend had done, so Buck peeked out. He didn't waste time with warnings or truce offerings. He aimed.

The first shot grazed the biker's clothing, but it didn't stop him from lifting his pistol. Buck didn't give him a chance to return fire; he loosed a second shot. The man jerked backward, his hand flying to his ruined shoulder. He tumbled from the step, hitting the ground heavily and rolling aside.

The overburdened truck hadn't gotten far in first gear; he'd only been able to pull his Peterbilt to the side of the VW.

He shifted out of gear and slammed on the emergency brake. *Save the cheerleader, save the world.* He didn't know why that catchphrase had jumped into his head, but it was there nonetheless.

Ignoring Mac's whines and his own screaming ears, he peeked at the far side mirror, then scooted into the passenger seat. His pulse ran wild and his instinct said to give it gas and never look back, but he had one obligation to perform before he could leave the lot.

Buck kicked open his door and leaned part of the way out. One of the men who'd gone back had now returned to the side of the truck as if to pursue the rig. The biker carried a ridiculously large chrome pistol, and he began to raise it when the door opened. Buck put the 3-dot sights on the man's Trash Panda logo and squeezed the trigger.

The guy slammed his hand on his chest where the bullet went in and shot several times into the gravel as he spasmed, then fell face first onto the ground.

"Nine rounds left," he said with unnatural calm.

"He shot Jack and Pete!" a biker shouted from behind the trailer.

Buck pushed the door open some more and looked almost straight down. The redheaded woman stood there like she'd been frozen by an ice ray.

He bellowed as loud as he was able, "You have two seconds to get up here if you want to live!"

His voice appeared to startle her, so he held out his empty hand.

"Come on!" He beckoned gently.

She blinked away the spell and climbed up the side of the truck. He didn't grab her hand to help her in; she was on her own for that. Buck scrambled back to the driver's side, expertly checked his mirror again, then leaned around the corner of his broken window.

The bikes were toast, but the bikers were trying to regroup to save their egos.

He fired at a partial profile of a guy at the rear corner but missed.

"Eight rounds left," he said to himself.

Buck glanced at the woman. She'd shut her door, but she was in shock. She sat with her hands folded on her sage green dress and stared out the front window with a look of terror.

"We're going," he said to her.

He plopped into his seat and threw off the e-brake, then dropped it into gear. The big Peterbilt lurched again as it strained to pull the heavy load. He tried to look back at the damage he'd wrought, but it was hard to see anything while guiding his truck off the lot.

A couple of men dressed like ranchers ran across the motel's front parking lot carrying shotguns. They had probably heard the gunfire and wanted to join in, but Buck didn't have time to see which side they'd support.

He had to look ahead.

There were too many cars already on the two-lane road, but Buck didn't bother to wait his turn. He turned in a tight arc to the right, forcing cars to stop so as not to hit him. Once he straightened out on the road, he tried to look to his right to see the bikers, but they were already out of view.

"Can you see them?" he asked the woman. "Are they following us?"

Like a good combat Marine, he tried to assess enemy capabilities. How many of the gang were still getting gas? What if they had fifty bikers in their club? Would they be more concerned with helping their injured brothers or finding him to get revenge? Buck guessed that two of those he shot would die without proper medical help. Maybe all three.

They'll want revenge.

"We've got to put some distance between us and them," Buck said to the woman after he realized she wasn't going to look outside her window.

The warm Beretta had fallen between his legs onto the seat, so he grabbed it and put it on the center console where he could easily reach it.

As he drove away, he felt certain he would need it again.

EIGHT

Search for Nuclear, Astrophysical, and Krono-metric Extremes (SNAKE). Red Mesa, Colorado

"This whole place runs on magnets," Faith said to General Smith on the tram ride. "Powerful magnets focus the energy beams as they go around the loop of the collider. It only made sense to have the *Silver Bullet* use magnetic levitation, too."

"*Silver Bullet*? Is someone afraid of werewolves?" The general was cordial, despite the feeling in the pit of her stomach that she was going to her execution.

"No, but this looks like a bullet, don't you think?"

The big car had sixteen seats in four neat rows, with equal room in the front and back for cargo. They both sat in the front row, but with one open seat between them.

"I suppose. It beats the crap out of what I use back in the caves of Cheyenne Mountain. My little tram has four tires and bounces along the concrete with barely enough room for me and a driver."

She didn't know what to make of that. "You work in a cave?"

"Sometimes. I've believed for a long time that the US military has become too complacent in our defense posture. There are fewer boogeymen who scare the politicians, which makes us vulnerable. These days most of NORAD's functions happen at Peterson Air Force Base in Colorado Springs, but I like to drill out of the old base in Cheyenne Mountain because it is underground."

"That actually makes me feel good, you staying prepared."

"For anything," he added.

Faith lived her life the same way. She'd taken martial-arts as a young girl, spent a lot of time outdoors staying fit, and passed on what she could to her baby sister, Dez. There was nothing more important than being responsible for one's own safety and well-being, which was why she felt a begrudging kinship with the military man sharing her ride. But there was still a divide between them.

The tram hardly felt like it was moving, despite how rapidly the lights of the tunnel passed above them.

"How fast are we going?" the general inquired.

"The maglev system can get up to three hundred miles per hour, but we have it limited to one hundred. That allows us to get to any flaw in the tunnel in about twenty minutes."

"And this is the same tunnel your beams use?"

"We used drilling equipment similar to what they used for the Chunnel between England and France. It made a tunnel big enough for two lanes of traffic to fit side-by-side in here, but we put a shielded wall down the middle so the tram didn't interfere with the experimental equipment. The wall also keeps technicians from walking into the tracks and getting hit by speeding bullets."

He nodded approval. "I can see that being an issue."

They sat in silence until the tram decelerated and stopped a few minutes later. When the doors opened, they revealed a chamber about the size of a school gymnasium. Emergency lights were already on, but additional lights engaged as she stepped out onto the low platform in the middle of the room. It took her eyes a few seconds to adjust to the brightness.

Stacks of crates filled the back half of the chamber to their right.

"This is the first insertion room, where they can start the proton beam and send it down the tube. It also serves the function of emergency exit." She pointed to the huge red word on the far wall to their right, beyond the boxes. EXIT had been painted in five-foot-tall letters over a well-lit door. "Stairs go up to the surface, which is about two hundred feet above."

"This place really *is* a vault," he said while following her out of the *Silver Bullet*.

"Don't remind me. The loop goes around for 62.5 miles, with checkpoints like this all the way. You are never too far from an exit, but it can get very dark in here."

"I bet," he said, sounding impressed.

"Those boxes are spares for all the equipment in this stretch of the loop—magnets, cryo tubing, wiring, and so forth. But the collider pipeline is this way." She pointed to the front half of the chamber.

Faith inhaled the damp, musty odor that never went away. No matter how exact their drilling and sealing methods, new leaks always showed up.

They went into the front half of the room, an area clear of boxes. The collider pipe came out of the tunnel about twenty feet to her left, crossed the empty region of the room, and continued into another tunnel about thirty feet to her right. Stout legs with a shock-absorption technology held it off the ground. To the casual viewer, it appeared like an ordinary metal pipe about three feet in diameter, but the insides were packed solid with high-technology components.

"So, that's the snake," she joked.

A metal staircase went up and over the tubing, providing an easy way for technicians to cross, so General Smith hopped up to get a better position. He peered back and forth like he was on the prow of a ship.

"General, there's nothing to see," she said. "It's just a pipe inside a dark tunnel. Each twenty-foot section looks like all the others. We'd have to go inside a few yards to get the motion-sensing lights to activate so you can see more of it, or I could call in and tell the lab to turn on the lights manually. Oh, wait, I don't have a phone. And the techs aren't there to answer the call," she needled.

There were wall phones every hundred yards inside the tunnel, but the general didn't need to know that. Her tiny dig was the only way she had to fight back against his draconian security measures.

He didn't seem to hear her.

"I said—" she began.

"There! What's that?" He pointed to his right, along the path of the collider.

He went down the steps on the backside, then ran along the pipeline toward the opening of the next tunnel. She followed as fast as she could.

"General, I assure you. Nothing is on here except the cryo. If we shut that down completely, it will take a month to re-cool the loop. I kept it on because I'm hedging my bet that we'll restart soon." She continued in a voice only she could hear, "Or someone will."

The general went directly to the next segment of the stone-chiseled tunnel. He pushed aside a washing machine-sized cardboard box.

"Please don't move things," she said weakly.

He pointed at an object in the darkness near him.

"Tell me, doctor, what do you call this? Is it for the cryogenics?"

She caught up but stopped about ten feet away. He stood next to a new piece of equipment she'd never seen before. The other boxes had been blocking it. It looked like a metal refrigerator.

"This is what I came to see," General Smith said. He pointed to a faint blue beam about six inches wide. It appeared to come out of the side of the fridge and zap into the collider at a shallow angle.

"I don't know what this is. Nothing like this should be here," she replied weakly, but she could feel the anger build. "How did you even see this? I've checked every foot of this loop. It took me two weeks to do it, but I wanted to be sure it was all in tip-top shape for our first experiment. This wasn't in the design." She hadn't checked it since they started the Izanagi Project, but no one could have added equipment while the beams were active.

"Well, it's here," he said matter-of-factly. "And my people tell me similar energy readings were found at three other locations around your ring."

The revelation shocked her. "There are more of these?"

General Smith nodded. "I ask again—what aren't you telling me?"

She gritted her teeth in fury—not at the general, but at someone else.

. . .

Canberra, Australian Capital Territory, Kingston Station

Getting off the train in Canberra was like going back to normal Australia. The train station was the size of a kiosk compared to Sydney, and it backed up to a dusty grass field rather than a big city. It was a relief to not see panicked people everywhere.

She stepped onto the platform with the other passengers and moved toward the building. A few people milled about, probably to catch the train back to Sydney, but that was about it for activity.

Before she went inside, five or six men came out of the train's middle car. They were dressed in old fatigues like they were hunters or mercenaries.

Or poachers.

As a naturalist on one of the wildest continents on Earth, she'd seen good and bad hunters her whole career. It was impossible to know one from the other by looking at them, and poachers sometimes didn't even think they were the bad guys.

These men carried large black duffels and walked toward the other end of the platform rather than into the station.

She turned her attention to the brightly lit station house and went inside to check it out. A dozen men and women in business suits came off the train and walked through the far end of the station at the same time she went in, but went directly out the front doors. A pair of waiting black vans slid open their doors and the travelers boarded.

"You must have come in with those hoity-toity types," a man said to her.

Her friend sat by himself on one of the bench seats, but he jumped up when she looked his way.

"Zandre!"

"Hey, Dez." They hugged. "I didn't think you were going to bloody make it, mate. They lost the Canberra to Sydney train last night, and they couldn't tell me if your train was coming in, either."

"What do you mean, they lost it?" she asked.

"News says it made it to Moss Vale, but it never showed up in Sydney. Don't ask me where it went. Nobody knows."

"There's been a lot of strange shit going on," she replied. "The opera house is gone. Did you know that?"

He nodded as they walked out the front doors of the small terminal. "Yep. We haven't lost anything in the Capital Territory, but I've heard of missing landmarks in Sydney, Brisbane, and other places up the Sunshine Coast."

"What about the rest of 'Straya?" she asked.

"Haven't heard much from Perth or the West, but you wouldn't expect much from out there."

"No, I guess not," she replied. The middle and western half of the country was about as populated as the moon.

They got into a modern pickup truck with clean seats and a lovely smell. Compared to Christian's beater ute, it was like sitting in a million-dollar sports car. She felt bad that the guy's Commodore was probably burned to a crisp now, but it made her feel a little better that she had helped save the man's life.

"So, tell me about the Wollemi Fire. Heard it was a beaut."

"Yeah, it was a total fuckup," she said a bit distantly. "Maybe some other time. Right now, I want to know about this extinct bird you've found."

"I'll tell you on the way. You simply won't believe me, though, until we get there."

Highway 395, California

Buck spent almost as much time watching his side mirrors as he did watching the road ahead. The two-lane blacktop highway widened to four lanes as it went up a steep hill. The higher he went, the better he could see Mono Lake down in the basin behind him, but it was slow going. The Peterbilt struggled to pull the heavy payload faster than thirty-five miles per hour on the hills.

I could drop the trailer.

When he'd talked to Mr. Williams yesterday, the company owner had mentioned that some of his drivers had dumped their loads and bobtailed home with no trailer behind them. Buck assured his boss he wasn't going to be one of those guys, but now that he had a pack of thugs hunting for him...

He could get lost on side roads without the heavy trailer, but it would require pulling off the road to unhook it. That didn't seem like a winning proposition, either.

Cars and trucks whizzed by as they went around him on the uphill. Fewer vehicles came from the north, which might have been a good sign. Nothing was chasing people away up there.

Buck checked his mirror once again, certain a pack of motorcycles would appear at any second and surprised when they didn't.

"Holy shit!" the woman yelled with sudden passion. "I almost died!"

Her volume startled him and his head spin almost gave him whiplash, but he refrained from saying anything insensitive like, "What the fuck?" Her teary eyes made him realize he'd almost ignored her for the past ten minutes as he concentrated on driving. "Hey, it's all right. You're okay."

She brushed locks of red hair out of her eyes and opened her mouth to say something, but she was unable to speak further. While she didn't openly sob, her chest heaved like she held back a lake's worth of tears.

He searched for the correct thing to say. "It's normal to be scared shitless after being in a life-or-death situation."

I'm shaking too, he thought to himself. He didn't dare lift his hands off the wheel or she might see them trembling as the adrenaline high died down. It had been a long time since he'd experienced the rush of combat, and it was just as bad as he remembered it.

"Those men," she said with a choked-up voice. "They took my keys and told me they'd shoot me if I ran. Oh, god..."

He worried she was going to descend into uselessness, which would have been normal after anyone's first time in a gunfight. He hoped she wouldn't and waited patiently, opting to say nothing instead of the wrong thing.

"I'm sorry," she went on, "for getting you mixed up in this." She absentmindedly spun one of the wide bracelets she wore on each wrist. The worn silver matched her necklace as if they were a set.

He croaked a tense laugh. "Getting *me* mixed up? You probably didn't realize I was the one who stirred up the hornet's nest when I asked them to move their bikes. Besides, I owed you one for backing me up outside your door."

Was Fred okay? He'd lost track of the motel guy during the chaos. For a millisecond, Buck felt guilty that he didn't know how the guy was, but he had threatened Buck and been no help in the fight. Buck had thrown in with the woman to save her from the violent bikers, so if he had a duty to anyone, it was her.

The woman. He didn't know her name.

More cars passed them on the uphill climb, but they were getting close to the top. Fred's motel was getting farther and farther away with each turn of the wheels. The biker gang could have been anywhere from Fred's to just around the last corner.

"Thank you," she said in what was barely a whisper. "For saving me."

He smiled and pulled his right hand off the wheel as a test. It wasn't shaking anymore, so he reached over to her. "I'm Buck. Pleased to meet you."

She took his hand and squeezed surprisingly hard. "I'm Connie."

The warmth of her hand drew him to her like a comforting fire on a snowy night, but he pulled away before he became "that guy."

"Why did they have to park behind my truck? Why did they have to start the fight?" Buck wondered aloud.

Worse, he thought back to the riot at Walmart. Buck figured it was his talk with the World War II veteran that had kicked it all off. Now, in some dumpy motel parking lot, he'd done the same thing with Connie. If he'd jumped in his truck first thing, he would have avoided Fred and Connie both and would have been on his way.

Connie's situation was all his fault.

Every bad choice he made delayed his trip back to Garth.

"Oh, no!" Connie said with fear in her voice. She pointed to her side mirror.

Buck looked in his.

Three motorcycles came up the hill at about seventy miles an hour and weren't more than a quarter of a mile back.

"Is that them?" she asked.

Buck picked up the Beretta from the center console. He already knew the answer.

NINE

Staten Island, NY

Garth had learned from his dad that once you choose a course of action, you should stick to it and give it everything you've got. When he decided he wasn't going to stay in his house and wait for the radiation to get him, he committed one hundred percent in carrying out his flight.

He'd put several of Dad's ARs in the trunk of the taxi parked behind Sam's house. He also tossed in a case of bottled water, some random food he pulled out of the pantry, a tent and sleeping bags, and a backpack labeled Bug-out Bag his dad kept in the garage.

The cab was stolen by a man named Dawson, who'd tossed a bunch of "weapons" into the trunk when he went on his quest to kill a fake dinosaur. Garth left one hammer and one shovel at the bottom, but he also kept the wooden guitar. He had no idea why the crazy man considered it a weapon, and Garth couldn't play, but it was already in the trunk, so he left it there.

When everything was ready, he sat in the cab's front

seat and paused for one final assessment. Once he drove off, he wasn't sure when he'd return.

The storm was over three hours away, so he had some time, but he didn't want to waste a minute. The news didn't seem to know when the radiation would arrive, because they claimed it was hard to detect. Their best guess put it in his backyard at the same time as the storm, but they advised people to stay indoors for twenty-four hours to prevent exposure.

"Dad, freaking pick up!" he shouted at his phone when another call failed.

"Sam, I hope you are there." He texted his best friend, not without some misgivings. He might have tried to go pick up Sam and his parents, but traffic would make that an all-afternoon affair. He sincerely hoped they already had other plans to get out of town.

'Sam, look at the news! Radiation cloud headed for NYC. Have to evacuate!'

Do I tell him what I'm doing?

He hoped it wouldn't look like he was abandoning his buddy, but he couldn't just leave without giving him a warning. What if Sam fought across town to get back to him, only to find he'd taken off to safer spaces?

'I'm taking the taxi and going south. Get your parents to a safe zone.'

The tornado sirens cranked up again, first far away, then closer to home, like a wave of noise coming his way.

His phone vibrated as a message came back. 'Dude! You are leaving without me? WTF?'

Garth laughed. 'You want me to wait?'

Sam didn't text back right away. It meant he was thinking of something to say. 'No. My parents have arrived. We're good. They'll know what to do.'

'We good?' Garth texted.

'Yeah. We'll catch up to you, bro. Promise.'

He hoped they would but knew that was unlikely—mostly because he had no idea where he was going, other than south. First get off Staten Island, then get out of New Jersey.

'Good luck, dude,' he texted to Sam while experiencing a wave of nostalgia and emotion for his friend. It felt like he might never see his buddy again, something that was as incomprehensible as it was crazy. Sam's parents would take care of him, just as Dad had given him the tools to take care of himself until he got back.

He started the engine, and his heart revved with it.

Dad had warned him about taking the cab out into the world because the police might frown on it, but he didn't have a better choice. His dad owned a pickup truck, but that was parked at some shipping terminal in White Plains. It was far to the north, and he needed to go south. The Yellow Cab might have been a bad idea, but it was the only way he could make some miles. He decided to take his chances.

Garth looked at the phone one last time, hopeful that his dad would text and tell him if he was doing something fatally stupid, but nothing came through.

He put the phone on the center console.

After backing out of Sam's driveway, he gunned the motor.

"Looks like I'm making a run for it."

Highway 395, California

Buck's grip on the Beretta tightened as he ran the odds. Hitting moving targets was a tough proposition, but it got even more difficult if you were also on the move.

Plus, if the bikers were smart, all they had to do was shoot out his front tires and he'd end up in a flaming wreck. If violence was coming, he had to fight back fast with the only asset he had while driving his tugboat on wheels: surprise.

That made him quite nervous because surprise worked both ways.

He spoke fast. "There's a rifle on my bed. Can you shoot?"

Connie shook her head. "I've written about guns but never fired one."

"Go back there. I'll need you to grab some ammo. It's in my bag next to Mac's crate." He'd taken it into the motel room just to be safe. Highway robbery was a real thing.

She hopped out of her seat and scooted by him. Her hip brushed his elbow and he flinched, pulling away quickly so he didn't appear to be trying to cop a feel. At the same moment, Garth's ringtone blared from the phone in the dashboard holder. Despite everything going on, he had to know what his son needed.

"Radiation?" he said in disbelief when he read the text message.

There was no time to respond. The bikers had closed the distance in seconds and were almost alongside his trailer.

"Fuck, we can't reload yet," he said to her. "Just stay down."

He'd shot six times back at the motel, which meant he had eight rounds left of his 13+1. There were three guys, but he was a huge sitting duck and they were nimble targets. It would not be a fair fight.

Once again, his heart rate launched into high orbit, but his sense of calm came down to Earth as battle approached.

He loosened his grip on the Beretta and visualized what he was going to do.

When they get close, I'm going to lean out and pick off the leader. The rest will fall back...

As the three riders attempted to pass his tractor and trailer, he leaned around the window frame and aimed at the first asshole. Buck met the eyes of the man—

"Fuck me!" It wasn't the Trash Pandas.

The rider jammed on the brakes and his two friends followed suit.

He brought the gun back inside but leaned toward his mirrors to see what he'd done. The three men skidded to a stop, narrowly avoided getting rear-ended, then turned around to head back down the hill.

"Aw shit, they think I'm some kind of nut job," Buck said to Connie.

He sat in shock for a minute while he contemplated how close he'd come to shooting an innocent man. When he snapped out of it, he set the pistol back in the center console and picked up his phone.

Connie returned to her seat carrying the 10/22 take-down and a box of ammo for his Storm. It impressed him that she didn't cower in the back but was grabbing guns and hanging up front where she'd be in greater danger.

"Just a second," he told her. "I have to figure out what my son wants."

He held up the phone to read it aloud. "Dad, nuclear fallout is headed this way. Should I shelter in the basement or get out?"

"Get out," Connie said immediately.

Buck checked the mirrors out of habit and turned to his passenger. "You don't even know where he is."

"When radiation comes, you go. That's bad stuff."

He couldn't argue about it being bad, but he had plenty of gear back at the house to build a relatively decent fallout shelter. Also, his kit included iodine tablets to counter the effects of low levels of radiation, plus gas masks, protective suits, and all kinds of goodies. Garth might need some instruction on how to use it all, but it was doable.

While he thought about his reply, Big Mac came out of his crate and shoved his way into the space under Connie's legs.

"Aw, he's so cute!" She rubbed both sides of his face like he was a stuffed animal.

"I think he wants his seat back," Buck said to lighten the mood. The three bikers had nearly been a debacle. No one had taken a shot, and no one had died. Buck had every reason to celebrate the tiny victory.

"I'm so sorry!" she said to Mac. "I won't be here long," she added.

That should have been good news, but Buck didn't feel it.

Looking at Buck, she continued. "I don't have a car to get back to New Mexico, which is that way." She pointed behind them. "But if you drop me off at the nearest town, I'm sure I can call a tow truck to get my car back."

Garth.

He held up his finger. "One sec." He was going to text something to his son, but he remembered a hundred lectures on texting and driving he'd given the teen boy. "Will you type something for me?"

She took the phone from his hand. "Sure."

"Stay at home. Will call you with instructions ASAP. Driving."

She keyed it in and hit Send. "Anything else?"

"No. He won't do anything without consulting me. He's

staying at a friend's house in New York City. Staten Island, actually. That's where we live."

"Well, I hope the radiation isn't too bad. What do you think that's all about? Was there an accident?"

Buck wanted the answer to that question, but another vehicle in the mirror caught his eye. It demanded his full attention.

He shifted into a middle gear because they'd finally gotten near the summit of the incline. All of Mono Lake and the surrounding basin was visible behind them. It would have made a nice photo.

But his eyes were on the yellow VW.

Search for Nuclear, Astrophysical, and Kronometric Extremes (SNAKE). Red Mesa, Colorado

"General," Faith said as she caught her breath. "As I stated before, this is the most complex piece of machinery in the world. There has to be a reason this is here." It was a deflection, because she was ninety-nine percent sure it should not have been there. It wasn't in any of the plans.

Who would have added something? SNAKE was supposed to be an open research facility, not a maximum-security prison. Just about anyone could walk in the front door by signing their name, although it did require a keycard to activate the *Silver Bullet* and go down the tunnel.

Unless they walked.

Unable to figure out how it had gotten there, she turned to the machine. "There is no way the power for this is coming from inside this facility. I mean, look at it! There aren't even any wires."

The general leaned around the box to look at the other side. "It must have a battery in the casing."

"Yeah, maybe," she replied.

General Smith chuckled. "I never would have thought we'd get seven miles in without you admitting to this. You had to know I was going to find it. Why didn't you move it?"

Faith held out her wrists. "Just take me in, general. I give up. My life's goal was to screw up the world doing illicit experiments in the name of physics. I specialize in time travel and quantum teleportation. I would have gotten away with it, too, if it hadn't been for your meddling ways."

"Scooby Doo?" he asked with a full helping of sarcasm.

She nodded gravely. "I have two Ph.Ds, three Masters, and two undergrad degrees. General, I know there are book smarts and street smarts. I've got a lock on books, but I'd like to think I do all right with street smarts, too. If I knew this was here, it would make no sense for me to voluntarily bring you right to it. Someone put this here, perhaps not understanding what would happen. Whatever it does, it's still doing it. We have to figure it out."

"Can we just move the box?" he suggested. "That will turn off the beam, won't it?"

She laughed a little. "You are trying to trap me into admitting it will, aren't you?"

He shrugged his shoulders. "It couldn't hurt. Figured you'd get sloppy."

"What's it going to take to earn back your trust?"

"You never had my trust, doctor, so don't feel bad. My job is to save the American way of life, not avoid hurting people's feelings. I know you are a very smart woman, and I'm just a run-of-the-mill general who got Cs in high school physics and felt pretty good about it. I have to assume you are trying to pull a fast one on me. I live for paranoia so our citizens don't have to worry."

"That's terrible," she replied.

"It's my life right now." He whipped out a phone and ordered his scientists to come into the tunnel. She hoped she could bring people too because no one knew the collider raceway better than her team—present box excepted.

The general hung up, and she saw her chance. "May I use the emergency phones to contact my staff, so they can also bring equipment to help?"

He stared at the faint blue beam coming out of the box.

"How many do you need?"

"Six?"

"I'll give you three. And I'll have six of my own, plus security. No one touches this device without me knowing about it. I'll put a detail on the others too, once we locate them down the tunnel. And I think I'll order a room-by-room sweep of the entire complex. We'll see what other oddities pop up."

She was crestfallen to suddenly be a second-class scientist under threat of being searched, but she tried to see things from his perspective. She would probably have mistrusted her too. It would have been nice to have more of her team on hand, but three would be enough to get things going.

She found the phone and called the administration wing.

The general stood close so he could hear her talk. When she hung up, he invited her to come over to him as he stood by the mystery device.

"No bullshit, doctor—what do you think this is doing?"

"No BS? I don't know. The light goes into the collider at an angle, and might not even be lined up with the beam inside. That suggests it is going somewhere else." She took a moment to reflect. There was no way someone could have snuck anything inside the collider channel. It was built to exacting standards across all 62.5 miles.

"You mean this beam goes beyond the tubing?"

"This tube has high-powered magnets and extensive shielding, so I have no reason to believe it could go through—"

Faith wore nice slacks and a silk blouse but got down and slid under the collider pipeline like a professional mechanic. Sure enough, the blue beam came out on the other side and went into the concrete wall about five feet away. She estimated it angled underneath the tram tracks, so no one would see it on the tram side of the tunnel.

"Holy shit! Uh, it comes out on this side." She didn't dare touch it since she couldn't imagine what it was. Her radiation badge was silent, so that threat was minimal, but the light's behavior would best be characterized as exotic, given the way it penetrated metal and concrete. It meant it was likely dangerous.

"Come on up. Get off the ground, doctor." He held out a hand to help.

She slid out and got to her feet without his assistance. It made her feel good for doing it, but the general continued speaking as if nothing happened.

"What if this beam was on yesterday during your experiment? And what if it got inside the collider when everything went to shit? Could it have been responsible for the blast of energy we saw?"

She straightened a few loose strands of hair. "Everything here at SNAKE runs with computer guidance. If we saw even a trace of unexpected activity, the computer algorithms we monitor would have paused the entire project.

These collisions take place at the atomic level, and the precision needed to achieve that would blow your mind. But..."

Faith paused as she thought about what to say next.

"If the person who put this here knew enough about those guidance issues—and knew how to get around them—perhaps this beam could have been inserted without anyone knowing about it. As to whether it caused the blue light? Right now, it's the best theory we have. It is the one thing that doesn't belong."

What else is here I don't know about?

She shivered for a second. It was chilly in the subterranean chamber, but the vastness of it gave her reason to worry. There were sixty miles of hiding places. Could there be more of these mystery boxes beyond the four the general claimed to have found? More importantly, who had put them there? It had to be someone on her team, didn't it?

Had she just invited the culprit to come assist her?

TEN

Highway 395, California

"Look behind us," Buck told Connie. "Is that your car?"

He had to be sure this time.

She expressed frustration despite leaning over to her window. "I can't see anything from this side." She hopped out of her seat and stood to get a better look at his mirror. "It might be."

The yellow VW Beetle raced up the hill, weaving through the slower-moving traffic. It even swerved into the southbound lanes to avoid two cars climbing side by side. The act showed desperation, but it wasn't yet proof of who was inside.

"Maybe they won't know it's us," she added in a downcast voice. "Your truck doesn't have any markings, and we blend in with the other big rigs."

"It's a good thought, but I highly doubt they wouldn't recognize the rear crash-under bar. I'm sure it's bent to shit after crushing their bikes."

"Oh, yeah." She sighed as she returned to her seat.

He looked back one more time as the roadway crested a

scrub-covered hilltop. The car had a clear path in the next lane, and they would be next to them in seconds.

As he started downhill, he hoped to see a means of help, but there was nothing but desolate, treeless hills in all directions. The rocky peaks of the Sierra Nevada lined the horizon to the west. I-80 was somewhere far to the north. If there were towns or police stations out there, he couldn't see them.

Buck shifted into higher gears to put off the inevitable passing maneuver, but that presented new challenges. The heavy load that had slowed him on the climb was going to be hard to control on the descent unless he kept his speed low.

That wasn't an option.

Buck got the Peterbilt up to speed, but the VW still caught up easily. He was about eighty-five percent sure two bikers were in the yellow car, but the morning sun glared off the windshield. That made it hard to see in, so he wasn't able to guarantee it was them.

"Sit tight," he told Connie. Then, as he noticed Mac still at her feet, "And you, too."

He let go of the shifter, wiped his sweaty palm on his jeans, and picked up the nine-millimeter pistol.

I have to be sure.

Buck timed it so he could peek out the moment the car was parallel with him, but he planned to duck back into his seat rather than fire the gun. After almost killing those other men, he needed visual confirmation of the enemy before engaging them. Unless they fired first. Then it would be go-time.

Aim at the tires.

The car didn't slow down as it approached, which led him to believe it wasn't the bikers. As the little yellow bug sped by, one of the Trash Pandas held a gun out his window and brandished it in the stiff wind. Buck snarled and leaned away from the window, assuming he was about to be shot.

"New Mexico plates! That's my car!" Connie said at almost the same instant. She'd stood up to get a good look as it went by. "Shoot it!"

He gripped the gun firmly but didn't stick it out the window.

The driver of the VW didn't slow down.

"They stole my damned car," Connie said angrily as she adjusted the 10/22 on her lap. For a moment, Buck thought she was going to start shooting at the guys, but all she did was watch them drive away.

Her car cruised down the hill, passing slower vehicles just as it had on the climb up. The VW went around a distant bend. The brake lights never came on.

"This has to be some kind of trap," Buck suggested. He checked his side mirror again, certain there was going to be a wave of angry bikers at his back door. There were lots of cars, but no motorcycles. "The guys in your car are going to set up a roadblock up ahead."

He thought back to the abandoned Yosemite roadblock, but the circumstances were different on this road. One car couldn't effectively block a four-lane highway.

Is that their plan?

"You'll just ram him, won't you?" she said after a moment of thought. "I mean, the truck is big enough, right?"

"Yeah..." His voice wavered. Even a controlled crash could damage his Peterbilt in the process, and it might also increase their odds of a breakdown. If the choice was between ramming them or getting shot, it would be worthwhile, but the act would put his whole trip at risk. Getting to Garth would be delayed, possibly for a long time, and that didn't even get into the financial problems a major fender bender would cause him.

Connie played with the bangle on her wrist again. "I'm sorry for all this."

Buck was sorry, too. He felt terrible that he'd had to shoot the bikers, but he comforted himself with the knowledge that they were the ones who had first brought out the guns. He had acted with honor, although that quaint notion was less important now. Once the shooting had started, there had been only two options: Life, or death.

He would do whatever it took to carry out his mission of getting back to Garth. Begrudgingly, he acknowledged that he would also do anything to protect Connie, now that she was riding shotgun in his truck. She also seemed like a nice person. She had expressed sorrow at what happened, but they didn't want to think of themselves as victims.

"They started it," Buck said out loud, as much for himself as Connie. "I'll take the rifle, please," he told her. "I'll trade you."

Buck handed the PX4 Storm to her, and she gave the rifle to him. Connie held the pistol in almost the proper way. She didn't put her finger on the trigger, which made him think that she wasn't a total gun newbie, even if she had never fired one.

To free both hands, he jammed his legs under the steering wheel while they were rolling in a straight line. He quickly pulled out the long magazine and held it and the rifle so Connie could see. "The bullets go in here. You just push them in one after the other. It holds twenty-five. When full, you stick this mag into the housing, like this." He rocked it in. "Then you pull this handle to load the first round."

Buck simulated the action. "There is already a round in

the chamber, so I don't have to do it. You have a total of twenty-four shots until we reload." He'd used one round on the rabbit the previous day, and he was now a little upset that he hadn't plugged in a replacement cartridge last night. "Finally, you tick off the safety here, then point and shoot."

After grabbing the wheel with one hand, they swapped weapons again.

"I swear, as soon as we find a town, I'll get out of your hair."

He chuckled. "Connie, I hope you didn't have impor-tant plans today, because I think we are going to be stuck in the cab for quite some time. I have to admit that I don't want to waste my grand efforts at saving our lives, only to risk yours by dumping you at some choke and puke in the middle of nowhere. Me and Mac won't let you out until we get you somewhere safe."

"Thank you," she said softly. "But I feel pretty safe right here."

Staten Island, NY

Garth made it to the end of his block when he ran into trouble. A pair of gray-haired men cradled shotguns in their arms as they stood at the intersection. He'd spent a lot of time carefully hiding the guns he'd put in the trunk so no one would see what he was up to. These guys carried guns right out in the open. On Staten Island.

One elderly man talked to a car coming onto the street, but the other neighbor came up to his window as he rolled it down. "Hey, Garth. Where's your dad? Never seen you drive without him."

"Hey, Mr. Silas. Dad is on the road. I'm heading out to get clear of the radiation. What are you doing?"

"We're watching for looters. Power doesn't want to stay on, which brings out the bad guys. Last night, people started evacuating when it looked like the storm was heading this way, then more went out this morning at first hint of the nuclear problem. We're making sure no undesirables come back in."

"You mean people have been evacuating for hours?" His voice was full of surprise. He had thought the sirens were the start of it.

"Yep. Hard to get everyone off an island this size. It's going to take time."

"Has most everyone on this street already left?" he asked.

"No way of knowing. Me and some of the other old-timers are sticking around to make sure the properties don't get ransacked. A little radiation won't hurt us."

"Is it only going to be a little?"

The man winked. "We'll know in a few hours. Don't you think about staying. If you got a good ride, and it seems like you do, get the hell out of here. Come back when they tell you it's clear. We'll hold down the fort until you get back."

"Well, thanks. I've got to go."

A large older woman shuffled across a nearby lawn. "Are you going to the city? I need a ride, young man!"

Garth shook his head forcefully. "I'm not. I'm headed south."

The woman scowled. "You should go where the customer wants."

"I'm sorry," he replied. Then, looking up at the man standing close, "Can I go?"

The guy carried a shotgun that was probably eighty or ninety years old, but it didn't diminish the intimidation factor. The wooden stock was worn and faded almost to gray, but his wrinkled hands gripped it comfortably like he carried it as a friend.

"Sure. Be careful, son." The man pounded the roof of the cab in a friendly way. "And you might want to turn your service light off. People will think you're on duty."

Garth studied the dashboard until he found a button for it.

"Thanks!" he said as he gave the cab some gas.

As an afterthought, he hit the brakes again and leaned out the window. "My dad would want me to thank you for looking out for our house."

The statement was worth it to see the man's eyes light up. "My pleasure, Garth. Give your dad my best when you catch up to him."

"I will."

When he left the roadblock of old timers, he couldn't help but feel he was headed into the middle of a gang war. He was positive the next roadblock would not have a friendly neighbor who would wish him well.

Canberra, ACT, Australia

Zandre and Destiny bounced along one of the endless stretches of dusty road in the wilds of Australia. Cattle grazed pastures that sprawled in all directions.

"I'm glad you could make it out here this quick, Dez. You won't believe the types of animals guys are bringing in."

"I thought you found a *dromornis stirtoni*?"

He laughed. "I've seen one, yes! This morning I've seen other things you won't believe. They aren't even listed as game, so it isn't technically poaching, but…"

Zandre knew her well enough to suspect she might not want to hear about illegal culls.

"It's okay," she reassured him. "I killed a Tasmanian Tiger yesterday during the fire. I thought it came out of the woods because of the blaze, but I got a text message from a... friend. She suggests time is all messed up."

He nodded as he steered around a small animal carcass in the road. "Yeah, I would agree with your friend. The Tasmanian Tiger is from the last century. The *dromornis stirtoni* is from the Pleistocene era. I looked it up. We need your skills at identifying even more ancient creatures."

She stiffened at the implication. "You haven't seen dinosaurs, have you?"

"Crikey! No. That would beat all, don't you think? Then we'd become the hunted. No, nothing quite so old, thank God."

Destiny sat in contemplative silence for the rest of the ride. She also nodded off for a brief time, immediately dreaming of a fight with a toothy dinosaur. When she lurched back to full awareness, they were on the driveway to the house.

"Place looks nice," she said to be polite.

His home stood alone in the barren wilderness. The wooden structure was about twenty meters square, with many windows. It had a steeply-sloped shingle roof shaped a little like a pyramid with the top half lopped off. The roof extended about three meters outside each wall, which created a wrap-around porch.

A half-dozen trucks were parked in front of six trailers off to one side of the main house. The decrepit old mobile homes served as lodging for Zandre's business, and a handful of camo-clad men unloaded an SUV parked at one of them.

"I recognize those guys," she said, making a sour face. "From the train station."

"Yeah. After yesterday's weirdness, one of my customers called his buddies to come in from Melbourne. That's part of why I called you. I'm going to be swamped with business, which is great, but I can't be held responsible for what they are hauling in, can I? None of these things are on the bloody permit schedule."

In her circles, hunters were often regarded as people with two heads and twenty eyes. She was a bit more pragmatic after spending so much time in the bush. Some hunting was necessary, like dingoes and wild boar, to tame the pest populations.

"As long as they have Territory hunting licenses, I think they'd be fine. Of course, I haven't seen what they are killing yet."

They both hopped out of the truck and Zandre strode briskly for the side of his house, waving at her to follow.

"Come on, I'll show you!"

ELEVEN

Search for Nuclear, Astrophysical, and Krono-metric Extremes (SNAKE). Red Mesa, Colorado

"We are definitely broadcasting."

Faith heard the words come out of Dr. Sunetra Chandrasekhar's mouth but couldn't process the meaning.

"Doctor, did you hear me?" Sun continued. "Whatever else this blue beam is doing, it powers a band of energy attached to the outer casing of the collider ring."

"I knew it!" General Smith added. "Your equipment is broadcasting the blue energy to the world."

Sun, ever the perfectionist, corrected the general. "Energy has no color, sir. Viewers most likely saw blue caused by haze, pollution, and air particles as the wave passed by. This would explain—"

"Yes, fine," he replied. "I don't care about any of that. Can it be turned off?"

Faith finally regained her bearings. "No. We can't touch it until we know what it does. I know it is here, and I see it passing through the casing of the collider tubing, but we have no idea what is going on inside. Thus, we have no clue what turning it off will do."

She glanced at the general, sure he was going to order the box turned off by any means necessary, but he remained silent. Instead, a shaggy-haired NORAD scientist spoke up.

"I agree with Dr. Sinclair. If we can establish a baseline of what it is affecting, it could at least give us an indication of the risks of shutting it off. I don't see how it can be doing much of anything, all things considered, but it would seem prudent to play it safe." The man smiled at Faith, but she refrained from smiling back. She didn't even know his name.

The general had been pacing nearby, endlessly talking on the phone, while his group of six science advisors poured over the machine. He put his phone in his pocket before addressing the scientist.

"Dr. Sinclair, do you concur with your colleague? Is the machine on?"

She bit her lip as if willing her mouth not to admit defeat, but she couldn't fight facts. After a few seconds of restraint, she had to give in. "I can see her laptop, General. There is a trickle of energy, but what's inside this tubing is not some *Star Wars* laser, like you might imagine. The total energy output of the operational collider isn't more powerful than a clap of your hands, and what we're showing on the casing is less powerful than the flap of a mosquito's wings."

"But something is there," he coaxed.

"Yes."

General Smith eyed her with his X-ray glare, and while Faith didn't back down, she didn't fight it, either. Someone had set up complex equipment right under her nose and run a concurrent experiment that none of them could fathom. She was both furious and embarrassed.

The general looked at the scientists gathered around the box. "In the half-hour since I brought you all here to see this, I've lost contact with two important assets in our space program, an early warning dish in northern Canada. Also, a missile frigate in Norfolk ran aground--" He stopped abruptly. "Dammit, I keep forgetting some of you eggheads don't have the clearance.

"Each minute we delay," he continued, "more things go wrong out there. You should also know that I'm a four-star general. I normally have lieutenant-generals order majors and colonels to fuck around inside remote basements like this one, so the fact I'm here should tell you how seriously the United States government takes this crisis. I need to know if this fridge-box is responsible. If it is, I'm going to kick it over myself."

Bob Stafford stepped in front of the box, appearing worried that the general would make good on his threat. "Sir, we've only just found this. We need time to study it. It has to be going somewhere, right? We can use our instruments to guess that location. If we get a few more clues, perhaps we'll know if it's safe to turn it off."

"Your own man agrees," Faith added.

"I don't see how it could be dangerous. Dr. Sinclair has admitted that the energy involved is less than a butterfly's wings or whatever." General Smith stepped to Bob's side like he was letting the scientist know he could go around him if he desired.

"Think of it like a firehose with a microscopic nozzle," Bob replied. "The amounts of energy are very small, but when they build up enough speed and collide with opposing forces, the heat generated can be hotter than the center of the sun."

Faith didn't say it, but Bob was leading the general away by talking about separate scientific extremes as if they were the same. The heat sounded impressive, but it was so minute as to be practically invisible. That was why they needed five-story-tall sensors to detect and record the sub-atomic impacts. Bob wanted the general to use caution, as did she. It was a rare alignment of their motivations.

One of the general's scientists looked up from a pile of equipment. "Sir, we think we know where it goes."

General Smith zeroed in on the man.

"Where?" he demanded.

"Sir, I took a picture of the beam coming out of the box relative to the floor and sent it to my peers at MIT. They used the SNAKE construction survey to assign a point on the Earth representing this location. From there, they figured out the angle of descent and created a curve of possible endpoints." The man pushed his thick glasses up the bridge of his nose.

"You know where this light is coming from?"

The man seemed uncertain. "Well, maybe, but I'm having them re-check it for me. I brought it up because I didn't want the SNAKE team to duplicate my efforts."

"Don't tease me, son. Show me what you've got."

The young scientist fiddled with his glasses again. "The margin of error is huge, so we have to wait for better data and—"

The general stopped him. "The next words out of your mouth better be the location. Where is this light going?"

"MIT's best guess is Geneva. In Switzerland."

"That's not possible!" Faith exclaimed.

General Smith looked right at her. "Do you have any idea what is in Geneva, Switzerland?"

Yes, sir, I do. It blew up twenty-four hours ago.

Highway 395, California

"Break 19, highway 395. Anyone hear this?" Buck called into the CB.

Connie cradled the 10/22 in her lap with the barrel pointed out the far door. Mac nosed the gun out of his way as he tried to also get on her lap. The dog's head gave her something to stroke while scanning forward and backward on the highway.

"I gotcha, break. Come on," a male voice returned on the CB.

"I just cleared the ridge coming out of Mono Lake, northbound. I'm being shadowed by a yellow VW, New Mexico plates. Two men, one flashed a gun at me."

Buck let off the microphone, then held it off to his side as he waited for a response.

"Why don't you tell them they shot at us?" Connie asked.

He wasn't sure of the right answer. Was he endangering other drivers if he got them more directly involved? Was he screwing himself by not doing so?

"Right now, I only want to figure out who else is on the road. If we can keep track of your car, we may not need to get others involved directly involved with the bikers."

"I guess it makes sense, but I would be asking for everyone out there to run those jerks off the road."

He smiled. "That isn't what us truckers do. These trailers are expensive, the tractors even more so."

Connie stopped petting Mac and patted her rifle.

"Don't all you guys carry guns? You could do a citizens' arrest."

He feared the police wouldn't answer the phone. Everything he'd seen since the state trooper had pulled him over suggested the authorities were no-shows out here. The police should have been at that Walmart long before he rolled off the lot. They should have been up at Yosemite. They should be passing his truck even now, heading in the opposite direction of Buck and Connie on their way to the motel. Surely Fred had called them after a shooting in his parking lot.

"We're just people, ma'am. I happen to be a little more prepared."

If she only knew.

A female voice broke into the channel. "I see a yellow VW Beetle. New Mexico plates. It overtook me heading north on 395 toward Reno. Currently a mile south of Bridgeport."

Buck clicked Freddy the GPS on his dashboard and zoomed the map out. Bridgeport appeared a few miles ahead, at the bottom of the hill.

"Thank you," Buck replied.

Connie scratched Mac behind his ears. He ate it up.

"Don't let him fool you," Buck said to relieve the tension. "He gets plenty of attention."

"I bet he's going to be a big dog. Won't he be cramped in here?"

"He's a gift for my son. When I get back to New York, this monster will have a huge house to play in." He reached over to scratch his friend's ear but bumped Connie's hand instead. "Sorry."

"No problem." She smiled. "How old is your son? Mine's eighteen."

"He's fifteen going on eighteen. He lives with our almost next-door neighbors while I'm on the road, which unfortunately is most of the time these days. They have a kid the same age. You can imagine that keeps me as nervous as a worm at the fishing derby."

"I know. Believe me. Mine is off to fight Saddam Hussein with the US Army. At least, I thought he was." She pulled out a phone and showed it to him. "I haven't been able to get hold of him since I woke up this morning."

He laughed, but jovially. Her phone was ancient and clunky, like something out of a museum. If her son was fighting Saddam Hussein...

"You know we went in and kicked the shit out of Saddam in 2003? Found him and hung the bastard. He's dead, ma'am."

"Please call me Connie. I heard you and Fred talking. I also heard him going around scaring people, asking about the date. What year do *you* think it is?"

"2020." He pointed to his phone in the cradle. When it turned on, it displayed the date on the screen.

"I see. That would make me...fifty-three years old." She didn't sound happy.

"Well, I'd say you were talking crazy." He glanced over and admired her youthful beauty without being dirty about it. "If you have an eighteen-year-old son, I'd say you weren't a day over thirty-seven."

"Thanks. I had my son when I was too young. I'm actually thirty-six. At least, I was in the year 2003."

We're about the same age.

They looked at each other for a few meaningful moments.

"You came from the past," Buck said as if reading her epitaph.

She faced forward and never let up kneading Mac's head. "I was coming back from a writer's convention in Reno. I drove into the motel last night and talked to my son for a brief time. I heard you and the owner talk about dates on money this morning. I tried calling my son right after, but my phone hasn't had a signal since I woke up. It still doesn't." She gave it a half-hearted glance.

Mac picked that moment to put his front legs on her lap as if he wanted to console her—or he wasn't getting enough scratching from her.

He had a million questions, but a sign for Bridgeport was ahead. The small town couldn't have more than a hundred people, and it was the same type of beat-down dusty waystation as the "town" of Mono Lake.

"Break 19. Anyone still have eyes on the yellow VW bug?"

He waited impatiently again.

If ever there was going to be an ambush by the crazy bikers, it was a mile ahead.

"Break 19. Anyone? Come back."

All they heard was static.

TWELVE

Staten Island, NY

Garth headed south in his borrowed cab, frantically replaying his driving trips with Dad so he had a clear idea of where to go. Staten Island was shaped roughly like a diamond, and he lived near the top point. That was where the ferry to New York City was located, as well as the Narrows Bridge he and Sam had come across last night. Another bridge was at the southern tip, which was his next goal.

He'd been on the move for about five minutes when he caught a red light and had to sit behind some stopped cars. The interstate wasn't far ahead, but he needed to take surface streets to get there. Lost in thought, he stared at the red LED stoplight when a voice made him jump.

"Taxi!" a man shouted from outside the back door. "Open up!"

Garth gripped the wheel with both hands while he caught his breath, then he turned back to the guy. "I'm not in service!" He pointed to his roof. "My light is off."

"You're empty. Open up!" The guy was dressed a lot

like him. Blue Jeans, short sleeved t-shirt. Yankees ball cap. He wasn't much older, either.

Garth shook his head vigorously. "I can't! I'm out of service." He figured repeating himself would help it sink in.

The light changed, and cars started to move, but the young man grabbed for the handle on the front door. Garth had locked all the doors, so that wasn't a concern, but the man held on and tried to run along as he gave the cab some gas.

"Wait! Take me!" He ran for a few seconds, then let go. "Fuck you!"

"Sorry," Garth said without looking back.

As traffic got up to speed, he let himself look back. The man was okay. He stood in the street with his arm up as if to flag down the next taxi.

"That was a close one," he said to himself.

Traffic was stop and go for the next several blocks. Shops and fast food joints filled the suburban strip along the road, but no one was buying. Instead, citizens lined the roadway ahead like they were preparing for a parade.

At first, they stood in ones and twos, but as he got near the highway, they started to show up in larger groups. And each time they saw him and his empty cab, they held up their hands to flag him down. His light being off seemed to have little effect.

"Sam, where are you when I need you? These people aren't going to give up." It would have helped to have Sam take up space in the back seat so it was obvious he had a fare on board.

The sign for Interstate 278 pointed ahead. The overpass was only a few lights away, but the number of cars had increased greatly. The crowd on the side of the road had also expanded, as if they knew it was their last chance to hitch rides.

Some cars did stop and pick up people, which appeared to give the others hope.

Garth warily eyed the small crowds as he drove along the four-lane avenue, and he made several green lights in a row, which led him to think he was going to get onto the highway without needing to stop in the thick of the people. However, his luck ran out at the last light underneath the overpass. The signal turned red for the left-turn lane to get onto the highway.

"Taxi!" The voice echoed under the bridge where he was stopped.

Floor it, Garth, he thought to himself.

There was no way to get out of the line. He was the second car back, but he hadn't left himself enough room between his front grille and the car ahead of him. He looked over his shoulder, hoping there was room to reverse a few feet, but a huge red SUV rode his bumper.

"This sucks," he said in despair.

Three older men ran up and knocked on his door. He looked at them once to confirm they wore traditional robes of a foreign country, but he didn't want to know any more than that.

"Come on, light," he said under his breath.

Cars passed going the opposite direction, meaning they still had control of the intersection.

"Please!" a man yelled. "Big storm!"

The men were joined by two old ladies, each with babies in their arms. That melted his heart enough that he considered unlocking the doors, but the men began to beat on the back window, scaring him into second thoughts.

"I'm out of service! Sorry!"

Moments went by, and he felt drops of sweat run down his temples next to his eyes. He tapped at the air conditioner in hopes that if he ignored the people they might go away.

Several young men arrived from the other side of the street as if they'd been hanging out under the bridge for a while. They were dressed in shorts and t-shirts like local residents. A couple of those shouted at Garth to open up, and one of them tapped at the window next to his head.

"Come on, asshole! Help someone." He waved a wad of cash larger than Garth had ever seen. "We can pay!"

Now there were at least ten people around his taxi, and more were on the way.

The light finally changed, and the lead car peeled out like it was a race.

That got everyone in a panic. The foreign men pounded on the glass so hard he was positive it would break. The younger guys kicked his door and lobbed some massive F-bombs at him.

He put his foot down and took off.

"I'm sorry!" he shouted.

As he sped up the ramp onto the highway, he realized how bad of a decision it had been to take the cab. He lived in a land where most people didn't need to own cars, and now they had orders to get out of town in a hurry. The yellow cab would be a juicy target for desperate people until he could get well clear of New York City.

When he merged onto the busy highway, he saw more pedestrians walking the shoulder up ahead.

He wasn't home free yet.

Highway 395, California

"Break 19. Anyone? Come back." Buck had only moments before driving into the dusty village of Bridgeport. He tried calling on his CB again.

"I hear you, 19," a gruff man replied. "There is a yellow VW parked on the north side of town. Saw it just now behind a road sign."

"Thank you!" Buck replied excitedly.

A red Kenworth truck came around a corner as it left the town. A man in a straw hat waved to Buck as they passed.

"I see you," the other man added on the CB radio. "Good luck."

"Appreciate it. Watch for a motel back there. Lots of traffic. People think..." Buck let go of the talk button for a second. He looked over to Connie, then back at the town. "Hey, funny question. What year is it?"

"That's hilarious," the guy sent back. "It's 2020."

Buck sighed relief. "Thanks. Keep an eye for a biker gang coming my way. They shot up the motel in Mono Lake."

"Roger. Out."

Buck glanced at Connie again, unsure how she'd react to the date. To her credit, she didn't seem as upset as he expected. "You okay?"

Mac had worked his way until he was almost completely in her lap despite the gun. She didn't seem to mind.

While waiting for her to respond, he made a command decision to veer from the main road onto a gravel side street.

"What are you doing?" she asked.

He reached behind his seat to a small pocket where he kept the paper atlas. "Here, take this. Can you tell me if there are any roads that will let me skip this town? If we don't go past the sign, we can avoid the ambush."

She took the book but looked at him with grave concern. "You think they are going to keep after us? We're in a huge truck. They're in my dainty little car."

"At least one of those guys has a gun. Probably both do. We are in a big truck, but that makes us a huge target. Our best bet is to get lost in the backroads, but I'll have to think of something else if there are no other roads."

Freddy the GPS could have helped him, but it wasn't that good at impromptu changes. Once he drove off the plotted route, it would complain and ask him to return to the assigned course instead of recalculating a new path. He couldn't drive the truck and study the small screen either, so the paper maps were ideal.

"Yes," she said after studying it for ten or fifteen seconds. "This gravel street meets a paved route a block ahead. If you go left, it goes into Nevada, but there is nothing for many miles."

It impressed him she could read a map with such skill.

They picked up the paved road and sped away as fast as Buck's hands and feet could work the controls. He kept his eyes on the side mirrors as they drove along the bank of a long, thin lake until they finally rounded a hillside. The VW wasn't in pursuit.

"Well, Connie, I told you, earlier. I think you're stuck with me a bit longer than you thought. Back roads are rarely faster than main roads."

"I don't care. I'm glad to be rid of them."

He shared her jubilation at their escape, but another problem reared its head almost immediately. They'd been traveling in a herd of cars and trucks ever since they left the motel, but now they were alone on the back road. They hadn't seen a car going in either direction in the ten minutes since they left Bridgeport.

Had that been the bikers' plan all along?

Bagram Airfield, Afghanistan

Lieutenant Colonel Phil Stanwick leaned against the window-mounted air conditioner, desperate for it to cool him after his run outside. His Ranger training had him in peak physical condition, but no amount of preparation helped him resist the punishing heat of the drought-stricken country. It was also why he chose to run at eleven at night.

He stood up when he heard someone come into the makeshift changing room of the Army gymnasium.

"Great run, sir!" one of them said to him.

He waved dismissively, although he was inwardly pleased he was able to keep up with the youngsters.

Maybe they went easy on you?

That was unlikely because it went against the Ranger code. As he got older, he had to train harder. So far, he'd managed to hold his own. His men wouldn't let him go soft, because it could get someone killed.

Another man came in and stood nearby.

"Sir, you asked to be informed if NORAD followed up on their inquiry. They just did." Specialist Matt Carbon was one of the communications liaisons from Regimental HQ.

"Thanks, Matt. Come back here. Let's talk."

Matt came into the locker room. It was only the two of them.

"Sir, NORAD was interested in how we brought in those Russian tanks, but they've also sent word that they believe there will be other strange sightings. They want us to report anything...unusual."

"More unusual than what we've already found? That will be the day."

Phil Stanwick had been in and out of the Afghan theater his whole career, but he'd never seen anything like the missing Russian tanks. When the Air Force drone had spotted the unusual unit, his Rangers were sent out to capture the tanks. They had them rounded up and placed in a couple of the aircraft revetments at Bagram until someone up the chain could figure out whether the operators were prisoners of war or just lost.

He couldn't imagine what else might show up.

"My boys will report anything they find. The colonel knows that."

"Of course," Specialist Carbon replied. He leaned closer. "I think something big is happening, sir. The signals people are in a tizzy over at HQ. How NORAD got involved, no one knows."

"Thanks," he replied.

"I'll tell them we spoke. Whatever happens from here on out, at least we can say we prepared ourselves."

Matt left, and Phil headed for the shower. With luck, the water wouldn't be a hundred degrees. The geniuses who had built the place had put the giant water tanks out in the sun, so they seldom had truly cold water except in the winter.

He spent his shower trying to imagine what could be bigger than finding a platoon of Soviet tankers who looked and acted exactly like they were from 1989.

THIRTEEN

Highway 182, California

Buck and Connie traveled at least ten miles beyond Bridgeport and still hadn't seen a car going in either direction. The hilly desert country revealed no human presence other than the highway, and he wanted to take his mind off all the things that could go wrong.

"So..." he drawled. "What were you doing before you got wrapped up in this mess? You mentioned being at a writer's conference?"

Connie shook her head. "I'm sorry. I can't think about that right now. It's just a lot to absorb, you know? I'm in a different time. I've lost years of my life. I wonder what happened to my son."

He brightened up. "That will be easy. Once we get somewhere with the internet or a cell tower, we can look up the number..."

"Can I try now?" She pointed to the phone attached to the dashboard.

"Sure, but it hasn't been working reliably for me. Do you know who to contact?"

She grabbed the phone and dialed. "I'll start with my son's number."

While she held the phone to her ear, he got Mac's attention by pulling down one of his jerky treats. "Here, boy. Let's leave the pretty lady alone."

The Golden was a sucker for those treats. He slid off Connie's lap and made his way between the seats to where Buck held out the meat stick. Just before Mac grabbed it, he tossed it onto the sleeper bed.

"Go on back there," he said in a friendly voice.

It wasn't long before Connie put the phone back in the cradle. "The line went dead."

"Yeah, communications are in the toilet. When we get to a bigger town, we should be able to get a better signal. We can even use a landline as long as those bikers aren't around to jump us."

She brushed the dog fur off her dress.

"I figured you could use a break," he added, pointing into the back. "Big Mac can stay off you for a few minutes."

"You told him to get off the pretty lady," she said in a hard-to-read tone.

Buck sat up straight like he'd been caught napping at the wheel. "I didn't mean it like that. Well, what I meant was..."

Connie laughed. "I know how you meant it. Thank you for getting me away from those assholes. It looks like we made it."

Buck gripped the wheel like he was wringing out a towel. Even his clumsy attempts at a compliment didn't distract him from the sense he was wasting time at the expense of his son.

"You're welcome, but I don't think we're free yet. This road was a mistake."

"Are you sure?" She looked in the mirror and then up ahead. "It's nice and empty."

"That's what worries me. What if the VW parked where it was going to be seen so I'd do this exact thing? The guys in your car could link up with chasers on bikes, and they could come out here and harass us without fear of being stopped by other cars."

She thought for a second. "I guess it makes sense, but I haven't seen any of them. Are you sure?"

"No," he admitted. "But this road could go on for a hundred miles. They wouldn't need to be in a rush to catch us, because I can't go as fast on these curvy back roads."

"Well, what do you propose?" she pressed.

"Turn around. Get back on the main road. Face those dirtbags in the open if we have to."

She seemed uncertain, so he turned to his pal. "Mac, should we turn around?"

He barked once, which was what he almost always did when he heard his name.

"See? He agrees."

Connie turned to the dog. "Should we keep going forward?" After a brief pause, she added, "Mac."

Big Mac barked again.

Buck gave her a sideways glance. "How the hell did you figure that out?"

"I know a thing or two about dogs," she replied with a wide smile that made him wish it was safe ahead.

"I need to turn around," he said dryly.

Connie didn't complain, as he had thought she would. She adjusted the 10/22 on her lap now that Mac wasn't there. "It's okay. I recognize a man in deep thought. You haven't stopped thinking since I climbed aboard. I know you're trying to keep me safe."

"I have a son I'm trying to get back to. He's counting on me to get this rig all the way across the continent. It was hard enough with just Mac and me, because the world has changed. It hasn't been right since the blue light yesterday."

"It's okay. I get it. You can let me out fairly soon; I'm sure of it."

He reached over and touched her gently on the arm. "No. It isn't that. I know you feel lost and alone because of the time issue, but please don't. Whatever has screwed up the world for you has also done it to me."

Buck got his hand back on the wheel, eyeing a place up ahead where he could turn his Peterbilt around.

His focus was on the U-turn for the next minute. Connie was quiet. He couldn't tell if it was a good or bad thing.

Once the truck was faced back toward Bridgeport, he got up the nerve to say what was really on his mind.

"There is safety in numbers, Connie. I know it means a greater risk of running into those guys in your car, but we can't cross Nevada on remote backroads with no one to call for help."

He wasn't Mad Max, and this wasn't a movie. Connie was a survivor, like him, and getting her to safety made him think in more dimensions than only about himself. As he drove back toward the town and its meager population, he steeled himself for what was coming.

Mac came up and sat between the two front seats, looking at the dashboard as if it were interesting to him. When Buck noticed, he reached for him out of habit, but Connie had done the same thing, so their hands bumped again.

"Sorry," he said.

"Don't worry about it. He's a fine dog."

The lone wolf part of his brain went back into his den. He glanced over at Connie. A new instinct gripped him, and he knew it wasn't only because she was a beautiful redheaded cowgirl.

She was a mother fighting to learn what happened to her son. She was part of their shared drama with the bikers. She was willing to stick around and help him.

The sheepdog part of his psyche came out and took a seat where the wolf had been.

I'll get us all to safety. "We're both going to find out what happened to our sons."

Search for Nuclear, Astrophysical, and Kronometric Extremes (SNAKE). Red Mesa, Colorado

Over the next hour, Faith's team confirmed the beam went directly to CERN, in Geneva, Switzerland. It did answer one mystery but created many new ones. The general ordered a meeting in the administration conference room to discuss their next course of action.

Faith ensured everyone was inside, then shut the door for privacy.

"Thank you, Dr. Sinclair. Before I get started, I have some news." He looked at the men and women at the table. "Summer Storm Audrey gained strength overnight as it straddled the coastline in North Carolina and Virginia. It wrecked towns in the same way the giant California storm destroyed parts of Sacramento and Modesto yesterday. Today, Audrey has been upgraded to a Category Four hurricane. Please keep Washington D.C., Baltimore, and New York in your thoughts."

"Now," he went on, "what were the results of the interference test?"

Faith almost asked what he was talking about, but one of the NORAD scientists spoke up. "We tried putting six inches of lead into the beam, but it had no visible effect. The beam passed through it like it wasn't there, same as it does for the metal loop."

"And what time was that experiment run?"

The scientist looked at a notepad. "10:05 am."

"Wait?" Faith raised her hand, though it wasn't required. "I wasn't told there would be an experiment of this nature. Why wasn't I informed? I'm still in charge here. General, your people may be smart, but they don't have the experience in this facility. They could damage something. I—"

General Smith held up his hand and looked at his phone for a few seconds. "Point made, doctor. I think we know enough now to restore you to the top of the chain of command within the science community. We can't afford to politic the shit out of this program."

"Well, thank you," she said slowly but with appreciation.

"And I'm releasing your people back into the main complex, doctor," he said to Faith. "But no one leaves until I get more answers. Is that understood?"

It was a victory for her. Despite the complaints to the general, she didn't want her staff released from the auditorium so they could head home. She wanted them to stay in SNAKE. If things were as bad on the outside as she had been told, her critical scientists might never return once they left the property. That could be detrimental to solving the giant riddle.

And the traitor might be stuck here, too. She regretted keeping them from their families, but she was driven and single. She only sympathized so much. To her, the job always came first.

"We'll get everyone working on this. I promise you."

"I expect no less." He stood up at the head of the table. "You guys are the tip of the spear in this fight. Tell me how this collider device became a weapon. Tell me what that link to CERN is doing. And for God's sake, tell me how we can fix all this."

Everyone nodded in agreement.

"I need immediate options," he went on. "The first question I want answered is whether we can turn off or otherwise disrupt the metal box in the tunnel." He looked at his aide over by the door. "Did we find any others?"

The aide motioned yes. "We dropped off men at each subway station and had them fan out in the tunnels. Our first pass revealed three other devices."

"Shit," Faith mumbled under her breath.

"Anything else, Lieutenant?" the general asked.

The aide went on, "They are aligned so that the beams from the four boxes create a plus sign when seen from above. We are also exploring other cavities inside the SNAKE complex, but so far we haven't found any additional illicit hardware. The search is ongoing, however, and may yield more."

The general looked at Faith.

"Four devices. Someone inside this base is a traitor to your research, Dr. Sinclair. Each had to be placed in your collider ring, apparently at extremely specific locations. Someone wanted things to go nuts outside. If I had unlimited time, I would fire you and every person in this place and scrub it clean of these devices. As it is, I have to put my trust someone because I can't do it alone."

The general didn't seem pleased with his decision.

"We'll figure it out," she replied in a firm tone. "Even if it kills me."

"Uh huh," he replied indifferently. "I need answers. Meanwhile, you don't mind if I interview some of your key staff, do you? Did anyone leave the facility yesterday before we arrived?"

"I don't mind if you interview my people. I want to get to the bottom of this as much as you do." She screwed up her face in distaste. "I'll ask my assistant if we had any early departures yesterday. Most of us were here all day to analyze data."

"Great. Fine. Look, I think we've got a plan. You all can go, except Dr. Sinclair. I need a word."

She waited until everyone had left, then shut the door. Bob gave her a wink just before the door closed, making her wonder what his game was.

General Smith spoke first. "I hate to say it, but you were right. I brought these young geniuses in to help out, but they are going to get someone killed. That experiment with the lead bar was their idea, and I let it go because I trusted they knew what they were doing."

"I wouldn't have authorized it, but it was good data. At least we know there was no harm in it."

"An optimist—I like that. I didn't say anything in the meeting, but something *was* harmed. Before I say what, I want to point out that while I have given you more responsibility, I don't fully trust you, nor do I have any trust for the other members of your team. However, a general has to go to war with the army he has, not the one he wants. This thing will go belly-up if I rampage through here like I want to."

"I think I understand," she replied.

"You are in charge of your people, but I'm in charge of

this facility. If you do anything that suggests you aren't playing for my team, you're gone. I'll put Dr. Stafford or the Indian woman in charge. It doesn't matter to me."

Not even Bob could have orchestrated this to enhance his own career.

She redirected the conversation. "You were saying that something happening?"

"Yes, thank you." He pointed at his phone. "10:05. That was when he tried to block the signal with the lead bar. At exactly the same moment, I lost twenty-five of the thirty-one GPS satellites from my constellation. It could have been a coincidence, but I doubt it. Do you know what it means?"

She sat heavily in the closest chair, which happened to be the one she had been sitting in when she scratched her name off the table's surface yesterday. Back then, she had believed it was her career going down the tubes. Now the general was showing her that much more was at stake.

"It means we're all screwed," she whispered.

FOURTEEN

Highway 182, California

"Connie, would you mind trying my son again? I really need to talk to him."

She grabbed his cell phone from the cradle and took a moment to study it. "This does look futuristic compared to my Blackberry."

He chuckled. "Garth would tell you this phone is yesterday's garbage. Nothing is ever good enough for him when it comes to tech. He's always asking for the latest gadgets, laptops, and phones, but I can barely afford the monthly cell phone plans, much less the newest models."

"Well, it sounds like you are raising him right. You give him what he needs, not what he wants."

"Yeah, I guess." He didn't want to get into his recent change of heart about how he'd been raising him. Spending all his time out on the road. Having his boy stay with another family. Once he was back, he'd have a heart-to-heart with Garth about their future. Connie wouldn't care about all that.

"I should press this?" She showed him the redial button

and he nodded.

After they'd turned around and backtracked on the blacktop, he figured it was the perfect time to try to catch his son and answer some of his questions.

"It's ringing," she said with excitement. "Wait...no. It went dead."

"Shit," Buck replied. "Not even voicemail?"

"No. Just silence."

It didn't surprise him. He told her the number for the landline and she dialed that next, but it also failed.

He took a deep breath and looked at his two companions. The redhead diligently pressed redial, brushed aside her long, wavy hair, then held the phone to her ear. When the line went dead, she tried again.

Mac stood between the seats next to Connie as if unsure if he should wedge himself in front of her as he'd done earlier. Maybe he was okay with this new person in his seat.

"All right. Forget about the phone for now. We've got to get back to civilization, and we have to go that way to do it." He pointed south toward Bridgeport.

Connie sighed. "It's kind of like calling a radio station. I was hoping to get through."

"I'll have plenty of time to try once I'm on interstate 80. Reception should be better up there. Thanks for trying."

She placed the phone back in the cradle on the dashboard.

"He's young. I'm positive he's safe," she said. "My son would have hopped in his car and gotten into trouble."

Buck felt a sinking feeling but tried to keep it out of his reply. "Yeah, my son is fifteen and doesn't have his own car, so I think I'm okay."

He doesn't have his own car, but he does have access

to one...

As he gave the Peterbilt more gas, he took comfort in thinking that Garth was most likely in the basement practicing with the guns. He was proud he'd divulged that information in dramatic fashion for his son. The shiny objects would keep Garth distracted until he could get through to him on the phone. He was sure of it.

Staten Island, NY

Garth joined the procession of traffic headed for the bridge off Staten Island. He wasn't the only taxi on the interstate, so he didn't stand out as much as he had in his neighborhood. However, numerous people walked along the shoulder of the highway and tried to flag down every cab that passed, including his, so he had to stay vigilant.

"I'm sorry, people," he said to himself.

The cloudy skies became darker as he went south, and a gentle rain began a few minutes later. It immediately made it more difficult for him to see the sad-looking people walking next to the road, but the rain also caused some brake lights up ahead, which slowed everyone down.

A mile later, his speedometer needle hovered around twenty as the cars and trucks trudged along the slippery highway.

"You said I had three hours!" he complained. The news broadcast had advised people to escape or stay inside because the hurricane was about three hours away. He'd barely been gone fifteen minutes before the rain began. That either meant the storm was bigger than they thought, or it was moving faster than they predicted. Either way, he needed to make up time.

He patted the pistol in his pants pocket and wondered if

he'd done the right thing by going out. He hadn't been able to ask Dad in real time what he should do, so he had taken the initiative. He tried his best to anticipate what he'd need on his journey, and he was loaded down with guns, food, and water, but the sudden rain squalls and crowds of desperate people made him think he'd underestimated the danger.

"You can never predict what people are going to do," he mumbled. That was something Dad always said. Normally his father reserved the statement for the lighter side of humanity, such as when people took dumps next to toilets in the subway stations rather than in them, but this time the lesson was more serious. Garth already had encounters with several desperate people trying to get into his car. Hundreds more walked in the nearby breakdown lane, and he had no idea what they'd do.

I could turn around.

As if to suggest it was a bad idea, a wave of nausea and dizziness washed over him. It passed almost immediately, but he had no time to think about it because a silver car on his left nearly veered into his lane. He mashed the horn to alert the guy, but his warning was drowned by hundreds of other horns from inside the traffic jam.

"What the hell was that?" he said breathlessly.

The rain increased from a light sprinkle to cascading sheets of water in the snap of a finger. Visibility reduced to almost nothing. Ahead, the highway filled with fuzzy red lights.

"No, don't slow down," he demanded of other drivers as he fought the fear. The men and women on the side of the road had no shelter from the storm. He was sympathetic to their plight, but he couldn't help them. His biggest fear was they would mob him and take the cab.

Dad would be pissed if I let that happen.

A crack of thunder made him flinch in shock because there was no flash of lightning to give him a warning.

"Dude!" He exhaled.

The rain clouds pressed in and turned the world green. The cars ahead slowed to walking speed, so Garth had to match it. He strangled the steering wheel in nervousness as he rode the bumper of the van ahead of him. He had to put on his headlights, which he realized everyone else had already done.

As soon as his lights came on, a man appeared as he ran across the highway in front of Garth's nearly-stopped taxi.

"What the hell?" He tapped the brakes, but since he wasn't going more than a few miles per hour, he stopped instantly. A horn complained from behind.

The dark shape ran around the front fender and came up to his window.

"Let me in!" The man tapped the glass with something metallic. It was difficult to make out in the torrential downpour, but he was almost certain it was a gun.

"I'm out of service!" he shouted back. It would take a miracle for the guy to hear him because of the rain beating on the car.

The soaked person looked like he could have been a serial killer from the local summer camp. Garth instantly knew terror.

What do I do?

The man tapped again, and he was joined by people pounding at the rear passenger window. Garth whipped his head in surprise to see who they were, but he only saw two indistinct black shapes in the murky rainstorm.

The man on his left shouted to the new people, and deep male voices shouted back.

Garth patted the pistol in his pocket again.

What would Dad do?

The closest man moved back a bit and brandished the metal object toward the newcomers. Those people cursed him, but Garth got a better look at the weapon when it flashed in the headlights of the car behind him.

It wasn't a gun, but a knife.

Garth pulled out the PX 4 Storm Subcompact. It was identical to the one Dad carried in his truck. He and Dad had fired them together the first weekend he'd brought them home. Never in a million years had he thought he'd need to use it in self-defense.

The highway crawled along at a few miles per hour. The pedestrians moved along with the cars, including the people surrounding his taxi.

Just go away, he said to himself.

He gripped the black metal weapon, but disappointed himself by how much his hand shook. He steadied his breathing and concentrated on the fundamentals he'd been taught.

Always keep it pointed away from things you don't want to kill. No finger on the trigger until ready to use. Always assume it's loaded.

He flicked off the safety and pulled the slide to rack the first round.

Dad always said the best deterrent during a home invasion was the sound of a shotgun racking a round. He wished something similar would happen in his taxi, but the rain beat down on his windshield and roof so hard that Garth barely heard the round go in.

The people continued to shout back and forth in the downpour. Garth sensed the desperation of both parties, and if he could have taken his time to pick up decent-looking stragglers, he might have let someone in. But not like this.

The man with the knife cupped his hands around his face and looked inside Garth's window. "You've got to let me in! These people have Ebola!" He pointed to the far side of the cab.

The two drenched figures trotted up to the passenger-side front window to defend themselves from the charge. "No! Let us in! Radiation is almost here!"

Garth kept the gun between the two front seats so neither party could see it, but he was ready. The cars ahead still weren't making better than walking pace, so he couldn't hit the gas and leave these people behind as he so desperately wanted.

His vision lingered on the two shapes to his right because they didn't appear armed. It was hard to tell if they were men or women because there was so much water dumping on them. The wipers swished back and forth like maniacs.

"Please, I'm not—"

The glass on his left shattered.

Garth jerked away from the window. "Holy shit!"

He accidentally fired the gun into the floorboard.

"Fuck me!" he screamed in reaction to what he'd done.

The man had used the butt of his knife to crack the side window. Pieces of glass were all over Garth, but the attacker ducked and ran after the gunshot at point-blank range.

He checked the other side of the car, but those people also disappeared.

The acrid smell of the gun blast filled the interior of the cab, adding emphasis to what he'd done, but it quickly dissipated due to the broken window. Diesel fumes and the stench of gasoline mixed with the odor of gunpowder and rain.

Steady, Garth. At least you didn't shoot your foot off.

He would have never lived that down.

Garth breathed in and out like he'd run a four-minute mile, and his ears rang from the surprise blast. He tried to look for where the bullet had gone into the floor but put that task aside as the cars started moving again.

The silver car to his left moved along as if nothing had happened. He didn't know what he'd expected. Was the guy going to roll down his window to see if Garth had been shot? That didn't seem likely. Not in New York City.

"Nothing to see here," he quoted from a movie.

There were no police lights visible in the darkness of the storm, which gave him mixed feelings. They weren't going to arrest him for shooting the gun, but they weren't going to arrest the knife-wielding window breaker either.

Since he was on his own, he stayed alert for his attacker as best he could. He kept a sharp watch out his shattered side window since it was his weak spot now. The roar of rain and booms of thunder sounded distant and muted, even as his left side became soaked with rain.

He never stopped checking his mirrors until they were moving fast enough that no one could catch him on foot. He let out a deep breath many minutes later, when he felt far enough away from the scene of the crime.

Finally, thirty minutes after the attack, as he was on the bridge crossing from Staten Island into New Jersey, he put the safety back on and pushed the pistol into his pocket.

He allowed himself to chuckle when he realized his greatest fear wasn't that he'd been attacked with a knife, or that the police might pull him over. It was that he'd broken one of Dad's rules about guns.

FIFTEEN

Bridgeport, California

Buck watched the empty road leading back to the small town. Somewhere ahead a yellow VW waited with two gang members inside. Both were armed. Buck had his nine millimeter, and Connie carried the small caliber rifle. Buck counted the eighteen-wheeler as an added asset. The VW didn't stand a chance against the big rig if it came down to a game of bumper cars.

They passed the first house. "Here we go," he said as matter-of-factly as possible. He turned onto a cross street and quickly reached the main drag.

Bridgeport consisted of one major street with about five blocks of shops and motels. The wide street had four lanes of traffic through the business district, but the two north-bound lanes were the busiest.

A few people walked the streets and waved at traffic as if curious to see the parade go through their sleepy town. The VW had last been seen behind a sign on the main road leading out of town. Buck hoped they were still there. He needed to reduce what he didn't know.

"This town is tiny," Connie commented. The last house was already in sight.

"I don't see them," he replied.

Buck spotted a little girl fifty yards ahead standing in a small park. She continually pumped her arm in the universal "please blow your air horn" request.

At that moment he was the only truck on the strip, so he had gotten her attention. She ran to the edge of the sidewalk and leaned into the road as if that would help.

He glanced at Connie with a wry smile, then laid on the air horn for a full five seconds.

The girl jumped up and down and flailed her arms in happiness as they rolled by. Adults in the nearby park also waved.

"Won't it give us away?" Connie asked as she waved to the girl.

"We're the biggest, baddest thing on this road. Those assholes won't miss us either way. I'm not going to pass up a chance to spread a little joy. Did you see her face?"

"I did." She giggled.

Buck laughed, too. "I should warn you: my ex-wife used to say I sometimes had a tendency to act like a little boy."

She snickered. "I can see why."

"And she didn't mean it as a compliment," he added.

"Some women can't handle the typical male. They want to beat the boy out of them." She sounded sympathetic, which made him want to ask what she meant, but as they left the edge of town, he saw them.

"There!" he shouted. The bikers were parked behind a large green highway sign. Most of the car was visible because it sat so low to the ground.

"What's the plan, Buck?" Connie asked.

"Do what we have to."

"Like at the motel?"

"If we have to. If you point the rifle at them, be ready to pull the trigger."

Buck's eyes went blurry for a second, and he slowed the truck in response. The sun went behind some clouds, and the sky turned dingy gray.

"Whoa!" he exclaimed.

"It wasn't just me?" Connie asked. "The world shimmered for a second."

"I saw it too." He regained his senses and ignored what had happened because he was about to engage the enemy. "Stay frosty."

The two burly men sat in the front seat, watching the truck as it rolled their way. "These guys wanted to be seen," he said to himself.

The gun was on his center console, but he had a more effective weapon. He needed to stop hoping for a good outcome. It was time to take charge and force the outcome he needed.

"Hang on, guys," he said to Connie and Mac. He pushed a couple of buttons on the dashboard.

He accelerated to thirty miles per hour as he approached the VW, and he saw the two men both raise pistols and hang them out their windows. They planned to fire as he drove by. That was the moment he knew he was doing the right thing.

Buck jammed the wheel to the right and pointed his 80,000-pound truck at the small sign and the tiny car behind it.

The driver opened fire.

"Shit!" Connie screamed as she ducked.

A single bullet went through the glass of his windshield almost exactly where the rearview mirror would have been.

Buck's reaction was to duck a little, but he stayed high enough to see where he was going.

A couple more gunshots clapped through the air, but Buck lost sight of the shooter because the VW went below the end of his hood.

His heavy truck plowed into the road sign, which crumpled over on top of the Beetle. The Peterbilt continued through the sign's moorings like they were made of plastic, then bashed into the nice yellow car with the two thugs inside.

The impact made him and Connie lurch forward in their seats, but he'd pushed the buttons to deactivate the airbags so they didn't deploy. Mac had it worse because he wasn't buckled in. He slid on the floor and ran into the shifter with a yelp.

The VW shot off like a yellow billiard ball crushed by a powerful break. Buck hit the brakes after contact, and his truck stayed upright as it slid on the shoulder of the road for thirty or forty yards. The car rolled many times because of its ball-like shape, and Buck imagined it would have kept going forever if it hadn't tumbled into a small creek, out of view.

Buck thought about getting out of the truck and making sure the guys were good and hurt, but he worried about getting unlucky. If one of the guys was still alive and still able to fire a gun, he could just as easily get a round between the eyes for his effort.

The safe play was to back up his truck, rejoin the flow of traffic, and disappear.

He reached down to check on Mac. He'd gotten on his feet and stood looking at his human with curiosity, as if to say, "Drive much?"

Connie was fine, too.

"I should have asked you if that was okay to do to your car," he said with some regret. "I figured it was safer than either of us getting shot."

"I'll send you a bill," she said in a deadly serious tone before giggling to reveal it was a joke. "For the second time today, you protected me. Do it a third time, and you might have a permanent passenger. What do you say we get the hell out of here?"

"My thoughts exactly." Buck maneuvered the truck out of the impact zone, listening and feeling for any mechanical changes in his truck. To his relief, the truck responded when he backed up. Nothing was jammed in the axles, and no tires were blown. There were no creaks or squeals.

He entered the traffic lane and ran through the gears until he hit the highway speed limit.

"Let's hope that's the last we see of those scumbags," he replied with as much hope as he could summon.

They had to slow two miles down the road. Buck couldn't believe his eyes. Traffic had come to a stop, but not because of a fantastic crash.

It was June in the Nevada desert, but snow was coming down like cotton-candy whitewash.

"What now?" he asked.

Canberra, ACT, Australia

Destiny walked with Zandre around the side of the house, but her friend tripped and fell as he reached the stairs to the wrap-around porch.

"Zandre!" she said with surprise.

A dizzy feeling forced her to kneel to avoid falling.

"Wow," she said as she blinked away the sensation.

"I'm all right," Zandre huffed. "Just nicked my ego a bit."

"I felt woozy too," she replied.

They both got to their feet and stood for a moment, but Zandre seemed anxious to forget about it. "Come on. You have to see what we've got here."

They went around to the back of the house to where half a dozen men stood over a long row of animal carcasses. They'd been lined up under the awning of the porch to keep them out of the sun.

She first noticed the Tasmanian Tigers.

A middle-aged man strode up to Zandre. "How the bloody hell are ya, mate? You've got a helluva place here. When are you fixin' to go out again?" He fidgeted with the gun slung over his shoulder like it, too, was anxious to go out.

Zandre was dismissive. "Soon. I've got to show my friend here what's been going on. This could be important for science."

The man seemed unimpressed. "Well, as long as I get one of these trophies. Other blokes say you can't miss out there." He pointed to the dead animals as evidence.

"Yes, yes. Soon." Zandre pulled her away from the man and went beyond the section of Tasmanian Tigers. There were a couple of large marsupials she recognized as recently extinct, and some smaller mammals she'd never seen before, even in books. They then came to a larger beast.

"This funny-looking thing is like a cross between a lion and a black puma. Its coal-colored pelt is totally inappropriate for Australia. We have no idea..."

The animal was beautiful and exactly as he described it, right down to the furry lion's mane, except its fur was all-black.

"All this stuff is just waiting out there to be taken," Zandre said with excitement. "A world of wonderful, beautiful, and very mountable animals."

Faith's words came back to her. Things were messed up with time. That suggested these animals had never seen human hunters and had no idea they needed to run away. If she could get out there and figure out where they were coming from, maybe she could protect them.

Don't do it, Dez.

She had to restrain her preservationist instincts in the presence of the hunters. Based on the little she'd seen, they weren't likely to want to give up this once-in-a-lifetime chance to bag more of the exotic creatures.

A man in his mid-twenties crashed through the rear screen door like he'd been thrown through it. He looked around until he saw Zandre. "Z! Radio just lit up. The second group up by Walker Hill swears they saw that fucking Duck of Doom again!"

A few men standing nearby looked at him with interest, but not much more.

The man seemed to figure no one believed him. "Richard Thompson is with that group. He says he'll pay ten million US dollars to anyone who can get him one. I'm going out!"

The bounty lit a fire under the hunters. The whole camp radiated excitement as the men ran around gathering weapons and gear. Destiny stood where she was, unsure of what to do. The dead animals on the porch were unique and rare, and very valuable to the research community, but if there was something unique and alive, out there, it could be priceless.

Zandre looked at her like he wanted to head out as well.

Destiny paced back and forth, trying to walk through

her options. She could wait until a specimen was brought in or she could go out and see one alive.

"Well, mate, I'm not here to fuck spiders," she replied with the common saying.

"No, that's not your style," he said with a laugh.

"You have a tranquilizer gun I can borrow?" she added.

He almost gasped. "You want to take one alive?"

"I have to see it, yes. You still have a four-wheeler I can use?"

He nodded. "Better hurry. Everyone is going out."

Her whole life had been spent studying animals. Now she had a chance to study something that had been extinct for thousands of years. Whatever magic Faith had done at SNAKE, she wasn't going to ignore the opportunity to observe it any more than the hunters could ignore the call to kill it.

"Bring the tranq gun down to the pond. I'm leaving right now so I have wheels."

"Okay, Dez, but I'm going after it with real bullets. Ten million would keep this place afloat for ten generations."

"Thanks, Zandre. I understand," she replied as she went toward the row of gas-powered four-wheelers. "You brought me here to see something amazing. Those bodies are part of that, but I have to see a living specimen."

More men came out of the trailers as she drove away.

SIXTEEN

Bagram Airbase, Afghanistan

After his shower, Lieutenant Colonel Phil Stanwick hit the rack, intending to get a solid four hours of sleep. The last thing he remembered was feeling a little dizzy as he stared up at the roof of his room, but he attributed it to running five miles with burritos in his stomach. It went away after a few seconds. *Hearty Army gut!* he thought.

He woke up to a sound he instantly recognized as the crump of a distant mortar launch. It was almost below the threshold of hearing, but multiple tours in the hot zone had trained his brain to listen for it, much like the chime of an alarm clock.

Sneak attack!

The Taliban were known for lobbing heavy mortar rounds from the backs of pickup trucks, then blending back into the population.

Phil jumped out of bed, grabbed his sidearm off the table, and rushed out his door. He went into the dark hallway of the officer's quarters shouting, "Incoming!" over and over as he ran. By the time he reached the end of the hallway, he was pleased to see the others stumble out of their doorways behind him.

He stepped outside to a beautiful if eerie sight. Several white flares blossomed in the sky over the two runways, dowsing the base in a soft light that made it look a lot like a snowy, moonlit field on Christmas Eve. An instant later, the base's high-pitched mortar siren spun up and shattered the illusion.

When he started toward the headquarters building, the anti-mortar Phalanx guns sent thousands of red-hot rounds into the sky in long, thin streams like celestial whips. They fired in five-second bursts, and each one sounded like God ripped at the sky itself. His teeth rattled in his head as more of the guns sought out the falling mortar shells.

The intense noise shook him to the core because he was a small cog in the massive war machine, but it wasn't his first time in battle, so he didn't let it delay him. He waved at his men as they ran by, trying to be the stoic leader they expected.

Phil ran too but didn't get far. A man in dark local clothing smashed into him, and they both careened backward and fell to the ground.

When he looked at the other man, he was ready to chew him a new one, but the Taliban soldier's AK suggested this wasn't just a mortar hit-and-run.

Somehow, the attackers were already inside the core defense of the base.

Time dropped into slow motion as he and the other man raised their weapons. The sirens, phalanx cannons, and mortar explosions were sounds from another reality. The billions of dollars of defense technology surrounding the base had failed. Everything came down to who could pull a cheap mechanical trigger before the other guy.

Kill or be killed.

Search for Nuclear, Astrophysical, and Kronometric Extremes (SNAKE). Red Mesa, Colorado

"Donald, may I come in?" After getting her job back from General Smith, she went right to her mentor. There were many things she needed to chat about, but mostly she wanted to ensure that he felt better after the excitement of the day before. He was the only person the general hadn't forced to stay in the auditorium last night.

When he pulled the door open, she couldn't conceal her concern.

"I'm not in my grave yet," he said with a broad smile.

"Sorry, Donald. You look, uh, better?"

"Come in, you kind liar."

They sat side by side on the sofa, as they had the day before. Without his scratch pad and pen, Donald looked like a tired old man rather than a tired old scientist. She feared for his health.

"What is it? What's wrong with you?" He hadn't been right since he'd come back from getting more of his heart medication.

"I think my pacemaker has gone on the fritz. They say you can't feel a pacemaker inside your body, but I know when my heart isn't beating correctly. It's acting like it did before my heart surgery. It's been like this ever since yesterday when I had those dizzy spells in Castle Rock."

"Outside the collider perimeter," she said almost to herself.

"Yeah, why?"

She didn't know if it meant anything, so she changed the subject and quickly explained what she and General

139

Smith had discovered in the ring. She described the four mysterious boxes and the four beams that linked Red Mesa with CERN. Finally, she mentioned General Smith's ultimate goal.

"He wants the beams turned off," Faith explained. "Not that I blame him. He asked us to work up ideas on what might happen to the system."

Donald patted his thigh. "This is all very exciting. You are going to be able to write papers about this for the rest of your career. I wish something this interesting had happened when I was your age."

"Not me. I was perfectly happy writing papers about the same old science we always have. Tiny advancements at a safe speed. This new development scares me. The general made it clear that our facility is affecting the whole world. That's too big a responsibility. I don't want it. I just want things to go back to the way they were."

"Science does its best work when the world depends on it. The atomic age, including ancillary technologies like our dear supercollider, was born out of the destruction of World War II, you know?"

"I know."

"Okay, so tell me about this link. What's your theory?"

She drew a deep breath. "I believe it's causing the ripple effect of the blue light. That energy, whatever we want to call it, is interfering with time. How? I have no idea, but it is, based on observations of cause and effect. General Smith told me the GPS satellites in orbit were losing time relative to the surface, and it is getting worse by the hour. He also said that twenty-five of his satellites went dark when one of the scientists put a lead shield on one of the CERN links."

"So, there are four links around the outer edge of our snake," he said as if studiously examining the evidence. "I wonder how they are getting to CERN? Do they all go to the same point?"

"We only know the beams are pointed there, but they go into the ground and disappear. Obviously, we don't have anyone on the far end to confirm they come out."

"Hmm. Does this general know what happened to our friends in Europe?"

"Only what he's seen on international news. I don't have a phone to try anyone who may have been off-duty at CERN when it exploded. That could really help." She ticked off a mental note as another reason to ask the general to return their phones.

"I have read papers on quantum entanglement and quantum teleportation, but most of the bleeding edge in that field concerns the transmission of data, not mass. Is anything being sent through to this end, like a doorway?" He giggled like a schoolboy. "I don't even know what it would theoretically look like."

She smiled. "The light coming from CERN enters the metal boxes on our end. We can't tell what's inside them, or even how they're powered. Someone had to place the boxes there. Someone on my team."

He nodded gravely, his face suddenly serious. "Is the beam coming or going, or can't you tell?"

"Not by looking at it. I'd need more sensitive equipment."

Donald pressed both hands on his knees, as if his back were sore. "I'll have to think about who has the know-how, but it could just as easily have been a grad student following a floor plan. It didn't have to be a super-genius placing them."

"No, I guess not," she admitted. It suddenly made perfect sense that the real mastermind would probably never be found. "But who would do such a thing? It's like a terrorist attack."

Donald tapped his leg some more. "If someone wanted to destroy civilization, they sure picked an esoteric way of doing it. I wish they would have left a manual for how they accomplished it, though. I'd die a happy man if I knew someone had figured out time travel."

She patted him on the elbow. "You could travel backward in time and be young again."

"Perhaps, but Einstein and his successors have been very stingy about time travel. Forward, relative to contemporaries, maybe. Backward? I very much doubt it. Maybe the beams of energy affect space-time in such a way that objects only appear to come from the past. It might be as likely they are coming from nearby parallel universes. Who knows?"

She didn't expect Donald to have all the answers, but the fact he wasn't quoting formulas or furiously drawing examples on a napkin suggested he was more tired than he let on.

"If it is a doorway," he continued, "then I'd be worried about what happens if we try to close it. If CERN is gone, and we have every reason to think it is, maybe the doorway can never be shut. Or perhaps we'll blow ourselves up if we try to close our side of the door. Makes me wonder if Geneva tried that exact thing, and that's what did them in. If a slice of lead can take out satellites, what would a full stop do?"

Donald put his hand on his chest as if to signify he was done talking. "I would look for other signs, Faith. I wouldn't be surprised to learn that more was affected by the lead bar than just his satellites. That's only what the general knows about. Much as we did with the news yesterday, you should keep track of what has changed today, in case he wants to stick any more lead bars into the experiment."

She would ensure no more blockages would go into the light, but she was already thinking of the possibilities brought out by her short talk with Donald. Even if they found nothing beyond those failed satellites, there was still a whole world suffering under the effects of their broadcast. All the evidence suggested things would continue to get worse if they did nothing.

Stopping the link to CERN could be dangerous, but leaving it alone might be catastrophic.

Highway 395, California

"Do you think we could go back and get my suitcase?" Connie deadpanned a few minutes after the destruction of her car. "I don't have anything to wear."

He'd only known her a short time, so he couldn't tell if she was serious. However, after the tension they'd shared this morning, and given her manner of asking the question, he was almost certain she was pulling his leg.

"Sure. Would you like help rolling your car onto its wheels so you can get inside?"

Both of them chuckled, but it set off a chain reaction of laughter that soon had both of them in tears.

"Can you imagine what those assholes were thinking when we hit them?" she asked at one point.

"Yeah!" he guffawed. "You mess with the bull, you get the horns. This rig is 80,000 pounds."

The laughter took ten minutes to burn off as Buck drove north from Bridgeport, and they never looked back at the Volkswagen in the ditch, despite Connie's mock request. Buck also made contact with several truckers on the CB,

143

and they confirmed there were no bikers in pursuit from the motel in Mono Lake. That only added to their sense of joy and relief.

None of the other drivers could explain why it was snowing like mad in Bridgeport but sunny and hot twenty miles behind. The weird weather forced Buck to do less laughing and more driving.

"Buck," Connie said in a soft voice after she'd settled down. "You could have left me in that town. I'm sure I could have found a ride home. Eventually."

For a while, Buck continued to stare at the brake lights of the cars ahead as he focused on driving in the snow before he finally looked over to her. This time her humor was gone, so he tried to be serious as well. "Did you want to be left there?"

She considered it for a few seconds. "I don't want you to feel obligated to watch over me, but you saw how I was. I couldn't protect myself. You, on the other hand, seem more than capable, although after all that incredible shooting and driving, I think you get some help from Jiminy Cricket."

He laughed. "You believe Jesus can get us through this?"

"I prayed for my son when he went off to war. You said we won against Saddam. I'll take it as a sign."

He furiously worked through her "watch over me" words. If he let her stay and things got back to normal, it wasn't unreasonable to think he'd drive her back across America, much as he'd done with Big Mac the previous two weeks. However, he was hesitant to come out and say that because it might sound creepy to her. Some trucker guy picks her up and wants her to ride shotgun for a few weeks...

Buck opened the door a little.

"Well, I can always use more divine help, but it wouldn't hurt to have an extra set of eyes in the truck. Now, don't get me wrong, Mac is a wonderful lookout, but we've had nothing but setbacks when I try to train him to hold a rifle."

She tested a chuckle. "So, it would be okay to stick with you for a while?"

He had to make sure they were both doing it for the right reasons. "The thing is, I'm heading east, not south. I don't think I can get you home myself. Not right away."

"It's fine. Really. After the motel, I'm more worried about staying alive."

Ever since she had climbed aboard, he'd had a calling to help her. Maybe that was what he required to get his truck across the nation and back to Garth, especially if things continued to worsen outside. Garth was the mission. She was willing to help him achieve it. He accepted that at face value. He couldn't argue with having an extra set of eyes.

He tried to sound nonchalant. "I'm more than happy to have you on board, knowing where I'm going, but it's a big country. Are you sure you want to go to the East Coast at a time when things might fall apart? Don't you have family who will worry about you?"

"If I'm in the wrong time, it doesn't matter where I go, since I don't belong. I'm comfortable in here," she pointed at her seat, "and don't like the madness out there." She gestured expansively through the windshield. "Plus, you risked yourself and your truck for me. Even the police wouldn't go that far. And I love how you protect this little guy." She rubbed Mac's ears with such vigor that his tail started pounding the back of the seat.

"Well," Buck said dramatically, "I guess if he likes you, it might be possible to let you stick around a while."

She reached over and bopped him on the arm.

"I like you both, as well. I could sense it the minute I got in. You two are the good guys, and I'd be honored to join your team."

That sealed it.

Ahead, cars shifted partway out of the lanes as they slid on the snow-covered road. Soon, the two-lane highway would require a plow to keep open.

They had to get beyond the snow before it got that bad. They were still too close to the Sierra Nevada mountains. He was sure that was the reason for the freak storm.

"I think we're going to need chains on the tires." He sighed because they would take a lot of work and time to get on.

She didn't sound as disappointed as he was. "How can I help?"

SEVENTEEN

Somewhere in New Jersey

Garth's sense of direction was good. He managed to cross the bridges and navigate the highways to get him deep into New Jersey, but he fast realized his knowledge of the state was derived from a few trips to the Pine Barrens with his Dad. He didn't want to pull over to check a map on his phone for fear he'd be attacked again, so he went with his mental map from those earlier journeys.

"I'm lost," he said when he finally admitted his internal map had turned blank.

His clothes were soaked from the rain pouring in through the broken window, and he wasn't sure how to block it. Maybe a trash bag and duct tape, if he had them, but then he wouldn't be able to see outside. Any fix would also require a stop, which was still a "no-go," as his dad would say.

The two-lane road took him through endless trees, so he figured he was close to where he and Dad went to shoot, but he needed to go farther south. The news said to get out of

New York and New Jersey, and his goal was to reach the southernmost tip of Jersey and get out that way.

He'd been on the road for about an hour.

Traffic was light in the forest. He had misgivings about taking the crowded highway, but he had no idea where the forest road would take him. Maybe it went directly into the path of the radiation. Instead, he kept going south, toward the middle of the state.

The road wind chilled his wet skin to the bone, despite the summer heat. It had never occurred to him to bring rain gear, although it now seemed obvious he should have dressed for a rainstorm.

The bright side was, the rain came and went. It was often heavy, but never as torrential as the first few minutes back near home. The people on the radio kept saying Hurricane Audrey was getting close but wasn't yet there.

"I can still make it." He wished again that Sam had come with him. His buddy was probably sitting in front of a fire at some posh resort paid for by his parents. While he didn't begrudge his friend's fortune, he did begin to wonder if he should have stuck with Sam after all.

Being in the Pine Barrens reminded him of Dad, however, and the feel of the gun in his pocket and the rifles in the trunk made him appreciate that he had to man up. Dad would demand no less.

"Dad, I hope I'm doing right by you." He kept his phone on the far seat, out of the splashing spray coming through the broken window. Now he leaned over to check if his dad finally left him a message.

There was nothing new.

"Dammit!"

Garth drove for another fifteen minutes, and the number of passing cars dwindled to almost zero. It didn't matter to him, except he was going in a direction no one else cared to go. That sounded alarms in his mind.

He considered turning around and trying a different way or pulling into a gas station to ask someone which way to go, but before he made a decision, a green sign put him back on the right path.

"Eureka!" he shouted. "Garden State Parkway. That's the ticket."

The rain got steadily heavier, which made him think about pulling over in a remote hiding spot, but the echo of the sirens at home kept replaying in his mind. The radiation was coming. He feared that more than any hurricane.

The big highway crossed over the two-lane road up ahead, and the on-ramp veered off to his right. His sense of direction said going right would take him south.

The ramp was designed like a swooping S-curve. Visibility was poor, but he was used to that now. However, about midway through the turn, the steering wheel seemed to stop working and the car drifted to the right. The engine raced like the tires were spinning but not gripping.

"Holy shit!" he screamed as he wildly pulled at the wheel. He was barely doing twenty miles per hour, but the car had a mind of its own and went into a shallow ditch next to the road, stopping a little short of some trees.

The engine sputtered for ten seconds, then quit.

"Oh, hell," he exclaimed in rising panic. The muddy grass outside his window looked close because the car sat in a shallow drainage ditch. He turned the key to try to re-start it and jumped in surprise when it cranked right up.

"Yes!"

His excitement was short-lived, however, when he tried to put it in gear and back up. The wheels spit mud all over the side of the taxi, and some of the chunks came inside and splattered the interior of the windshield.

"Shit. Shit. Shit." His heart raced as his situation dawned on him. The car was perfectly fine, but it was bogged in the mud. He would need help getting it out.

A couple of cars passed while he fought to get the wheels to grip. Another vehicle was parked on the ramp about fifty yards ahead. It hadn't been there a moment ago, and the brake lights were on, like they were waiting to see what he did.

Now he experienced true panic. He was a sitting duck. A beached yellow duck.

The wipers kept enough of the rain off the windshield, so he saw the lurking vehicle. If they were nice, maybe they'd help him out of the ditch and he'd be on his way. If they weren't...

"They can't all be bad guys," he told himself. Dad had reassured him that the world was filled with good guys. Unsung heroes who wanted no recognition for their actions. Folks who would help you out of a jam if you were stuck on the side of the road after midnight.

But he had also warned him about the bad guys. Wolves in sheep's clothing, always in search of the next easy score.

And he sat in a car full of guns and ammo. The wolves would want all of it.

"Make up your mind. Choose a course of action. Stick to it." Dad would be proud that he'd remembered his lessons.

Garth opened the driver's door...

Highway 395, California

The snow came down hard and heavy, but the great

number of warm engines creeping along the pavement prevented accumulation below his treads. Buck kept moving forward without needing to break out his chains.

Driving on the slippery roads was nerve-wracking, so he didn't dare handle his phone himself, but Connie was more than happy to dial the numbers every five minutes for him. After an hour of their routine, she placed the phone in the cradle, then pulled the 10/22 from where she'd jammed it next to her door.

"Mind if I stick this behind my seat? I don't want it to fall out when I open this door."

"Sure. Just as long as you know where it is." He left unsaid that if she needed it, they'd be in real danger. "It has a strap, so you can carry it if you get out. Whatever you do, don't go outside without your gun. If nothing else, it will make people think twice about bothering you."

"Or they'll attack me to get it," she replied in jest.

He remained serious. "That's always a risk of open carry. I tend to believe the bad guys operate under the assumption that people with guns are not to be fucked with. There's easier prey out there."

She lost her humor. "Is that what I am? Prey?"

He laughed it off. "We are both prey, ma'am. Don't think anything of it. It's the benefit of sticking together. If we both have guns, it means we're willing to back each other up. That counts for a lot, even if we don't look like a couple of BAMFs."

"BAMFs?" she asked.

"Bad Ass Mother Fuckers. It's what you are now, okay? Nine-tenths of it is looking the part. You survived a gunfight. You survived an assault. You survived being ripped from 2003. And, last but not least, you didn't even flinch when your car was totaled."

"I did tear up when I got into your truck. That doesn't sound like something a BAMF would do." She laughed a little, suggesting she wasn't totally writing herself off.

"Everyone starts at the bottom. I was a mess after my first engagement in Iraq. I didn't cry, mind you, but I almost pissed myself a river when I realized some of those bullets were aimed at me. It's perfectly normal to be scared out of your skin in these situations. Trust me, you handled yourself as well as anyone possibly could. In fact, I'm glad you cried a little. If you hadn't, I might think you were some sort of psychopath. That would suck."

They shared a warm laugh.

Ahead, the road went through rocky terrain with steep cutouts on each side. The snow didn't cover the red rocks, which made them contrast with the half-foot of snow everywhere else, but red brake lights came on as they traversed the rocky chokepoint.

The road went downhill and curved to the right, and was also covered with snow. He recognized the potential for disaster right away. Buck's legs tensed as he feathered the brakes to keep his truck at about walking pace around the bend.

"They must have been going too fast." Buck barely had time to rubberneck a dozen cars and one big rig in a ditch next to the road. They were piled up like a bunch of kid's toys. Some of the small vehicles had been crushed beyond recognition.

"Holy moly," Connie declared as she gawked at the scene. "Shouldn't we help them?"

Don't get involved, he thought.

There were no ambulances or police cars. A lone eighteen-wheeler was pulled to the side of the road, facing the direction Buck traveled. It would be easy to justify that someone was already there to help.

Don't get off mission.

"We should at least see if we can help, shouldn't we?" Connie's tone suggested she thought it was a good idea.

At the last moment, he pulled onto the shoulder in front of the other trucker. It would ensure he had room to maneuver if he had to leave in a hurry. He would never again let himself get trapped like he had been back at the motel, although he committed to ramming his way out if necessary.

"You wait here," he said to Connie as he threw on the e-brake. He left the motor running, which was standard practice for him.

"I thought we were a team?" she replied with a little disappointment.

"And right now, I need you to watch my, uh, *our* rig. Don't let anyone in, okay?" He didn't want to scare her, but she had to know it was an important task. "If anyone tries to get in, you shoot them."

He picked up the small rifle and handed it to her. "I'll be back as fast as I can. I'm only going to see if help is on the way. That's all."

She took the rifle. "I'll do as you ask, but I don't even know if I can fire this."

He gave a quick refresher. "It's ready to fire. Simply press this safety release, then pull the trigger to shoot. Make sure nothing is behind your target, like me or Mac." He smiled, then slid out his door.

Mac jumped on the vacated seat and looked down at him. "Take care of Connie," he said to his friend.

Cars and trucks continued to pass him on the road as he walked back to the other truck. He noticed the man sat in the cabin of his Blue Mack, so he waved until he was recognized. The driver gestured for him to come over to his side step.

"Hey," Buck said as the guy opened his window. He shivered because he wore a short-sleeved Hawaiian shirt instead of a heavy coat.

"Hey, driver," the older man said back. "You going into that mess?"

Buck shook his head. "I felt bad driving by like we don't have a problem in the world. Is there anything we can do?"

The guy held up his CB microphone so Buck could see it. "I've been trying. I get plenty of trucks, but no emergency services within a hundred miles. I was able to relay a message through six different drivers up to Reno, but it could be an hour before anyone gets here."

Buck looked at the pileup. The long white trailer of the semi-truck had detached and flipped over. Plain cardboard boxes had been flung over the white snow like someone serving up pieces of bread to the birds. At least two of the cars were on fire, creating thick black smoke at both ends of the pileup.

Despite his misgivings, he felt obligated to get a bit closer and take a quick peek. "I think we should—"

Gunshots snapped in the cold silence over from the area of the wrecks.

"Aw, shit," the man in the cab exclaimed. "Things are getting hot over there."

More gunshots indicated it wasn't only one person doing the shooting.

Buck's mind switched faster than Houdini's hands. "I can't get into another shootout. Hey, I'm on channel 4. Buck Rogers. Let's stick together." He waited long enough to see the man give him a thumbs-up sign.

"I'm Clarence, but I go by Sparky on the squawk box. I'll follow you." He started to roll up his window but stopped. "*Another* shootout? You've been in one today?"

Buck waved. "We'll talk. I have to go!"

He ran back to his rig.

Being with her was already paying off. He realized her positive effect on him as he climbed into the cabin. As much as he wanted to help those in need, he wasn't going to voluntarily enter a gunfight. The old Buck might have considered it.

He resolved to tell the first emergency services person he passed on the road or heard on the CB. It was the only sensible thing left for him to do.

EIGHTEEN

Search for Nuclear, Astrophysical, and Krono-metric Extremes (SNAKE). Red Mesa, Colorado

"Doctor Sinclair!" Benny shouted. "Wait up!"

Faith had left Donald in his room and was heading back to Bob and Sunetra when the Denver newspaperman spotted her from fifty yards away.

"What are you doing back?" she asked as he trotted up to her. He'd spent all of the previous day at SNAKE and left with the other reporters when the general took over, but it didn't surprise her at all to see him back so soon. He was tenacious.

"I never left," he remarked. "I watched the Humvees in the parking lot to see what they were up to. Last night I slept in my car, but this morning I came inside as soon as I saw someone at the front desk. It surprised me that the military guards let me right in."

"Yeah, well," she said as she looked up and down the hallway, "you may regret that decision. You can get in, but I don't think they're letting anyone leave."

"Like Hotel California," he said dryly.

"Yeah, just like it." She smirked.

He pulled out his phone. "Should I call my wife and let her know I'm okay? I sent her some texts last night, but if I'm staying..."

Faith brushed his arm to get him to hide the phone. "Don't let them see it or they'll take it away." Then, thinking of the tenuous level of trust she had with General Smith, "Shit, Benny. I wish you wouldn't have shown it to me. Come here."

She led him into one of the many unused offices and shut the door.

"I can't knowingly let you run around with a phone, Benny. We've all had ours confiscated."

"Seriously? That's a massive swat at the Constitution. Did you mention it to the Army guys?"

"They're Air Force, actually. And no, I didn't interrupt their shakedown to quote the law. I'm not at liberty to publicly state what is going on here, but I believe it to be very important. All I can tell you is no other news organization that I know of is here. And if they were, they wouldn't get anything more than what I'm telling you now. I hope you understand."

"I've heard there is something important happening down in the collider ring. Care to comment?"

She pursed her lips to stall for time, because he must have meant the strange boxes they'd found. There was no way he could know about the link to CERN unless someone had fed it to him.

"I'm not sure I—" she began.

"Oh, come on. Everyone knows, doctor. I hear it discussed in the hallways. They are talking about shutting down the cryo, which suggests something major has happened. Doesn't it take two weeks to re-start and re-cool everything?"

"A month," she deadpanned.

"A month," he repeated. "And even if you are willing to spend a month offline, won't your benefactors get a little peeved? We're talking about a huge story. Come on! Tell me what's happening."

She was in a difficult spot, but she returned again to trust.

"Benny, do you trust me?" She gave the young reporter a hopeful look.

"Well, you did come through on getting me into the press conference yesterday." He said it like it was a stubborn admission. "But you didn't give me an exclusive."

She chuckled. "To be fair, my press conference was halted before I could offer anyone an exclusive interview."

"The military guys said there was a terrorist threat. It was a lie, wasn't it? If it had been terror, none of us would be here."

After a long pause, Benny kept talking.

"I take your silence as an acknowledgment of something big. You've got to tell me. The national news is swamped with unusual earthquakes and freak storms, and now there's talk about ice getting out of control at the poles. All planes are grounded, and road travel has become as dangerous as Russian roulette. Nobody knows what's going on, and it is freaking people out. If you know something, you have to share it."

Faith kept up her poker face. "Benny, if you trust me, I'll swap you the phone for a promise I will tell you everything I know as soon as I'm cleared to do so."

He stepped away from her. "But I need my phone. How will I contact my paper? My wife? How will I read the news? There's a ton of stuff going on out there. In the last few minutes, I've gotten fifty alerts! The world's gone apeshit."

"And you're in here, I get it. If you work with me, I'll do my best to keep you in the loop. It may not be "apeshit" quality stuff, and you may not be able to report on it in real time, but you'll have access other reporters can only dream of."

Another good reason jumped out at her, and it would make her pitch to General Smith much easier. "Frankly, I don't see why we need more than one reporter here. You can be our exclusive partner."

He appeared to think about it. "That's a generous offer, but the ape stuff is amazing. Did you know the Coors brewery looks like it did fifty years ago? It's only ten miles north of here."

"Well, they must not like changes," she replied.

"No. You're missing the point. The whole brewery reverted to what it looked like fifty years ago. The people didn't change. The machinery did. It got old."

The old came forward in time. Like a rubber band.

"Interesting," she said noncommittally, trying not to give away that she knew about similar events. Her abrupt wording got Benny's keen attention.

"Did the general kick us out because something in here is related to all that? Are you studying the phenomenon here in secret? What?"

Her options dwindled to almost nothing. She couldn't tell him the truth or it would betray her pledge to the general. Telling Benny a lie might hold him off for a bit, but then she would lose the leverage of truth. She needed to think bigger and longer-term.

She opened the door, signifying their private chat was

over. "General Smith is doing his job in my old office. You know where it is?"

"Of course."

She looked outside and saw some of the staff in the hallway. Turning back to Benny, she held out her hand. "Please give me your phone. I give you my word that all will become clear when we meet the general. If possible, I will get this back to you."

His shoulders slumped. "I thought you trusted me."

She understood completely.

"You have no idea how much I do. There *is* something big going down in the world, and I'm confident working in here will be worth your while, but I can only bring you inside if you trust me now. The alternative is sitting in the spectator seats with the rest of the press, if they are let in at all."

"You better not screw me over," he said as he surrendered his phone.

"Benny, I would never think of it. Truth be told, you and your phone may have just saved the world."

Canberra, ACT, Australia

Zandre delivered the tranquilizer rifle to Destiny as promised. He was in a hurry to get to his own hunt, so he didn't want to stop and talk for long.

"Thank you," she said once the handoff was complete.

"I hope you find something," he said with sympathy. "I didn't bring you out here to watch me shoot animals since I know you don't favor it, but the bounty is too large. The taxes are killing me, all right?"

"Z, you don't need to explain yourself. I made it, thanks to you. I would never have known these animals were back."

Inwardly, she wondered for how long. Faith said SNAKE had caused the time issues. Did that imply a fix would return things to where they had been? Would all the fantastic specimens disappear?

I have to study one before they go.

With that thought, she was in a hurry to depart as well. "Where are you going?" she asked him.

"Walker Hill, for starters." He pointed to a distant hill. The rest of the landscape was gently rolling terrain covered in grass and a few trees, but that hill was taller than the rest and a lot greener.

"I'll go a different way," she replied.

"Good luck," they said in unison as they split up.

Destiny had been to his ranch several times over the years, but she'd never gotten out on her own. It was liberating to be back in nature with the powerful little vehicle at her disposal. As for where to go, she figured Ducks of Doom were exactly like almost every other animal. Eventually, they'd end up at the watering hole.

She meandered across the open grassland until she started to climb a slight slope. After another kilometer or two, the slope led her to a thin line of trees running along a small creek. She drove slowly along the edge of the tree-covered hillock looking for an area well-suited for wallowing beasts.

This is the place. Destiny shut down the vehicle and breathed deeply of the air. She closed her eyes and felt the flora around her.

She carried her rifle to a small, mud-rimmed pool of water and took a seat in some brush. Cattle had come through the creek numerous times; hoof prints and piles of dried dung were everywhere.

Time got away from her as she sat in the morning sun

and excitement turned to boredom. Mostly, she daydreamed about the long line of dead Tasmanian Tigers, and how there must be more of them around, too. She saw nothing in her spot, however, and as the hours went by, she began to think about moving. The hunters could have bagged a dozen Demon Ducks in the time she'd been gone.

She wasn't one to give up so easily, however, and after waiting another thirty minutes, a throaty warble got her attention. A couple of other animals replied to the first, and, judging by the volume, they were in the tree cover not far away.

They sounded birdlike.

She waited to see if the creatures making the sounds would come to her, but they remained where they were: close, but not close enough.

Destiny picked up the rifle and made sure it was ready to fire. With as much stealth as was possible with her heavy boots, she got to her feet and tip-toed her way through the bushes down the creek bed.

When she arrived at another pool of water, she held her breath as she watched. A few giant, feathery creatures splashed in the swimming hole. At first, she was going to write them off as mundane emus because they didn't seem large enough to be "special," but as she peered through the leafy undergrowth, she knew that wasn't what they were. Their warbles were distinctive and unlike anything she'd ever heard before.

"Come on, girl," Destiny whispered. "Get a little closer."

She managed to take a few steps in relative silence, allowing her to get an unobstructed view of the beautiful light-feathered birds, but then she pushed her luck. With a final footstep, she crushed a small stick.

Two of the man-sized beasts sprinted down the shallow creek out of sight, but one remained where it was. From her new position, she got a much better view of the magnificent find. Destiny calmed herself and froze in place, remaining absolutely silent. She wanted to convince the animal not to leave through force of will alone.

Her eyes drifted to the bushes on the far side of the creek, behind the remaining beast. A familiar shape poked his head up and locked eyes with her, the blue steel barrel of his gun barely visible through the leaves.

The man froze in place, much as she had.

"Oi," she mumbled.

She wasn't the only hunter at the watering hole.

Highway 395, California

As the morning continued, Buck and the trucker known as Sparky followed the snowy highway over a few high hills on the outskirts of the mountain range until they came to a final ridge that took them toward a broad, flat plain ahead.

The snow started to taper off, which gave him confidence that he wouldn't need chains even though the temperature remained below freezing. His dashboard said it was twenty-eight outside. Along the way, he had Connie put a square of duct tape over the inch-wide bullet hole in his windshield to stop the wind noise and bitter chill.

"Weird weather we're having," Connie said like it was small talk.

"Yeah, no kidding. Yesterday I saw the worst thunderstorm of my life, but I think heavy snow scares me even more. I've heard of snow in June up in the higher elevations of the Rockies, but not down here. If it snows too much in one of these passes, it might be weeks before we could drive out."

"If my dates are all screwed up, maybe the weather is messed up, too."

Connie's statement surprised him by bringing the obvious into the open. It hadn't been obvious unless one was thinking outside of the calendar's constraints. "Yeah, that makes perfect sense. It would explain the surprise storm yesterday and the hurricane heading for New York City. Those things don't come out of nowhere, right?"

She shrugged. "I'm from New Mexico, where the weather is boring. I have no idea about hurricanes."

The CB chirped. "Buck, come back."

He keyed the mic. "This is Buck, go ahead."

"Tahoe is just up there," Sparky replied. "Are you planning to gas up or stop?"

Buck looked at Connie. "Need anything? A supertanker soda, perhaps?" He had no idea if she'd know about the 128-ounce monstrosities they sold at truck stops. "Or, better yet, I'm sure we can get you a nice John Deere hat at a gas-n-go. Might look nice on you."

She faced him with what could only be described as a pouty face. "If you are going to slather me up with your asphalt aphrodisiac and dress me up like one of your trucker lot lizards, maybe you should have left me back in that town."

Buck was stunned. His mouth fell open, amazed that he had missed saying something so rude to her.

Connie held stern for only a couple of seconds, then burst out in laughter.

"This is going to be fun." She giggled. "For the record, I could down a supertanker drink like nobody's business, but this redhead only wears cowboy hats."

All he could do was laugh with her. "What did you say you did for a living? Kick smartass truckers right in the ghoulies with your cowboy boots?"

"A writer," she answered. "It usually takes me ten minutes to think of the right thing to say, but with you, it comes easy."

"Glad I could be of help," he said with good-natured sarcasm. Then, he spoke into the CB microphone to answer Sparky's question. "We're going to keep on. I've got enough fuel in the tanks to go another 1500 miles, but I think Salt Lake is our next planned stop."

Salt Lake City was across Nevada and most of Utah, but once they got on I-80, it would go fast. He would have been there last night if yesterday had gone as planned. It was already late morning and he still wasn't on the interstate.

"I'll have to pay the water bill before SLC, but I'll do my best," the other trucker answered back.

"Water bill?" Connie asked.

Buck glanced over with a smile. "Stop and pee."

"Duh," she said while slapping her forehead. "I knew that."

"Of course," he said with mirth, "we can make better time if we use the old trucker trick of filling up Gatorade bottles. Then we wouldn't have to stop at all."

He waited for the snarky response, but she simply turned her head away from him. A few seconds later she seemed to think of a reply.

"I won't put that detail in my books."

Buck stifled a laugh as he spoke into the mic. "Keep your ear out for other haulers. Maybe we can find some friends going east and link up for safety." He'd never been in a real convoy. Sometimes he joined up with another truck or two, such as when he'd have to cross long boring states like Nebraska or Texas, but those broke up fast. Most truckers were independent and liked to be on their own schedule.

However, the bikers had him worried that unforeseen dangers were out there. Just like he'd joined up with Connie for self-preservation, he figured the same principle applied out on the road. They had always traveled in convoys back in Iraq, so he tried to transfer the thought-process to the homeland.

"Roger that," Sparky replied.

He checked his side mirrors. The sky was dark and cranky behind him. The snowstorm continued to work over the road in the foothills, but the wind and blowing snow suggested it was drifting to the northeast. His brain tried to draw I-80 in Nevada on his mental map, but he was at a loss.

"Connie, would you mind looking at the atlas for me? I'm curious if we'll run into that storm again."

He was on the lookout for trouble on the highway, but he also kept watch for the next zinger from his new passenger.

NINETEEN

Somewhere in New Jersey

Garth popped open the trunk and ran to the back of the taxi. All his gear was stacked neatly in the trunk. He'd jammed the tent way in the back, and a pair of sleeping bags were on top of it. Numerous other pieces of his dad's survival kit surrounded the tent and gun cases. Making it fit was a testament to his packing skills, but now he was in danger of losing it all.

"Take the irreplaceable stuff," he told himself.

The taxi had ended up in the ditch facing the way he'd been driving, so the lurking car was in front of him. However, the other person must have been scared off when Garth got out, because the car now sped away to get on the highway.

After accidentally shooting the gun inside his car, his body had shaken for a long time, like he was shivering from cold. He had thought it might have been because he was wet with the rain, but now his body shivered like before. It wasn't the cold at all.

"Holy shit, that was close."

For the moment, Garth was alone. He held open the trunk lid as he tried to calm his wild nerves and think about his next course of action. The pitter-patter of rain falling on the metal suggested he better hurry, because he didn't want to soak the gear.

Stay or go?

He couldn't push the taxi out of the ditch on his own, and it didn't seem like a good idea to sit inside the car and hope good people came to his rescue. That wasn't how Dad would do it.

Garth grabbed the bug-out backpack, which had some of the bare essentials for living in the woods: a tarp, a knife, fire starter, flashlight, and similar small items. Once it was over his shoulder, he grabbed one of the rifle cases, slid it out of the car, and set it on the grass. He did the same for the second one. There was no way to bring the cases of ammo because they weighed a ton. It would require a small wagon to lug those around.

Garth slammed the trunk shut and picked up both cases before checking for cars. For the moment, the highway and the on-ramp were empty, so he trotted into the woods with the heavy load. As long as no one saw him, there was no need to go far.

A dense clump of underbrush about twenty-five yards in provided the perfect hiding spot, and he shoved both rifle cases deep into the greenery. Once they were stashed, he pulled out his pistol and stood there for a few seconds just in case. The pine trees and other evergreens made it hard to see anything beyond twenty feet.

"Steady." Garth took a moment to savor the scent of the hardwoods, which reminded him of Christmastime. He also commanded his hands to stop shaking. Stress. And shock.

You're fine. Relax.

No one came storming into his hiding spot. He felt safe for the moment, but he needed a plan.

Rain steadily beat down on the trees around him. The hurricane was close, but his dread came from the other storm—the cloud of radiation heading east toward New York City and the surrounding countryside. He was still well inside the red bubble of danger he'd seen on the television.

"Find help," he muttered. "Free the car. Drive to safety."

It would be a simple plan if he could find anyone who wouldn't screw him over. His first thought was to flag down vehicles on the Garden State Parkway, but when the first car had pulled over after he crashed, it had put the fear of God in him. Leaving the woods and waving at drivers reminded him of all the people he'd passed back on Staten Island. He didn't want to be one of those guys.

Dad had often told him that if you looked and acted like a victim, you were more likely to become one, and he practiced it by always acknowledging strangers while he was out in public rather than keeping his head down and staring at the ground. He said criminals look for people lost in their own thoughts. Garth was a master of being distracted, but he tried to kick the habit when he traveled with Dad.

He was on his own. He had a car and supplies, but he needed a hand.

He didn't know if help was on the other side of the overpass; the raised highway blocked his view, and the trees didn't help. But experience had taught him businesses gathered at intersections, so there was a decent chance something was close.

What are the odds of finding a tow truck?

Garth pulled out his phone and bent over to keep it out

of the rain. After a long, defeated sigh, he typed a short message to Dad.

'Sorry, dad. Took cab out of city. In New Jersey. Ran into ditch. Getting help.' He hit Send but realized he'd forgotten the most important piece of information his dad would ask. 'I'm fine.'

He added a smiley face in the belief it would prevent Dad from blowing a gasket. Telling him he had wrecked a car was not a smiling matter for either of them, but he was already disappointed in himself. He didn't need Dad to feel bad.

If only he'd paid more attention, he'd be on the highway to the south tip of New Jersey and safety. Instead, he threw the phone in one pocket and the pistol in the other. He was now dependent on someone else to get him out of his jam.

Usually, that was what he did for Sam.

Before he got too far, he turned around and looked at the terrain.

He didn't want to forget where he'd stashed four AR-15s.

Search for Nuclear, Astrophysical, and Kronometric Extremes (SNAKE). Red Mesa, Colorado

Faith carried Benny's phone into another of the unfurnished offices. She didn't pull it out of her pocket until she was out of sight of any nosey staffers.

His lock screen was activated but his news feed sat above it, so she was able to scroll through it. She read through a few innocuous items until she came to one that suggested a time distortion. "South Pole ice sheet adds ten feet overnight. Ocean level drops half-inch."

No amount of clicking made the story open up for her.

"Dammit!" she hissed.

The next story was also one she would have liked to read. "Statue of Liberty only half-finished."

Two financial headlines came up next.

"Market falls two thousand points in one day. Shuts down."

The next one explained how several old companies had tried to put themselves back on the New York Stock Exchange.

"There goes my 401(k)," she said sadly.

Finally, she saw a story about the missing GPS satellites General Smith had mentioned. The headline gave no details, however, so she didn't learn anything beyond what he'd already told her.

She searched for the timestamps on the stories, but Benny's phone only put them in order. It didn't show the time they were published.

I need my phone back.

After scrolling through ten more stories, each more unbelievable than the last, she'd seen enough.

Faith already knew SNAKE was responsible for causing the blue light, and the NORAD guys had made things worse by putting that piece of lead into the beam. What she needed to know was whether things would get better if she managed to turn the beam off completely, or if the world would continue to get worse no matter what she did.

At least you're safe at SNAKE, she thought before taking a moment to consider it.

The blue beam had shot outward from her Red Mesa headquarters. No one reported any of the time weirdness inside the collider ring, so for a fleeting second, she wondered if it was safer to be where she was. She needed more data to build a more complete picture of the cause and effects.

She had to go face the general.

Carson City, Nevada

The snowstorm turned into whiteout conditions as Buck drove through Carson City.

"Hey, I didn't realize we were already in Nevada," Connie joked.

"The welcome sign was probably covered in snow back up in the hills," Buck replied. He tried to look at Fred the GPS to see if the California-Nevada border was on the screen, but the device interface was blank.

"Oh, no, we lost the signal," he said as he tapped the unit on the dashboard. "Lucky for us, we only take one highway to get to New York. We'll catch I-80 up in Reno and take it the rest of the way."

"Wow. That's lucky, since it looks like your technology is caput."

"Nah. If the power goes down on my digital version, I also have the book." He pointed to the tattered copy of the United States road atlas. "I like to be prepared."

"Boy Scouts?" Connie asked with interest.

"Yep. Eagle Scout and everything." The Boy Scout motto was "Be prepared," and it was one of the most important directives of his life. His troop leader would be proud to see him carrying guns and ammo in hidden compartments in his truck. Buck remembered him as a hard-nosed man who had spent a career in law enforcement, but he stressed self-reliance in the boys and made no secret of the fact that he wanted to move to the mountains and live off the land when he retired. Buck hoped he had made it, if only as a reward for teaching the boys what was important.

The Scouts were a big part of his prepper attitude and can-do spirit.

"My son was an Eagle Scout, too. Got it when he was sixteen."

"Before the fumes caught him," Buck said sensibly.

"Fumes?" she asked.

"Girls' perfume and the high-octane fumes of cars. It derails many a Boy Scout on their quest to get Eagle before their eighteenth birthday."

She laughed. "He was a lady's man, that's for sure." She stopped, then sounded concerned. "Not was. Is. Wherever he is today, I'm sure he found his filly and settled down."

Buck didn't know how to answer. He knew in his heart Garth was still at home boarding up windows and filling the tubs with drinking water, but he didn't know if he would sense if something happened to him.

However, he was less certain about Connie's son. The war against Saddam had been won in the first few months, but the War on Terror had dragged on for almost two decades. Who knew what her son did after that first attack? Garth was miles away, at the end of the road that was just up ahead; her son was removed by seventeen years. It made his challenge seem small.

"I'm sure he is, too," he said with a voice full of positivity. "Let's check the news," he added to change the subject.

They'd been trying his phone for the past hour, but the snowstorm apparently caused a total blackout of mobile phone service. His phone wouldn't connect with anything, even his voicemail. Connie's job so far had been to call both of their sons and try to establish contact. She'd come up empty on both.

Since the phones didn't work, they tried to get news and information on the radio, but they only found static from one end of the dial to the other. Even the AM band was white noise.

"It's like a total technology blackout," she suggested.

"I can't believe the storm is blocking cell phone signals or the GPS. It must have something to do with the time stuff. How could Fred connect to satellites of seventeen years ago?"

"It doesn't seem possible," she wondered.

"Now, anything is possible."

The storm had grown behind his Peterbilt as they drove north on Highway 395, but it had also closed in from the mountains in the west. At least ten inches of snow covered the grass and rocks next to the road, with a lesser amount on the pavement. It was a risk to continue, but he was going to press on as far as his wheels would turn because he had to stay in front of the storm or he might lose a week or more. He needed to get home.

"At least the bikers won't be driving through that," Buck offered. "That's the biggest damn moat I've ever seen around a castle. Castle Mac, isn't that right, boy?"

The dog heard his name and stuck his face between the seats so Buck and Connie could both give him head and neck scratches.

Buck picked up the CB mic because he wanted to make sure it still worked. "Sparky, you got your ears on?"

His trucker friend replied instantly. "I'm still back here. It sure is quiet, huh?"

"Your radio out, too?" Buck asked.

"Yep. Whatever is in this snow, it ain't natural. I've never seen anything take out the AM dial."

"We're with you," Buck replied. "I'm ready to get on I-

80 and get the hell out of here. Maybe things are better in other states?"

"I've been talking to two other bubbas up ahead. They're going to join us at a Reno park n' ride so we can convoy up. I think we'll have a few more by the time we get there. You think we'll need more?"

Buck wanted to ask if Sparky was armed since that would determine how many drivers could contribute to the convoy, but he wouldn't do that over an open frequency. That was a conversation best conducted in person.

After a moment of consideration, Buck keyed the mic. "Yes, Sparky, I think we're going to need all the trucks we can get." A line of massive tractor-trailers could cut through snow and keep the ball moving toward the goal line. Anything was better than stopping.

A convoy also played an important role in their personal safety.

He glanced at Connie. "Funny that he's worried about gathering more drivers. There's no such thing as a convoy being too big. I'd rather have a hundred trucks behind us than have to worry about the next big-balled bikers who feel the need to fuck around with good, honest people."

"I just hope a hundred is enough," she replied with an uncertain chuckle.

TWENTY

Bagram Air Base, Afghanistan

Lieutenant Colonel Stanwick pulled the trigger on his M9 Beretta as air brushed the top of his left ear. He hit the enemy fighter center mass, then unloaded six more when he realized the whistling sound was a bullet passing an inch from his melon.

"Fuck!" he screamed.

The crack-bangs near his ears muted the sounds of war from the rest of the airfield, but he retained enough sense to realize there must have been a hundred different calibers of guns going off. That upped the scale of what his men faced and pushed him to move.

Blood pumped through his veins at a million miles an hour while he slid on the rocks over to the other man. He ignored his scrape with death and focused on taking the terrorist's rifle. It was less effective in close quarters, but it was better than running through all fifteen rounds of his pistol and having nothing left to defend himself. He'd already spent seven.

Must get to the command post.

The peacetime lights of the base had been shut off and the aerial flares were dying out, so it was hard to determine if the scurrying shapes in the night were his men or the enemy. It seemed reasonable to assume there was more than one enemy infiltrator.

He got up and ran toward hard cover.

The dark battlefield was a case study in munitions. He recognized SCAR rifles and Mark-48 machine guns as his own, and the distinctive pop of AK-47s was everywhere. However, he did not recognize about half the others, which was a little frightening. He'd been in third-world deployments for most of his adult life, so he had learned to identify makes and models of dozens of small arms because it helped him survive.

This battle was different. He zigzagged the last of the way before ducking behind the sandbags protecting the entryway.

When he ran inside the aircraft bunker that served as his command post, he wanted answers from the officers on duty. Specialist Matt Carbon was closest.

"Carbon, who the fuck is shooting out there?"

"We don't know for sure," Specialist Carbon yelled over the background din. "We have reports of tanks, technicals, and fucking camels. They're throwing everything at us, sir."

"The Taliban may be a determined enemy," he replied, "but they don't gear up and attack en masse like this. You have to give me something better. Can this be more of those Soviet tanks we found?"

As the unit responsible for bringing in the old tanks, he figured it made sense they'd be targeted. Were the Taliban now working with the Russians? The tanks had been cleared of the operators, but perhaps they represented Trojan horses or rallying points inside the wire.

Carbon held up a finger. "I'm getting call signs that sound Russian. Fuck, sir, I need a translator."

His supply chief walked over and threw on a pair of headphones.

A repetitive thump echoed inside the walls, and different booms replied from far away. The closer ones were easily identified as Abrams tanks on his side, but in much of the battle, he wasn't sure who fired back. He wasn't even sure which American unit had the Abrams. Certainly not his Rangers.

"I need answers!" he commanded.

The supply chief finally came up for air. "Sir! It is Russian. I can't believe they're broadcasting in the clear, but it doesn't sound like they're attacking us. They're duking it out with entrenched Afghan Army units."

"That doesn't make any sense," Lieutenant Colonel Stanwick replied. "There isn't any such unit, not here."

The radioman pushed back his headgear. "Sir, Outpost Charlie Seven reports capturing a small unit of men with ancient rifles. They say they are here to conquer Kabul, but they speak with British accents and are dressed like Redcoats." He paused for a moment. "This has to be a joke, sir."

"Except for the live rounds," he replied, "I was thinking the same thing."

Phil studied the ten soldiers in his headquarters. "We have a lot of questions and no answers. Ideas, people. I need your best out-of-the-box thinking."

Reno, NV

Buck and Connie made it to the Reno commuter lot in late morning. He didn't want to stop before Salt Lake City, but the cause was a worthy one. They waited there with Sparky and two other tractor-trailers as more drivers expressed interest in joining their convoy.

Despite the early hour, he was spent. What should have been an easy hundred miles from Mono Lake to Reno had turned into a whole morning. Their escape from the bikers and the endless whiteout road conditions had zapped his driving energy. The only good news was that he was about to head east, toward Garth.

"I'd say we have about five hours of driving to get across Nevada. That might be all we can do today since we lost so much time due to the snow." Buck balanced the atlas on the middle part of the dash so Connie could see it. Big Mac sat on the floor between them and also seemed to study the book.

"If we don't run into trouble," she said evenly. "Or more snow."

"Right. If everything goes as planned and the weather gets back to the proper season, we might make it across while there is still daylight."

The snow was hit or miss. It had been heavy outside Bridgeport and lighter at some points on the drive, but now it was heavy and thick. Only a few cars dared head east on the interstate, but the highway wasn't officially closed, so he wanted to push on.

"Fewer cars means fewer assholes on the road. And the best part is," he said with flair, "there is almost nothing along the highway when we go through Nevada. A couple of small towns, but that's it. Very few people."

"Hopefully very few biker bars, too," she added.

"The snow and ice will take care of them. No biker is going to survive long on these slick roads unless they have a death wish."

She laughed while brushing her long fingernails down Mac's neck. "Just you, me, and your dog. No assholes. I think that sounds like a pleasant drive. Maybe this disaster isn't going to be so bad. How long should we wait here for more trucks to show up?"

He pulled out the lucky centennial quarter he had found when the blue light went by.

"Heads we go now, tails we're already gone."

Search for Nuclear, Astrophysical, and Kronometric Extremes (SNAKE). Red Mesa, Colorado

"I need some answers before I meet with the general." Faith looked at her core team. She'd taken a seat at the head of the conference table, far from the etching of her name. Bob sat on her right side with a digital tablet. Sun sat on her left with a stapled report neatly placed in front of her.

Sun spoke first, in her usual hard-to-hear manner. "My team and I have analyzed what we could, but we need more time to review the data. The CERN beam is not in a convenient spot to do a proper investigation, and we don't have the right equipment on hand to go crawling around in that tunnel. The other three containers are in similar conditions."

"CERN beam? Is that what we're calling it? Maybe it's a SNAKE beam?"

Sun's smile was miniscule. "I don't honestly know, but SNAKE has its own beam running along the collider ring. The two are interacting."

Faith hid her disappointment. "Don't you know anything else?"

"We don't know the energy source, the wavelength, or the direction. We detect no radiation with our handheld equipment, but I'm convinced there has to be some. It's like no energy source I've ever seen."

"Is it coming from CERN or going there?"

"As I stated, we don't know the direction," Sun replied.

"You can't even guess?"

"I don't guess. The experiment with the lead shield might have illustrated whether it is unidirectional or bidirectional, but they didn't have the proper controls in place. They might have done better to stick their face in the beam to feel which way it's going."

Faith spoke with confidence. "Well, the good news is that I've put a stop to those one-offs. We do this by the book and with the best equipment we have. The NORAD scientists are nominally under my control."

"If you believe the general," Sun chided.

"I have to, Sun. He's in charge."

"Of course," the quiet Indian scientist replied.

Faith turned to Bob, who continued to tap and swipe on his tablet. "Bob? Anything to add?"

He looked up like he'd forgotten he was in an important meeting.

"What? Sorry. I'm trying to get my department organized to help analyze Sun's data, but it is harder than shit when I can't call the contacts in my cell phone. Not everyone is at a desk, either, so the office land-line directory is useless. The wi-fi is working, for now, so I can text them, but that only barely makes it possible to manage people."

"I'm going to talk to the general after this meeting. I think I can get some of this communication stuff fixed, but I wanted to come to him with something helpful. You know, show him my all-stars can run rings around his scrubs."

Bob looked sideways at her and smiled for a fraction of a second before facing his screen again.

She deliberately placed her palms on the table in front of her. "He's going to order us to shut it down."

Sun and Bob both turned to her.

She continued. "The experiment with the lead bar served as the catalyst. He knows SNAKE is responsible for the unusual activity out there, and he lost his satellites when the lead bar hit the beam from CERN. The only logical conclusion he can formulate is that he has to kill the beam to save humanity."

"I don't think you should allow that, Dr. Sinclair." Bob spoke with uncomfortable formality. "Whatever these four links with CERN are doing, they obviously played a part in the tail end of the experiment yesterday. If we assume the experiment is still running, as the general believes, then perhaps we can argue that the four beams are keeping things from collapsing even further. Think of them as life vests on a sinking ship."

"The analogy only works if there is a rescue vessel coming," Faith replied. "As far as we know, CERN is gone. There is no help at the end of the ropes."

"You both indulge in fruitless speculation," Sun lamented.

"I deal in the impossible, doctor," Bob said to Sun, "although I think it's obvious that I don't have a computer model whipped up for this scenario. I'm using logic. If the beams are coming from CERN or going there and CERN blew up, then why didn't the beams turn off?"

Sun leaned forward in her chair. "They originate here."

"That's one option," he agreed. "But think of this: What if the beam is coming from the other end? What if CERN is wrecked but there are four boxes in the rubble still broadcasting?"

Faith's brow furrowed as she studied Bob's eyes. "Are you suggesting CERN is still there?"

He shrugged. "I don't know. Maybe part of it is. The news says there was an accident, but what if they were wrong? We haven't heard from our people. The ropes are still attached to the debris, if you like. I believe if the general tries to cut them, things will get worse, not better."

If only I could fly to CERN and look in the hole.

She needed to go to the general with a recommendation. It seemed like she had one.

"Are we in agreement we should not try to turn off the CERN beams at this time?"

Sun gave a curt nod. "Not until we've had time to run analysis on the paltry data we already have."

Faith turned to Bob. "And you?"

"I absolutely think we should give it a little more time. Someone should dial up the Geneva police and ask them if there are any survivors over there. That would go a long way toward finding out the status of the CERN supercollider. I'm sure the whole ring didn't disappear..." His voice faded as if he suddenly wasn't so certain.

"I'm sure it didn't," Faith encouraged him. "I'm going to get our phones back. When I do, the first call I'm making is to Geneva. I'll call the mayor if I have to, but we need to know exactly what happened to the supercollider on the other end. Was it running at the same time as ours? Is it still there? If we knew someone on the international team was still alive, we could ask them to take readings on their ring equipment. We might be able to establish whether they are showing the same low-level energy we're seeing here."

"Yeah, turning things off without knowing what it will do is always a bad scientific option," Bob said matter-of-factly.

She stood up.

"Okay, I'm off to see the general. Keep doing what you're doing, and find me if you learn anything new. Thank you both for working around the clock on this."

Sun walked out, but Bob kept typing on his tablet. When Sun was gone, he leaned over to her.

"Whatever you do, don't let the general shut things down, okay?"

His words rubbed her raw. "That's what I *just* said I was going to tell him."

"Yeah, but I know you. If the general pushes to shut it off, you'll do it. This is for real." He tapped his screen. "I'm sure it would be a mistake to interfere with the beams. Don't go weak on me."

She felt their old antagonism rise to the surface, but she stomped on it before it drove her to answer in kind.

"I'll be sure to tell him Dr. Stafford expressly forbids a shutdown," she said sarcastically.

He remained serious. "That would be wise."

TWENTY-ONE

I-80, Nevada

Buck's convoy of five trucks left Reno in a driving snow-storm. Normally, he might have waited around until the conditions were better, but he had reached the highway destined to take him all the way home, and it was a powerful draw. Fortunately, the other truck drivers in his group were equally anxious to get some miles behind them. They all reported spending hours in traffic getting out of California, and they didn't want to sit in more of it all the way across Nevada.

His black Peterbilt was the first in line and first down the entrance ramp to I-80.

"I'll take it slow," he called to his new friends.

Sparky went next.

He was an older gentleman with greasy hair and a short salt-and-pepper beard. He piloted a Blue Mack with a box trailer. Buck had peeked inside his cabin; he was a little jealous of his interior because it seemed a lot larger than his sleeper cab. However, Clarence only had himself. Buck's rig now had three occupants to fill the space.

Sparky checked in when he was on the interstate at Buck's back door. "Sparky here, radio check."

"You're good, radio check," Buck replied with a laugh. The man knew his radio was working.

"Monsignor is in line. Lord, bless us all."

Mel Tinker went by the handle Monsignor, which had confused them all. The young guy didn't dress religiously or talk like a holy man. Nothing about him suggested why he would call himself a man of the cloth, so they had to ask.

His reply had been sobering.

"If you carried the shit I do, you'd be praying all the time just like me." Mel pointed to the polished-steel liquid-hauler behind his rig. Flammable warning signs were everywhere. "If I ever spark up, it's goodbye to me and the nearest square mile of souls. I guess I like to be prepared."

His current assignment was to pull his tanker of acetylene to a chemical plant in Illinois.

"Who is in the rocking chair?" Buck called out on Channel 4, asking about the trucks in the middle of the convoy.

"It's me!" a perky twenty-something woman replied. Evelyn went by Eve on the CB. Buck hadn't caught her last name. She was a recruiter for the Parker-Point shipping company, and her bubbly personality undoubtedly convinced many young men to sign up and become over-the-road truckers.

She and her Peterbilt pulled a load of electronics bound for a terminal in Massachusetts.

"Beans is tail gunner," a man added.

Beans drove the last truck. The heavyset Hispanic man hailed from Southern California, but he'd lived and traveled all over the United States, so he had no accent. He was about fifty, which put him on par with Sparky in terms of years, but Buck thought he was the least serious of the four drivers. He joked about lunch several times even as they talked about their route across Nevada, so Buck assumed "Beans" referred to his appetite.

"Take it nice and slow, guys," Buck said to the professional truckers behind him. "This snow has to break soon, and then we'll be at the head of the traffic instead of the rear."

There were a couple of nice hills on the Nevada crossing, but nothing like the high snow-packed passes of the main mountain ranges. He was betting the snow would clear once they got farther into the desert.

A few miles out of Reno, he finally looked at Connie because there was a commotion on her lap.

"Hey!" he said. "Get down, you silly pup."

Big Mac, the fifty-pound baby, had curled up on Connie. The dog must have sensed his tone because he raised his head to look over at him as if to say, "Please, Dad, let me stay."

Connie laughed. "It's fine, really. He asked politely."

"Politely?" he replied with surprise.

Mac's eyes somehow got larger, and sadder. "Pleeeeease?" they said.

Buck shook his head. "That dog is smarter than he lets on. Garth is going to have his hands full."

Connie was rubbing the Retriever's flank, and he knew there was no sense interrupting.

"Fine. But you get down the second she asks you, okay?"

Mac's idea of saying thanks was slamming his head down so he could get back to basking in the attention of the new person sharing his seat.

The snow was nerve-wracking to drive through, but his soul soared ten feet above him as he appreciated how lucky he was. He'd found the perfect dog at the start of this trip. Connie was a great addition, despite how she came aboard. And now he had four truckers backing him up.

He wanted to say something to that effect to Connie, but he couldn't think of a way to do it without sounding weird. She even looked over at him, a softness in her eyes hinting that she knew what was on his mind.

Be cool, he told himself.

He almost got it out, but she spoke first. "Why are you in the front? Wouldn't it be safer to be in the middle? I mean, the convoy was your idea, and all."

Buck clenched his jaw. He had not expected that.

"You're right. The leader has the most dangerous position because he doesn't know what's coming and has to react to changing conditions faster than the others."

The thought of danger tempered his mood.

"So, why not be in the middle?" She asked it matter-of-factly, like it was a point of conversation rather than an accusation.

He shrugged while holding the wheel with both hands. "Linking up with the others was my idea. It wouldn't be right to ask them to assume the danger. Besides, do you want one of those other drivers up in the front if we *do* find trouble?" He chuckled. "I mean it in the nicest possible way. They all seem like—"

"Civilians," she finished.

Buck glanced over to get a read on her. "I don't mean it like that."

"I know you don't. I can tell you don't have a mean bone in your body. But it is absolutely true. I think you're wired to lead, not follow. I saw the same thing in my son. That boy was a handful."

He didn't want her to dwell on her missing son, any more than he wanted to dwell on how it had been too many hours since he'd been in contact with his.

"Why don't we play a game?" he suggested.

She perked right up. "Oh? What did you have in mind?"

He thought of some of the games he liked to play to kill the days.

"Let's see who can find the most states on license plates."

Connie thought about it for a few seconds and looked forward on the highway, then in her side mirror.

"Is that your idea of a joke? There isn't anyone out here but us."

He pointed to the side of the road. An abandoned car sat in a ditch. "Fine. Let's play count the wrecks."

"How about Slug Bug?" The Beetle was covered in snow, but its shape remained distinctive. Connie leaned across and lightly hammered Buck in the shoulder. Mac started to bark.

Buck laughed. "Don't make me get my gun, because you know I won't hit you back."

"I know," Connie said softly.

Canberra, ACT, Australia

Dez only had a split-second to decide what to do. The man on the other side of the creek seemed to be pointing his gun at her, and she had no cover besides the leaves of the bushes.

She aimed her tranquilizer rifle at him and fired without

thinking. The light snap of the gun was followed by the whistle of the dart crossing the creek.

The man's gun boomed, and a tree splintered just above her head.

"Crikey!" she shouted.

The man fell backward, his bolt-action rifle pointed at the sky, the spent round still chambered.

The Duck of Doom seemed frozen between her and the hunter, the two threats it had to compare and assess.

She shot it before it made its decision.

To her relief, it fell over in the shallow water, so she didn't have to chase it down.

The creek became still again, and she put her hand over her heart to feel how fast it was beating.

The bloody blow-in made me shoot him.

It was amazing to have shot the bird, but she couldn't take her eyes off the man's shape in the bushes beyond. She strode through the shallow water and went up the bank to check on him. She grabbed her dart from his shoulder and verified he was breathing, but that was as much attention as she was willing to give him.

She started to second-guess herself immediately. Had he truly been aiming at her? Had she intentionally misread his posture to enable herself to fire on him, so she could get her animal? Was this about the money or self-preservation? She wasn't certain, but she expected her subconscious drove her to protect the animal as much as herself.

Most of her fears went away when she made her way to the *dromornis stirtoni*. The animal looked like a cross between a huge Emu and a typical mallard duck. It was ungainly-looking, with black and white feathers that seemed more Dalmatian than duck, but it wasn't quite as tall as she expected.

The species of ancient bird was known for being three meters tall and up to 600 kilos in weight, but this one wasn't much larger than her. "You must be a teenager," she said to it in a quiet voice.

Destiny wanted to celebrate her feat with her sister, so she pulled out her phone and took a photo of the rare creature. Then she texted it to Faith, although she didn't know if the strange man still had her phone.

'Sis. You are right about time being messed up. This Duck of Doom is from at least 30,000 years ago. Maybe a lot longer. I captured it!'

She hit Send.

I've got to move fast.

She ran to her four-wheeler and grabbed the folding game-hauler cart. It would allow her to get the animal out of the creek and through the trees, so she'd be able to load it onto the gas-powered machine. Then it would be easy to return to the house.

Everything was planned out in her mind, but when she came back through the trees, two more hunters were already there.

"It looks like he shot it and then had a heart attack," one of them said when they found the sedated hunter.

Destiny wasn't one to back down from a fight, but she couldn't shake the feeling that first hunter really had meant to shoot her. Ten million dollars was a huge amount of money, and hunting accidents weren't uncommon, especially when there were no friendly witnesses.

She had to decide if she was willing to risk her life again.

Am I doing it for the money or the bird?

Her mind still wasn't made up when the men rolled their own game cart to the water's edge.

. . .

Somewhere in New Jersey

Garth hiked back to the road and went underneath the Garden State Parkway. The high bridges gave him shelter from the rain, and for a few minutes he stood there and enjoyed the protection.

However, he didn't dare stay long, so he took a few steps closer to the water dripping from the far edge of the bridge. Garth intended to set out into the rain, but he noticed movement up where the bridge deck met the slope of the earth.

"Hello?" he said. Almost without thinking, Garth put his hand in the pocket with his pistol so it would be easy to pull it out.

"Are you a ghost?" a girl's voice called out from the shadows.

He wondered if it was a trick question designed to get him into an ambush, but there was nowhere below the bridge where someone could hide. The two-lane road passed beneath it, and that was it.

"No."

"Oh," she replied.

He relaxed a little. It was probably a vagrant. They were not uncommon in New York City. "Do you know if there are any shops in this direction? I need to find help. I've had an accident."

The girl came out of the shadows and slid down the concrete embankment. Garth was surprised to see her dressed like one of those reenactors from an old-timey pioneer farm. He'd taken a few field trips to places like them, although he had no clue if there were any in this part of New Jersey.

She was also about his age.

Her light-blue flowery dress reached down to her leather boots, and a bonnet wrapped around most of her blonde hair. "You look like you came from that TV show *Little House on the Prairie*." He thought about his words when she showed no reaction. "I don't mean it as an insult. I think you look awesome. Where do you work?"

Her nose turned up. "Work? I work all the time, every day." She showed him the wooden stick she held. It had been trimmed with a blade and had a sharp point at the top. "I was in a cave looking for mushrooms and rats when I—"

"Rats?" Garth interrupted.

She put her hand on her hip in a posture he was familiar with from school. "Are you going to listen or not?"

"Sorry," he replied.

She pursed her lips. "No, *I'm* sorry. It's just that I've been here for a while. I was hunting in a cave when I got dizzy and fell over. When I woke up, I saw strange carriages pass under this bridge with ghosts inside. They moved at unnatural speeds with terrible howls. I crawled up into the topmost reach of this odd cave and waited there until I saw you. You are the first person who is not inside those metal monsters. Truly, they must all be dead?"

"They are inside cars, is all," he said dryly. "I drive one, too."

He squinted and gave her a hard glare to determine if she was having him on.

"What?" she asked when she saw his look.

"And you don't work at a pioneer farm? Is this some kind of gag?" It was probably his payback from the universe for leaving those people behind earlier.

"My pa and I were part of a train heading to our land out in Oregon. It was going to be our farm." Her shoulders slumped. "Until he died. Then my life turned upside down."

"What about your mom?" he asked.

"She died giving birth to me. It was only me and Pa up until we crossed the Platte River in Nebraska. Then it was just me."

He gulped heavily, still not sure if she was yanking his chain. There were kids in his school who dabbled with drugs. The little he saw of that made him wonder if this girl was high on something.

"I'm sorry," he said. It was a safe reply. "I'm Garth, by the way."

She finally showed a fragile smile. "Thank you. I'm Lydia."

They shared a moment of awkward silence when his phone vibrated in his pants pocket. He jumped at being startled, which caused her to take a step back.

"It's okay." He pulled out his phone. "It's this."

Her face turned wonderous. "What is it?"

He shook his head. "You really don't know? It's a phone. Here, look. I got a text."

"What's a text?"

Lydia came closer as he read the message from his father.

"Well, that bites the big one," he said with disappointment.

"What?" she said with curiosity.

"I sent a message to my dad earlier. I left home assuming he was going to tell me to get away from the radiation storm, but this is what he says: Stay at home. Will call you with instructions ASAP. Driving."

"I know I'm not being helpful, but every other word you

speak is foreign to me. It sounds like a radiation storm is dangerous. Is it?"

The intensity of the rain increased as if it knew it had him trapped.

"Very," he said, newly convinced that he'd made a huge mistake by leaving the house.

TWENTY-TWO

Search for Nuclear, Astrophysical, and Krono-metric Extremes (SNAKE). Red Mesa, Colorado

The general wasn't available to see Faith for several hours. Numerous scientists and staff from what she thought of as the NORAD contingent filed in and out of his office until shortly after lunch.

A young airman finally came to her makeshift office with an invitation to see the general. She picked up Benny on the way and had him wait outside the door.

"Come in, Dr. Sinclair," the general said as he rose from what was once her desk.

"General, I've been waiting for—"

He interrupted. "I'm sorry. I know I put you in charge, and time is critical, but I wanted more of my team in place before I felt comfortable making any decisions."

"And?" she said.

General Smith walked her to the large window facing out over the Hogback and the dry high plains beyond. He pointed to the parking lot below.

It was filled with Humvees and school buses, plus the cars and trucks of her regular staff.

"How many people did you bring in?" she remarked.

"Two-hundred and fifty. Every physicist I could find, order onto a bus, and ship here overnight. Most are from Colorado and surrounding states. I was lucky to get the first batch on an Air Force cargo plane, but there are no more flights. Everything is grounded except emergency military transports, and there aren't enough of those to go around."

She tried to think like the military man. "Isn't it a state secret? What if I go tell the Chinese or Russians our air defenses are down?"

It was supposed to be a joke, but General Smith had no sense of humor right now. "We know this is worldwide. Their air forces are down, too. Every plane in the world is stuck on the ground."

Faith sensed she'd stepped in it. "I wasn't implying I would, general. I was trying to lighten the mood."

"Don't worry, I don't think you're a spy." He directed her back to the plastic chairs, and they sat down next to each other.

"General," she began the second they were both seated, "I'd like to give you this." She pulled a phone out of her slacks.

He took it. "You've been holding out on me?"

"No!" she snapped. "I mean, no, not at all. This belongs to a reporter who spent the night in our parking lot. His name is Benny. Works for the Denver newspaper. Good guy. As soon as I saw him this morning, I confiscated this."

"Oh, that's different. Thank you." The general looked like he wanted to say something but didn't.

She nervously shifted in her seat. "General, I didn't do it out of altruism. I want you to trust me, so you'll give me...

give us our phones back. Sir, we need them to do our jobs. I have people on the outside I need to call to make simple observations about the causes and effects we're experiencing. If you—"

"Say no more," he cut in. "The horse is out of the corral already. You can have your phone back. Call whomever you need to."

"What do you mean about the horse?"

He pointed with his thumb to the busses outside. "We couldn't get all these scientists without someone asking a bunch of questions. They make it look so easy in the movies." He chuckled. "In reality, try sending some dark vans to pick up a professor or two from a college campus and watch the news hounds show up in droves. They followed the buses, so of course, it's all over the internet now."

"Reporters are outside," she said once she figured out the implications.

"Yep. All of them, apparently. Far outside, for now. But they're watching us."

She couldn't have planned it better.

"General, I would like to propose giving Benny full access to SNAKE in exchange for his silence. We can use him as our contact with the news services, so they can't complain about not providing information. We can tell him what we want him to know, and he can share that with his peers. One man. One message."

"Will he go for it?" General Smith sounded uncertain.

"May I invite him in? You can ask him yourself."

"Sure, why not? The press is destined to be a big thorn in my ass, so this would be helpful."

The general got up and went behind his desk, then

invited Benny to come in. Faith stood next to the reporter to introduce him.

"So, Dr. Sinclair says you two worked out a deal?"

"I report on whatever you've got going on here, hopefully with real information and not the fake stuff, and you tell me what I can share with the outside. Faith said that may be very little, but eventually, I'll be able to share more."

"And you agree to these terms?"

"I do. The only thing I ask is that you allow my wife to come here for the duration. I don't want her on the outside where it's dangerous."

General Smith didn't look happy.

Faith spoke quietly. "Benny, we didn't discuss this. Don't you think it would be more dangerous to be here, where things are..."

"I don't have time for this. Dr. Sinclair, do we have facilities for Benny and his wife?"

"I believe so. Our current numbers sit at about eight hundred, plus your two hundred and fifty. SNAKE was designed to support three thousand daytime staff, with dorms for one hundred. People will have to sleep on the floor, but if we need to sequester more scientists, we should be fine."

General Smith sat down. "Benny, you can bring your wife, but not your dog or your pet snake or any of that shit. She stays with you and out of my hair. Dr. Sinclair, my lieutenant will issue your phones back to you. I've lost a lot of time waiting for these scientists to arrive, and I need a solution to our—" He looked at Benny. "That will be all, son."

"You aren't going to let me listen in?" he said, sounding hurt.

"All information you get will come through Dr. Sinclair, is that clear? You will be the closest reporter in the United

States to what we're doing here, but you aren't the cock of the walk. Now please leave."

The door opened as if by magic. His Air Force assistant was there.

Benny left, and the general spoke the second the door closed. "Dr. Sinclair, these boxes of blue light are obviously important. I've got a hundred people telling me a hundred different things about what they could be. Half want to shut them down. Half want to keep them lit. I thought you scientists all thought the same way?"

"Sir, science is messier than you think. We seldom agree on anything unless it has been peer-reviewed to death, but there are people who claim to be scientists who believe the Earth is flat, so there are always going to be holdouts."

"I don't need Flat Earthers here. I need to know which way to go on this, on or off? Can you organize your cats and get them to agree on something? I'm thinking it needs to be off."

She thought of Bob's insult about what she would do if he wanted it turned off.

"Sir, you should know that my team strongly recommends we keep the beams on."

He peered hard at her. "Why is that?"

"Right now, a hunch. Once I have my phone back, I'm going to call my contacts at CERN."

"I thought CERN was gone?"

"That's what I thought, too, but has anyone knocked on the door?"

Somewhere in New Jersey

"Lydia, I'd love to stay around and talk, but I've got to get across the highway to find someone to help me get my car out of the mud." It seemed safer to leave the troubled girl behind, although he did feel a little guilty about it for some reason.

"Hey!" she replied instantly. "Please don't leave me. You're the first person I've seen here. I need to get back to the wagons, although they are probably already gone. I was going to be late, even before I got lost."

"Your people would leave without you?" he asked, shocked.

She nodded. "They do all the time. The wagon train is miles long. They can't wait for one lost girl. And without any family, I'm an afterthought anyway."

"I'm not sure why, but that pisses me off," he replied.

"Eww," she said with disgust. "You should not talk about pee." She said "pee" in a hushed voice.

He laughed. "No, it's a figure of speech. Where are you from? Really. Don't give me any bullshit."

"Manure is good for fires," she mumbled. Louder, she continued. "I told you where I'm from. Not here. My wagon train recently passed Tortoise Rock, Wyoming."

"What the fuck?" he blurted. "Wagon train? What year do you think this is?"

"1849, of course. What year do *you* think it is?" She did the thing with her hand on her hip, as if she were getting the better of him, but her eyes roved around like a lost dog's. She seemed uncertain of the world around her.

He held up his phone and showed her the big, bright screen. The date was right in the middle.

"2020?" she scoffed. "I think not."

He laughed. "That was what I thought a few seconds ago when you came down here. It isn't possible. People don't dress like you anymore. Look at the cars that have passed. Isn't that closer to the far future than 1849?"

She studied his faded orange gamer shirt. "They now dress like this? What does it mean? Your undergarment advises me that the cake shown on your front is a lie."

Garth almost lost it. His t-shirt was an old gamer meme. The piece of birthday cake was adorned with the words The cake is a lie. Sam had always made fun of his shirt, but Dad had gotten it for him, so he wore it well beyond its shelf life.

"It would take me a while to explain it to you," he said, stifling his laughter. "But this isn't my undergarment. This is just what I wear."

"It is a pretty color," she mused.

"Thanks," he replied, not sure if he liked wearing something a girl found pretty.

He made as if to head into the rain.

"Wait!" she said again. "Please. I've been here since yesterday. Will you help me catch something so I can cook it?"

Garth took a deep breath. He wasn't sure where a conversation with her would lead, but he decided to indulge her. "You'd cook a meal for me?"

"Well, I'd cook it for both of us, of course. A woman's place is at the hearth, I know, but I've spent a lot of time on my own. Perhaps with your help? I'm not selfish, but I *am* hungry."

He unslung his pack. "No girl I know would ever say something like that. There's no single role for any gender. I don't really care either way, but I can help you with this. You don't even have to cook it." He dug around for a pair of multigrain bars, pulled them free, and handed one to her.

She held it like he'd cut off her fingers.

"You tear it open like this." He demonstrated the simple act of opening and biting into a bar.

At first, she looked horrified, but it only took her a few seconds to catch on. She took a huge bite, then downed the small bar by stuffing the rest into her mouth.

"Good God! No one is going to steal it from you."

She was engaged in chewing the massive bite, unable to respond.

"I really need to go, Lydia. I have to get help freeing my car."

She held up a finger to make him wait. After she swallowed the food, she gave him a bright smile. "That was a curiosity! I even feel full."

"Well, glad I could help."

"Wait. Please. I have a lot of experience freeing wagons from the mud on the train. Some days that was the only thing I did." She brushed her thigh with her free hand as if wiping off mud. "I'm sure I can help you free your wagon."

"Car," he corrected.

"Right," she said. "Car."

Garth was in a difficult spot. If Sam had been with him, Lydia would already be part of the group. He would have fallen in love with the attractive girl and taken her back to the car, if only to let her watch him try to free it himself. But he tried to think like Dad, because he was in serious trouble. He had to get the car back on the road if he was going to escape the radiation cloud bearing down on New Jersey.

Was he thinking with his brain on this one?

Lydia apparently read his mind. "We got stuck in the Platte River. That was part of the reason Pa died there. He was overworked from freeing wagons from the heavy mud. Not just ours, either, but other families in our traveling circle. Before that, we got stuck in the mud three times in Missouri. Those were also real bad."

"Radiation is coming. I can't afford to make a mistake. If

you aren't strong enough to move the car, we might die out there."

She shuddered. "Radiation is really bad?"

"Yes. It's why I figured I'd go over there." He pointed along the road toward the far side of the Garden State Parkway. "Find some big, strong men willing to help."

"I promise. Take me to your, uh, car. I can help you get it out. I'd bet my life on it."

It was a tempting offer, and he took ten or fifteen seconds to mull it over. A distant rumble of thunder reminded him there were two storms heading his way. No matter what choice he made, there was risk. He had to make a decision. Try to find more help, or trust the ancient stranger?

"A bird in the hand is better than two in the tree," he said quietly.

"I've heard that!" she exclaimed. "I understood your speech."

He sighed heavily. Fate had spoken.

I-80, Nevada

Buck managed a steady fifty miles per hour in the snow. It was more than what the road conditions suggested, but the Nevada highway was mostly flat, straight, boring, and empty. The terrain partially explained why they saw fewer wrecks as they headed east. Even if a car ran off the road, it was so level that they could drive right back on.

Time seemed to stand still in the flatlands of the Silver State. The convoy inched across the map under a white sky on white roads next to the white desert.

"You okay?" Connie asked out of nowhere.

He blinked a few times, then looked at her. "Yeah, why do you ask?"

"Because you're staring at something a million miles away. Want to talk about it?"

His first reaction was to snap that he was fine, but she was sincere, so he tried to analyze his thoughts.

"I'm second-guessing shooting—and probably killing—those men again. I should have just waited for them to leave instead of stirring them up. Then they wouldn't have bothered me, and they wouldn't have seen you go to your car and bend over the trunk."

He felt his face flush.

"I didn't mean I saw it, too."

"My caboose?" she said, bewildered.

He scratched behind his ear. "Well, that was what got them interested."

Connie giggled. "For a tough guy, you sure are lousy with your feelings. And you were married to someone? Wow!"

"Hey, now. I do all right."

She rubbed Mac, who was apparently asleep on her lap. "Seriously, Buck, you have to let it go. Trust me, I write about this stuff all the time. If you'd stayed in bed, maybe you would have missed the bikers. Or, maybe you would have faced them later in the day, like now." She pointed outside. "Imagine if they surprised us out here in Nowheresville, USA."

"I can keep going. What if you had kept to yourself and they'd found me later in the day? You wouldn't have been around to help me. We can think about this from a million different directions, but in my view, they got what was coming to them. I'm glad you shot them to protect us, and

I'm happy you tipped my car into that ditch. You should have no regrets on either count."

Buck smiled because her words stroked his ego. He wanted to believe that he had acted properly, but it helped to have someone else confirm it.

"Thanks, Connie. I mean it. Ending a life isn't something I enjoy."

They looked at each other.

"It's like you said," Connie replied. "If you were the type of person who enjoyed that kind of thing, I doubt we'd be sitting here talking." She leaned back in her chair with a smile on her face.

"I'm glad you're still sitting there," he said.

"I know." She beamed.

TWENTY-THREE

**Search for Nuclear, Astrophysical, and Krono-
metric Extremes (SNAKE). Red Mesa, Colorado**

Bob was lurking in the hallway like a kid who was anxious to see if Faith got into trouble with her parents. "Well?"

"Well, what? I told him we recommend not shutting things down. He said all those other scientists on the buses are coming in to offer their ideas. The general wants us to come to a consensus."

"But he isn't turning it off right now?"

She nodded. "Unless he does something behind my back."

Bob ran his fingers through his dirty blonde hair like he was strung out and needed a cigarette. "Dammit, Faith. It wasn't supposed to happen like this."

"No shit," she replied. "If Izanagi had gone as planned, we'd both be sitting on our laurels right now writing boring papers. All the stuff we dreamed about."

Despite their differences, there had been a brief moment in time where they had been happy together. Now that the threat of his backstabbing had been minimized, she didn't feel bad about remembering those days, if only for a few seconds.

"No," he said forcefully. "You aren't seeing the point. It isn't about papers or tenure or any of that bullshit. It isn't even about the thing between you and me. Faith, this is much worse than you know."

"What are you talking about?" She studied his eyes. "What am I missing?"

He waved for her to follow, and she walked next to him in the hallway. When they reached the end of the hall, he looked back. "The general is bringing in his people because he wants to be sure that when he makes a final decision, he'll have the scientists back him up."

"That's logical," she assured him.

"No, not with him. Faith, open your eyes. Why do you think a four-fucking-star general is sitting at your desk? There's only one rank above him in the military, and I don't think they even use it."

She looked at him sideways as they continued down the hallway.

"They mentioned it on an episode of Jeopardy. There haven't been any five-star generals since the 1950s or 60s. I can't remember which."

"Okay, so he's important."

He took her to a section of the administration wing far from any of the other scientists.

"Faith, I have to tell you, I don't think you're cut out for this political bullshit, but maybe that was one of the things I liked about you. But you have to listen to me on this one. The general is here for a reason, and it isn't only because he happened to be in the area."

She sensed he was going to say more, but he intentionally dodged her gaze.

"Spill it," she demanded.

He waited a bit, then seemingly talked to himself. "This is going to get me in a lot of trouble."

She grabbed him and forced him to stop walking.

"If you don't tell me, so help me, I'll—"

"That won't be necessary." He laughed.

He stood closer and looked over his shoulder one final time.

"The military organized this whole thing. They paid for Azurasia's Izanagi Project. They probably paid for those boxes to be set up. And, I have no doubt they know what's going on between CERN and us."

Faith felt like a wide-eyed deer caught in the headlights.

"Don't be ridiculous. Why would they investigate themselves? They are the military. They can do whatever they want, and no one will ask questions."

"The why of it is not important right now. I'm telling you this because of how this was all set up."

She caught on quick. "You were helping them."

His nod was sheepish. "I swear I never saw any shred of evidence that the experiment would endanger people. I think someone fucked it up on the CERN side, or maybe it was sabotage. Whatever. None of that matters, though. I'm telling you with all seriousness that you cannot let the general turn it off."

"Why? You've got to give me more."

He put his arm over her shoulders and guided her down the hallway as he spoke in hushed tones. "My job was to make sure the CERN computers relayed their telemetry to SNAKE and vice versa. For the bulk of the experiment, that was dull work and hardly took any time at all. However, near the end, the amount of data kept growing exponentially. By the time we approached noon yesterday, we were transferring more data than we had bandwidth, so much of it was lost."

"Holy shit. Are you saying the crash came because of bandwidth issues?"

"No," he said quietly. "It was only telemetry that got lost, but the data could have been useful in figuring out what caused the blue light. Maybe it would even explain what happened to CERN."

She exhaled, trying to put the pieces together. "So SNAKE and CERN were in cahoots, and the whole thing was funded secretly by the military. Does General Smith know this?"

"I have no idea," Bob replied. "He sure doesn't act like it."

She snapped her fingers. "You have inside information on what those four beams are doing, don't you? Dammit, Bob, I'm going to strangle you when this is all over. Why can't we shut them off?"

"We're dealing with an area of science few people understand. Dr. Johnson's team in CERN were the experts. Whatever caused this disaster had to start in CERN, not here. We just got the blowback."

"What are they? What are the beams? Why can't we turn them off?" She was close to finally having her answer.

"Two words: Dark energy."

She thought about it for a second. "And I have two words for you. Horse and shit."

It took him ten minutes to convince her he was right.

He described how the world could end, and that was devastating enough, but he also hinted how time itself could come crash-landing into 2020 if they messed with the beams.

I-80, Nevada

Driving through Nevada was like watching the same piece of scenery repeated over and over again. The highway cut through the flat scrubland in long, straight sections and low hills remained distant, as if it were impossible to get close to them.

It was lonely country at the best of times, but the snow cover made it seem larger and far more empty than usual.

"Don't you live in the desert?" he asked Connie, remembering she lived in New Mexico.

"No. It's arid where I live, but not desert at all. I live in Taos, in the mountains."

"I've been close to there on my travels, but never made it all the way."

Mac was back on the floor, but he'd found a comfy spot in the tight space in front of Connie's seat. He yawned like Buck and Connie were keeping him awake.

"You are missing out. It's beautiful country. A lot better than this hellscape." She pointed out the window. "Though maybe this does have a stark beauty."

"This is Beans, come back," chirped the CB radio.

"Go ahead, Beans," Buck replied.

"In a few miles, there's a hamburger joint that is the best place to eat on this side of Nevada. What do you say we pull over and check it out?"

Buck wasn't hungry, although he imagined he should be. Instead of toast and eggs at the motel's breakfast buffet, he had started the day with a gunfight.

He looked at Connie but didn't key the CB microphone. "I'm not ready to stop. I've been losing time on my trip east since yesterday. Now we're finally moving the ball forward, and they want to stop?"

"You don't have to," she replied.

"I don't want to lose the convoy, either, but they aren't mine to command." Buck wasn't a wishy-washy kind of guy, but the combination of all the problems in his life conspired to make this choice more difficult than it should have been. "And, honestly, I think it's dangerous to stop. I saw Modesto rip itself apart yesterday, and you and I have both seen weird shit on the highway. Going into any town for a bite to eat seems risky."

"So tell them that," Connie said as if it were obvious.

He thought about it for another mile, but Beans called again. "Anyone? Can we stop at this exit?"

The emerald-green road sign was the only vibrant color from horizon to horizon. It informed them that the next town was three miles ahead.

It took him every inch of that three miles to decide what he was going to do. At the last possible second, he veered onto the offramp.

"Yeah, we can stop," he said without emotion. His goal was to get in and get out.

The five trucks rolled into the little town one after the next.

"The Shanty Town diner is the highlight of this place," Beans reported over the CB. "I stop here every time I pass this way. You should, too."

"I guess we are," Buck said to his two friends.

"I don't know why you didn't pass on this place," Connie declared. "It can't be that good."

"A convoy is give-and-take. If I ordered them around,

they might not follow me, and I admit that it is past lunch time."

"Maybe," she replied.

When they got into the small town, Buck knew something was wrong. Unlike Bridgeport, where the people had watched the traffic go by, this one-horse berg was empty. When they got to the Shanty Town Diner, it was even worse.

"Who the fuck would burn down a fine eatery?" Beans asked.

The small building Buck assumed was the diner was now a black smudge on the pavement. A nearby gas station had blown up, and the adjacent wooden buildings had burned to the foundations.

"We should go," he said to Connie. Then, realizing his role, he picked up the CB. "Guys, I'm rolling through town. Just keep going, okay?"

A couple of the truckers replied with alternatives that Buck didn't like, so he didn't respond. They followed him regardless. Sometimes, leaders simply lead.

"What happened here?" she asked.

"I don't know, but it scared the people into hiding. Maybe they have their version of the bikers to worry about, or maybe they no longer want outsiders in their town." He'd listened to books on tape for many miles of his travels. Small towns always had a dark side, and if the stories were based on any truth at all, they had to get out of there.

"Just drive," he said to restate his point.

"I saw bodies," Eve said over the CB.

"Where?" the Monsignor replied.

"Don't be gross," Eve shot back. "Unless you are some kind of sicko."

Mel laughed. "I guess I'm a little curious to see what I'll

look like someday. This mega-bomb is going to make a charred mess a lot like what we saw back there. I can see why people cleared out of the area."

Buck's Peterbilt went down the ramp at the next interchange, and seconds later the little town was a mile behind.

"God bless it," Sparky called out. "They were right about this stuff. The country is in some kind of civil war."

Buck was going to correct him, but Beans broke in first. "Local news, guys. I got something all the way to the left of the AM dial."

He tapped the radio on, then slid the needle to the left.

"Once again, we advise listeners to stay inside. If snow in June isn't enough for you, we have multiple reports of a prison break in south-central Idaho. Residents of northern Nevada are advised to stay indoors. Do not pick up hitch-hikers. Report anything unusual to local authorities."

"You were right," Connie said. "Our day should be about getting you to your son, not dicking around in roach-filled diners."

She picked up the mic before he could agree. "This is Connie. I'm riding shotgun with Buck. His instinct was to avoid any towns, and that's what we're going to do. We're all skipping lunch, and we're going to cross this state before anyone eats, got it?"

One by one the four other truckers agreed.

She sat back in her seat, seemingly satisfied.

"Not how I would have done it, but it needed to get done all the same. Thanks for that, partner." He laughed, never taking his eyes from the windshield, and made sure to loosen his fingers to keep from white-knuckling the steering wheel.

"I don't care what these other people do, but I'm better off with you than without. I hate to say it, but you're stuck with me and my big mouth. They should be happy to be stuck with you, too, if they want to survive."

"I'm sure I'll be hungry ten minutes down the road, but for now, I'm glad to shave off a few more miles. Besides, I have a dead squirrel in the fridge. We can eat that if we have to."

She looked back at his small refrigerator. "I'm not squeamish, but hearing that made my stomach turn over. I think I threw up in my mouth a little."

Buck chuckled. "Sexy."

She couldn't help but chuckle too. "You are one strange man. Isn't he, Mac? Mac?" The dog, who was wedged in front of Connie's seat with the floor heater blowing on his fur, didn't budge. He was out cold.

As the convoy's point man, Buck was already looking ahead to the next bend.

TWENTY-FOUR

Somewhere in New Jersey

Garth had time to talk to Lydia as they walked. "So, what do you do for fun?"

"There isn't much time for that on the journey. We walk from dawn until dusk most days. I guess the fun comes when I get to talk to other kids my age. It at least distracts us."

They were back out in the rain, which had picked up considerably since he'd left the taxi. Lydia's bonnet did a good job of keeping water off her face, but Garth hadn't even brought a hat. The rain ran down his head, and he kept one hand over his brow as a visor. He felt like a moron. What would Sam do?

"Do you have games or anything?" Garth blurted. He couldn't imagine anything fun back in 1849.

"Oh, we chase each other around or tell stories. Those can become games."

She didn't do a very good job of selling him on it. He thought about what she was saying. He was interested but didn't want to come across as a jerk. He also didn't want to be the one doing all the talking, like Sam would have done while he tried to impress her. Garth had seen the looks on the young women's faces, so he knew it wasn't a tactic that worked. Ever. Garth wondered what his dad would advise. Dad. How to talk to women.

Garth chuckled, but the rain drowned it out. "Let's get a better look and see what kind of options we have." Garth pointed to a clearing between the onramp and the main highway. They started trooping in toward the spot, which was in the general direction of the car.

"I've told you what I do," Lydia said softly. "What do *you* do for fun?"

"Wow. When I think about my days, I see most of it as fun. I spend a lot of time with my friend Sam. You'd like Sam. He's hilarious, and he can tell some stories. Anyway, Sam and I play on our phones most of the time. Usually with each other, but sometimes not."

He patted his pocket to signify what he spoke about.

"How can that be fun? Does it roll on the ground? Maybe it spins?" She smiled and clapped like she'd figured it out.

Garth shook his head, wondering whether she was still yanking his chain about where she was from. While she acted like she was from the distant past, he had no way to verify the truth of her claim. Deep down, he was sure the teen girl was manipulating him into believing something as silly as time travel, although he had no idea why.

The bottom line was, he needed her.

"No. But I'll show you when we get some time." Turnabout was fair play. "Sometimes we go into the city and spoof people. You know, pretend to be something we're not. Or wear egregious amounts of cologne and stand in crowds to see how people react. Spoiler alert: it isn't pretty."

"'Spoof?' I haven't heard that word before. If you mean playing roles in a theater? I've never seen a show since we never had any money, but I've heard they were incredible."

Garth watched her face. She sold it well. What would it hurt to let her have her moment? If she was spoofing him, so be it. Lydia was making it interesting, and she wasn't beating a pistol against the window of his cab.

He looked into the sky. "There!" He pointed to a dark bank of clouds to the northwest. The sky was already overcast and wet so the darkness didn't look like anything special, but he'd been paying attention to the broadcasts. "That's got to be the radiation storm they warned about. Shit! We've got to move."

Lydia was facing to the south. "What about those? I think they are worse."

Garth looked where she pointed. Another dark area swirled menacingly underneath a top layer of rain clouds. It was as if the two violent storm fronts decided to slip in beneath a third, calmer, storm. He and the girl were in the path of both.

"Come on!" the car is right over here.

They ran together for a couple of minutes, and she easily kept up with him. If her words were true and she walked every day of her life, it would make sense.

Nah, can't be true.

"Why is one storm worse than the other?" Lydia asked as they ran. "We should go back! We can stay in my cave and avoid the rain."

He thought of his dad. The delayed text reply had told Garth to stay home and wait out the radiation storm. Dad was going to be angry about him having taken the cab, and he would be super-pissed that he had run the car off the road. He would go supernova if he let himself get caught in the rain out in the open.

The yellow-colored taxi came into view ahead of him, so he continued to run. "Come on! We're there."

She followed him to the car, although she seemed reluctant to get too close. "This is your wagon? It is the same as those shrieking machines under the bridge. It has no horses." She looked inside the rear window, but then positioned herself to see inside the broken one by the steering wheel. "There are no ghosts inside yours?"

Garth tried to think of it like a tv show or a movie. He had to convince her to help him, or they were both going to get very sick and die.

"Look, I don't have time to tell you everything. You've missed almost two hundred years of technology. This is like a...a boat. A boat doesn't have horses pulling it, right? They use steam." He had no idea if she'd even seen a boat, but he figured that was reasonable. He also had no idea if her boats used steam power, but he'd read about steamers in school and they looked pretty old, so he took a chance.

"This boat on wheels will take us away from this place and allow us to escape both storms. However, we have to get it out of the mud right now." He pointed to the mud-drenched rear wheels. "They just spin and the car doesn't move."

"I still don't see why you are worried about the rain—"

"It isn't the rain," he interrupted. "I told you before. There is radiation..."

Again, he had to think of a translation.

"The rain has little fireballs inside each drop. I know it sounds crazy, but those fireballs will get inside your skin if they touch you. I've seen movies of nuke tests on YouTube. It is horrible stuff."

Cars sped by on the Garden State Parkway. In his head, he thought there had been an increase in traffic since he'd met Lydia. It was as if more people were moving out at the last minute to escape the looming threat.

He walked over to her. "Please? I need your help to free my car. After that, I won't stop you from going back under your bridge if you want, although I'm happy to give you a ride."

When she looked at him, her blue eyes struck him as ancient in some way, as if they'd seen a lot more than he had. The rest of her face was youthful, tanned, and a bit dirty. Maybe she'd spent a lot of time outside at the pioneer farm.

"You'd really let me ride with you? You don't even know me."

He got close to her, intending to start begging for her help, but she held up a hand and put it on his chest before he got too close.

"I'll help you," she said, looking beyond him. "I want to know what it's like to ride with the ghosts."

He mentally smacked his head. She was going to be disappointed when she finally understood how cars operated, but he'd deal with that later. Right now, he had to see if his gamble paid off.

"So, do you know how to get my car out of the mud?"

She smiled.

I-80, Nevada

The snow seemed to break, and the sky brightened as Buck's convoy got well into Nevada. Miles upon miles of snow surrounded them on the flat desert floor, and the distant hills appeared as nothing more than snow drifts on the horizon. It was white everywhere.

Soon after the weather cleared up, his phone vibrated in the cradle. He looked away from the snow-covered highway for a moment to confirm it was Garth.

"Hey, can you pick this up? It's my son. Tell me what he says."

Connie plucked it from the holder and read it, but didn't relay it to him right away.

"What does it say?" he pressed.

"It says, 'Sorry, dad. Took cab out of city. In New Jersey. Ran into ditch. Getting help.'"

"What the..." Buck sucked in a deep breath. "What is that...*kid* doing out on the road? I know I taught him better. Oh, God. He's going to be out there when the radiation hits."

He frantically spun the radio dial. "Damn. I've got to know where the storm is now. Maybe I can still help him get out of the path. Shit! He could be hurt or bleeding in his ditch. Does it say anything else?"

She looked at the text. "No. I'm waiting to see if more comes through."

Buck practically ripped the steering wheel off the dashboard. "Dammit! I told him to stay home!"

His anger came out like a flamethrower. First, he aimed it at Garth, although he couldn't carry that heat for more than a few seconds once he realized his boy was in legitimate trouble. However, he next directed hells-hot anger at the mobile phone company he and Garth used. It hadn't worked right since the blue light yesterday; it was down more than it was up. He was sure the system delays would cost Garth's life. Finally, to his dismay, he turned the flames on himself.

"Buck, you've really done it this time. You should have been there."

"There was nothing you could have done," Connie reasoned. "I know you tried. I typed in the message told him to stay put. It got to him too late. Maybe he was already out the door by the time you received his message asking for advice. You should be proud that he didn't text and drive."

He didn't want to tell her he was thinking along entirely different lines. If he'd been in New York with Garth, none of the delays would have mattered. However, he set that aside. It was pointless to imagine what could have been, just as Connie said it was pointless to wonder about all the different alternatives with the bikers. Garth needed his help. Now.

"Connie," he said in a measured voice, "will you please type the following?"

"Ready," she replied.

"Garth, get to shelter as soon as you get this. Do *not* get caught out in the open. Radiation will kill you." He hesitated. There was no way to convey all his expertise with radiation drills and how to survive. The only surefire answer for his son was to get out of the rain. He'd deal with the rest later; hopefully he'd have a better signal when they got close to Salt Lake City.

"Anything else?"

"Tell my son I love him."

"I will," she replied softly.

Buck was still almost twenty-five hundred miles from his boy, but he was getting closer with each passing minute. When the weather outside improved, he intended to push the limits of his Peterbilt.

. . .

Search for Nuclear, Astrophysical, and Kronometric Extremes (SNAKE). Red Mesa, Colorado

After speaking with Bob and learning of his treachery, she threw herself into her work. The general finally returned everyone's phones, so people could communicate within the facility. She tried to piece together an explanation for the general so he wouldn't shut the boxes down.

She tried the numbers of a few colleagues at CERN and tried to contact the authorities in Switzerland, but international calls didn't go through. She also tried Dez, down in Australia, but that didn't go through either.

All in all, having her phone back did almost nothing for her, but eventually she did get one important message.

It was the general.

"Already?" she wondered.

'Dr. Sinclair, please join me in your office. Decision time.'

She got there to find a dozen other scientists already inside.

"Let her through!" the general called to his associates when he noticed her at the door. "And close up back there."

Someone shut the door after she was in the room. The general was already talking by the time she reached the standing space up front.

"The 50th Space Wing reports that the calibration error is now off by six years. *Six years*, people. Now, I don't know what those beams are doing down in the supercollider ring, but this is unacceptable. We have to stop it."

He took a deep breath.

"I need options."

The room broke out into a chaotic churn of voices. The general tried to listen for a few moments but then held up his hand. "One at a fucking time!"

Faith hovered to the side, content to observe until she got a feeling for what the new scientists wanted to do. None of her people were in the room, which weighed heavily on her.

"We can run a cable to their tram car," a man suggested.

"Is there a way to crush them?" another asked.

A dozen different people had ideas, and they all involved destroying the equipment broadcasting the blue beams. As she had feared, she was on the wrong side of consensus.

"Are we all talking about destroying the equipment now? Sir, you can't shut it down. I have strong evidence suggesting the links to CERN are what's holding things together. If we turn the boxes off or destroy them, we risk making things worse on the outside."

That got his attention. "You mean outside this office?"

"No, I mean anywhere beyond the SNAKE collider ring. I figured out after talking to Dr. Donald Perkins that he was affected by the time distortion when he left the collider ring yesterday. That's why he is sick today. Other evidence suggests the power is broadcasting outward from the ring, not inside it."

One of the NORAD scientists scoffed, but when the general looked at him, he shut his mouth.

"Dr. Sinclair, it's wonderful to know we're safe here in your special circle, but the rest of the world is in danger. It also doesn't change the fact that the satellites are six years out of alignment. Who knows what that means for people on the ground? I think the only safe play is to shut off the power coming into SNAKE by any means necessary."

The NORAD scientists nodded in agreement. Even the shaggy-haired man who had originally supported her back in the tunnel was now on board with a shutdown.

She was tempted to reveal Bob's role and the involvement of dark matter, but in a room full of hostile scientists and their take-no-prisoners commander, she didn't want to come across as the lone wacko. Then he'd never listen to her.

Faith tried another tack.

"A little more time is all I need," she asserted. "Give my team and me a few more hours to piece together a solution we can all live with. We have our phones. I've tried to contact CERN, but haven't reached anyone. There's so much to learn."

General Smith held up his hand, and everyone got quiet. "I've learned enough. You eggheads go to your Hobbit holes and talk about what comes next. I want a solution in fifteen minutes that we can kick off within the next hour. We're shutting down all of the blue beams. That's final."

"General!" Faith blurted.

Smith practically rolled his eyes at her, confirming his lack of respect.

"Sir, please give me permission to evacuate my staff. If we blow up like CERN, we'll have no scientists left to pick up the pieces."

The general stood at the desk, then bent to put his hands on the wooden top. He seemed to think about her request.

"Agreed. They can wait on the front parking lot."

"But—" she began.

"That will be all," he told her, his face blank.

She ran out in a hurry. There was only one card left to play.

Bagram Airbase, Afghanistan

Lieutenant Colonel Stanwick had assumed his intelligence picture would flesh out as the night fight wore on and give him a better idea of the battlefield, but it didn't. It only grew more confusing. An old combat adage of every first report was wrong was coming true, but the second and third reports, along with the succeeding follow-ups, seemed to be wrong, too.

Battalion headquarters as well as the Air Force staff at the airfield didn't know anything more than he did.

He stared at a dust-caked whiteboard and tried to give a briefing to the soldiers who remained. The fundamentals of warfare hadn't changed, and his first priority was keeping his people alive. Information was their shield. If it was wrong, it increased the risk. That was a long way from his intent.

"This is us in the middle." He pointed to the center of the crude sketch of the rectangular air base. "We know Soviet heavy tanks are positioned on the high ground north of us." Phil drew some mounds to represent hills. "Their gear is shit for night fighting, so we assume they are using pre-designated coordinates to hit the airstrip."

"The Russians are still our allies, aren't they?" Matt Carbon asked.

"Of course, but these are Soviets; I'm not sure how, and I don't care. We fire back when we get hit. I've been trying to get the dipshits in Kabul to get us a Russian liaison so we can get these guys to stop firing at us, but they say they haven't been able to raise anyone in the Green Zone since about seventeen hundred."

"So who is firing back at the Soviet tanks?" a voice called out. "There's no allied armor on base."

"That's an interesting question," Phil replied. He marked an X on the map and held the marker there. "They belong to the Marines. Delta Company, 1st Tank Battalion, 1st Marine Division, to be exact."

"Whiskey-Tango-Foxtrot, sir?"

"I know. They shouldn't be here. Neither should these men." He drew a circle to the south of the base, "This area is where we've found British Redcoats."

He went crazy with circles. "And this is where the Northern Alliance is dug in. And this is where Mohammed Zahir Shah—the deposed king of Afghanistan--is holed up. And we think these are Chinese forces."

"Sir, are we at war with everyone?"

The base rumbled from a ground explosion. Phil had to lean against the whiteboard because of the shift beneath his feet. Dust rained down from the concrete ceiling.

He waited for a second for the air to clear.

A jet screamed overhead.

"Yes, I think we—"

The ground heaved as the air got sucked out of the room. "Cover!" Lieutenant Colonel Phil Stanwick yelled as he dove to the floor. His whiteboard and the wall behind it were sucked inward by the force of the nearby explosion.

TWENTY-FIVE

Search for Nuclear, Astrophysical, and Krono-metric Extremes (SNAKE). Red Mesa, Colorado

The alarms in SNAKE began their shrill warning as she left General's Smith's meeting. He was nothing if not punctual.

She sprinted down the hallway to catch the one person who could put a stop to the shutdown. When she arrived at his office, Bob was still at his desk, as if the alarms were of no concern.

"I appreciate the sentiment of your running to get me, but I'm not leaving," he said, patronizing her.

"What?" She was panting after her run. "You really think highly of yourself. It's a wonder your head doesn't need a sidecar to carry your ego as well as your brain. No, I came here to put you back to work. He's shutting us down."

"So I've gathered. I'm assuming you told him what we discussed and he ignored you?"

"I told him everything but what the experiment was exploring. He and I have been butting heads since he showed up, and he stacked the room with his own scientist like you said he would. A second-hand explanation wasn't going to sway them. I saved the heavy lifting for you."

"You want me to explain quantum entanglement and dark matter to a general?"

"Just enough so he understands, dammit. Come on, you can't be this dense. He has to be stopped."

"Ah, so at least you believe me? That's a start, I guess."

She got the sense he enjoyed having her up against the wall, but it was the truth. Whatever else she had to say about Bob, he wouldn't lie about what was unarguably a brilliant experiment, even if the end result had been so disastrous. SNAKE had tapped into dark energy. He would do everything in his power to live long enough to get the accolades from his peers he knew he deserved. The leadership of SNAKE might even come with it, although she wasn't ready to dangle that in front of him.

His ego was his weakness, however, so she unabashedly baited it.

"I do believe you. The fate of the whole planet may hinge on whether you can make the general believe you, too."

Bob studied her for ten or fifteen seconds.

"Fine," Bob said melodramatically. "Let's go. I'm sure I can do a better job than you did."

Whatever, she thought. Anything to buy a little time.

They marched down the hallway together. Faith ignored the claxons blaring from every corner as well as all the people running for the exits. When they got to the general's office, he was on the phone. She was fortunate his door was already open because none of his assistants were nearby to do it for her.

The general waved her in but didn't hang up.

"General, you have to stop the shutdown." Faith pointed to Bob. "He has information you need to hear."

The military man put his hand over the receiver of his phone. "I told you, we're doing this. I don't want any more scientific debate."

Bob stepped up. "Sir, if you shut down even one of those beams, I assure you things are going to get worse outside. Shut them all down, and the world's magnetic poles might shift dramatically, almost instantly. The inner core of the Earth could seize up. That would be game over, as they say."

The general still held his phone askew while looking at Faith. "Is he for real?"

Without crunching the math, she had to trust Bob.

"Sir, he's the head of modeling. I trust him to know what he's talking about on the science, but I brought him here for a different reason."

Faith turned to Bob. "Tell him."

General Smith seemed to recognize that the tone had shifted. "I'll call you right back," he said to the person on the phone.

Then, to Bob, "You have one minute to wow me."

Bob brushed his fingers along the side of his head. "I worked on the Izanagi Project from its inception, and I know how and why the metal boxes were installed. The experiment—"

"Are you fucking kidding me? You were down in the tunnels and didn't think to mention this?" The general stood up, obviously upset. "I thought you and I talked about trust, Dr. Sinclair? Is this your idea of telling me the truth?"

"Sir, I just found out, I swear. But there is something more serious that I think you already know about: the military paid for the Izanagi Project. They were the ones who installed the boxes and altered the parameters of the experiment, so maybe *you're* the one who hasn't been forthright with *me*."

She crossed her arms, hoping the pose conveyed her sense of moral superiority.

The general shook his head and faked a smile. "My dear Dr. Sinclair, you should not give me that self-satisfied look. I told you I don't trust anyone, and you've proved me correct."

She relented a little. "I've been nothing but honest with you. Bob was working for the military. I had no idea."

"False. I know you sent a message to your sister in Australia."

Fuck. How did he find out?

"You told her SNAKE was the cause of the world's problems. How many times did I ask you if anyone on the outside knew?"

Faith was blindsided by his accusation, but it did explain why her phone had been kept for so long. They had searched them all to see who knew what.

"Are you going to hurt her?" she asked with reluctance.

The general's eyes grew wide. "Hurt her? Who do you think I am? No, we're not going to hurt anyone. Besides, it hardly matters now. Everyone knows something fishy is going on. That's why all those reporters are out there."

He took a deep breath. "I only brought it up because I can't trust anyone at your facility, Dr. Sinclair. You might be making up this story about military contracts and further destruction to stop me from shutting you down. I can't take the chance."

"But sir!" she insisted. "You and I talked about this before. His experiment involves the biggest mysteries of the universe. Dark matter. Dark energy. Quantum flux. Time

231

travel. But he didn't need a supercollider as big as the solar system."

The general stood ramrod straight behind his desk and picked up the phone again. Initially, she was relieved that he was calling it all off, but that wasn't it.

"I can't trust you, Dr. Sinclair. Better evacuate with everyone else if you believe SNAKE is destined to blow up. I think that's an exaggeration too."

She was in shock.

"Do it," the general barked into the phone.

I-80, Elko, NV

Buck's convoy maintained an even eighty miles per hour across what remained of Nevada. The weather continued to improve, and the snow on the ground was mostly gone. By the time they reached Elko, the temperature was back up into the fifties, and for once there were no storms on the horizon. That also improved their radio reception.

The news was all bad.

His main concern was the two storms converging on Garth, although the broadcasters said little about it. However, the rest of the country shared the weird weather. Another hurricane had popped out of nowhere in the Gulf of Mexico, and there had been a devastating tsunami along the southern coast of Alaska, as well as dozens of reports of strong tornadoes.

He and Connie were also interested in any news related to time travel. Just as she and the others showed up out of the past, people were starting to recognize that it was happening all over the country.

Dead relatives were suddenly alive.

Old buildings appeared next to new ones.

Some towns went back to the way they had been fifty years ago.

When the convoy went through Elko, several big piles of tires were on fire, as if the town was in turmoil. That spooked his fellow drivers.

"Hey, guys," Monsignor said on the CB. "I'm thinking this is a little too much fire for my taste. I'm considering dumping and running."

Eve replied. "I'm with you. If consumers want their TVs, they can come out to Nevada and get them. I'd rather turn around and go home to Seattle."

Buck looked at Connie. He was already on edge because Garth hadn't replied despite the better weather, so having his people freak out around him was unsettling. "I've heard of guys dropping and running. My boss said some of his drivers did it yesterday. They must have already been seeing this time shift wherever they were. It's only getting worse, apparently."

"Can you make better time if you drop the cargo? I would think so because of all that weight."

"Not as much as you think. Big semis like this aren't aerodynamic at all when they don't have a trailer behind them. I'm not sure it's the real issue, though."

He picked up the CB mic. "Hey, guys, Buck here. Look, I know you are hearing weird shit on the radio. I saw lots of it coming over the Sierras down by Yosemite and the Nevada border. Hell, my co-pilot is from 2003."

Buck paused to look at his partner before going on.

"I'm worried, too, but we all have a job to do. Whatever is happening outside, it might be a blip on the radar that disappears tomorrow. How stupid will you feel if you get home to find company people asking for compensation for losing a trailer? Can your pocketbook survive such a hit?"

There were provisions in every contract for such eventualities. The safety of the driver was always paramount over the contents of the haul, but he was trying to make a point, so he avoided the law.

"I love what I do," he admitted. "I've never missed a delivery, and I'm not going to let jacked-up weather or craziness in the news force me to give up this job. If we stick together, I believe we have a great chance of riding through this rough patch and making it to our destinations. Then, instead of quitters, we'll be heroes."

He didn't know if he was making sense, but he saw how to close his speech. He knew truckers, and most of them were always on the lookout for the next easy dollar.

"You guys can write your own checks if you don't drop and run. Companies will kill to hire someone who didn't give up even when time travelers came to America."

Buck listened for their reply, but he'd accidentally hit upon a troubling fact.

If things did get back to normal, would Connie disappear from his life?

She reached over and put her hand on his arm.

"You did all you could. I hope they'll stick with you."

He didn't answer. He had just found someone he liked who liked him. He wasn't ready to lose that. Was it selfish to want things to stay as they were?

TWENTY-SIX

Canberra, ACT, Australia

Destiny watched as the hunters loaded her bird onto their four-wheeler and drove it away. A second four-wheeler arrived and took away the hunter she'd tranquilized as well. There was going to be a shitstorm when the guy woke up, so she furiously thought about what she needed to do to protect herself.

She didn't need to reveal herself to the hunters by driving behind them. They were on Zandre's equipment and would go back to his house, so she plotted her own way. She arrived a couple of minutes before they did because they were hauling heavier loads.

"We got one!" they screamed when they pulled up to the house.

A lot of hunters, including Zandre, were still in the field, so there were fewer men around to welcome the arrivals at the lodge. That was fine with her, because her anger had grown with every minute of her drive.

They stole my bird.

She parked her four-wheeler away from the others and

took her time walking over to where the men had tossed the Duck of Doom onto the grass. She stopped at each of the hunters' rides to see if they'd shot other animals, thankful they had not.

When she approached the celebration, she went over to the downed creature, although a solidly-built hunter kept her from getting next to it.

She pretended not to care, but then she noticed the sedated hunter propped up next to a step.

"Oi. Is he all right?" She pointed to the man.

"Heart attack," the protective hunter replied. She recognized him as the man who had pulled the Duck of Doom out of the water and put it on his cart. "Called triple zero, but they said it will be a while. We're on our own, I guess."

She knew it wasn't a heart attack, so she didn't waste more attention on him. However, she found it fascinating that the injured guy had received no medical help from his friends. They seemed more interested in the bird.

That upset her almost as much as the initial theft.

"I shot that bird, you know," she explained. "You guys found it in a creek, didn't you? I was away getting my hand-cart when you came in and took it."

The lead hunter glared at her. "Sorry, Sheila. No one was there but Dave. We figure he shot it and then had a heart attack. Poor guy."

The others grunted in support of their comrade as if they believed his story without exception. She saw it would be fruitless to lay claim to the bird, but she'd expected that.

"Well, it is a beautiful creature," she said, looking it over.

"All I see is ten million dollars," the big hunter replied. His friends laughed.

"Dave's ten million, right, mates?" she said innocently.

If she wasn't going to get the credit, she would at least make sure the big lying asshole didn't get it either.

The man glared at her. "Dave's injured. Maybe dying. Me and the others found it and drove it here, so who's to say who really brought it in?"

She checked the Duck of Doom once again; some of its feathers were fluttering. That would easily be mistaken for the effects of wind, but she knew better.

"I shot it," she insisted. "And I'll prove it to you."

"We'd love to see it," the angry hunter taunted.

She held up her finger to signal she needed a second. "Be right back."

When Destiny reached her four-wheeler, she sat at the controls to catch her breath. Her heartbeat was running wild. After surviving the forest fire and a brush with being shot, she was no fool when it came to surviving in the outback. At the same time, she couldn't let these hunters get the best of her. It wasn't in her nature to be someone else's doormat.

If she timed it properly, she would prove the truth of what she said and make it clear to the rest of the hunters who was lying.

She started the gas engine.

Destiny was careful to keep the engine revs at a minimum as she slowly drove across the large grassy lawn toward the group of hunters. She paused about ten meters away but gave it a little gas to get their attention.

All eyes were on her.

You can do this, Dez.

A few seconds went by before she saw the Duck of Doom stir. It wasn't the wind moving its wings. It was waking up.

"I can prove I shot that bird," she said in a raised voice.

"It's really easy, actually, because you don't know what type of weapon I used."

She revved the engine louder, praying she knew animals well enough that she could anticipate what would happen next. It was an educated guess based on her experience with sedating other animals over her career, but it was still a guess.

No one could predict what a thirty-thousand-year-old bird would do.

Destiny let go of the brake and lurched toward the men. They spread out as if fearful she'd run into them, which was what she wanted them to think. One of the men fell over the prone body of the bird, which caused it to hop up.

She continued forward, revving the engine to drive up the noise.

The bird was confused and squawked bloody murder as it bumped into a couple of the hunters. Once it saw an opening, it ran for a clump of trees at the edge of Zandre's yard.

"I tranquilized it!" she shouted as she avoided hitting any of the hunters.

Destiny chased the white-and-black bird with her ride, and she was amazed by how easily it got away from her. It departed in a fast waddle-hop before it jumped into the brush with a final passionate warble. It was almost like it knew it was free again.

I can't protect you, little guy, she thought. *I need the military.*

The Demon Duck of Doom didn't stop at the trees. It ran beyond them into the open expanse of the Canberra bush, destined for parts unknown. She followed it, content to have won a small victory, but plans were already forming in her mind about what she would need to do to help all the new arrivals. As a naturalist, it fell on her to take care of the time-shifted visitors and get them to safety.

She had just proved to herself that she'd go to almost any length to get it done.

Destiny wondered in those first seconds if the hunters were going to shoot her for scaring them. After staring down the barrel of a loaded rifle at the creek, she feared it might be easier to shoot her in the back. However, she assumed no one would want to kill her in front of witnesses.

Or she was being paranoid.

It didn't matter to her what the hunters wanted, and they would not be chasing her anytime soon.

She had the keys to their four-wheelers.

I-80, Nevada

The drivers behind Buck still hadn't made up their minds about staying, but most of his attention was on Garth. He was now receiving an AM station out of Salt Lake City, and the male talk-radio host was discussing the situation on the East Coast.

"As we said last hour, the radiation threat remains high from the Susquehanna River where the Three Mile Island reactor is located, all the way to the eastern tip of Cape Cod. The nuclear regulatory people have been hush-hush about the levels of radiation in the air. Well, radiation in the rain, since it seems that a giant storm is blowing it toward the coast. What do you think is the real story here?"

A woman guest replied to the host. "I believe the main issue is that Federal authorities have no way of knowing where the radiation will blow, and thus they have no way to issue realistic evacuation orders. We're talking about something like twenty million people in a narrow band between the origin point and the coast. There will be lots of casualties if people head out into the rain. Their best bet is to ride it out."

"Unless Hurricane Audrey gets there first."

"True. It could push the blast zone to the north, outside the limits of New York City, maybe to the north of Boston as well. Of course, the new path will create new problems for upper New England and eastern Canada."

"Is that what you're seeing on the weather forecast?" the host asked.

"Right now, the cutoff line is in the middle of New Jersey. Audrey is pushing north at a high rate of speed, but I'm not sure it will be enough."

Buck shut off the radio.

"Fuck," he drawled. "I should have tried harder to get hold of him."

Connie held up his phone. "I've been dialing his number every few minutes. It never goes through, nor does the number of my son."

He felt terrible for both of them, but it helped that she was trying.

"Please let me know if you get—"

"Wait!" she exclaimed. "A message came through just now."

He let off the gas in his excitement. "What does it say?"

"I'm fine," she replied.

"That's it?"

She watched the screen as if more was about to pop up, but a minute went by and nothing appeared. "Yes, he only said he was fine."

"I can live with that," Buck commented, returning his focus to the road. "He's still in the game and unhurt. It means he's going to be okay, like us. I'm sure he's back on the road and heading for shelter."

"Buck," Monsignor called on the CB. "We've made our decision."

He glanced at Connie and the oversized puppy at her feet. "Well, let's see if they're going to stay with us."

Search for Nuclear, Astrophysical, and Kronometric Extremes (SNAKE). Red Mesa, Colorado

Faith had been pushed to the sidelines because of her white lie about Destiny and her failure to offer compelling alternatives to a shutdown, but she tried to stay close to the action.

She was in the room when the scientists went into their Hobbit hole, as the general had called it. They talked about a variety of ways to destroy the boxes, including smashing them or blowing them up, but she saw the huge flaw in their thinking.

"Won't that damage the collider, too?" she asked the group.

When they gave her blank stares, she continued, "Does anyone have a come-along? We could use one to pull them away rather than destroy the cases.

The solution was something she had learned from her father back in Australia: a hand-held winch that was designed to pull off-road trucks from obstacles on the outback roads. It turned out that the general's Humvees each carried one.

When she walked into the control center an hour later, the general surprised her.

"Good thinking about the winches. You'd make a

decent government employee, Dr. Sinclair. Your solution cost us nothing. I respect that."

"Well, your idiots were going to use C-4 to blow up the boxes and a good chunk of my ring, so I had to think of something."

He gave her a hard look. "It was good that you were there."

She stepped over to him. "General, this is my last plea. I want nothing more than to protect the world. This is a global situation. I know we've cracked heads, but I want to start over. I didn't see how my sister could threaten our security from the far side of the world, but I was wrong to keep it from you."

His glare burned into her retinas, but she held firm in the belief honesty was the only thing that could save her. If she as the leader needed to fall on her sword, she'd do it in an instant.

"Sir, you can put Bob in charge. I don't care anymore who is at the helm, but you have to listen to *someone* on my team. A total shutdown is going to kill everything."

He didn't appear to have been swayed, so she got even closer.

"General. You can kick me out. Kick my whole team out. But if you have one ounce of respect for any of the work we've done in our lifetimes, please only destroy one of the boxes and then see what happens. If I'm wrong and life goes on normally, you can destroy the others at your pleasure."

"You really believe your shifty friend, don't you?" he asked.

"Sir, you have no idea what he and I have gone through in our lives. We were together a long time, God help me. He's arrogant. Selfish. And his ego? You can see it from space." She let out a small laugh. "But he would not endanger us by giving us the wrong information. More importantly, he would not injure himself. Sir, he's telling us the truth about this. Something bad is going to happen if you shut it all down cold turkey."

"I guess it couldn't hurt to do a staggered shutdown."

She brightened, although it was still a defeat. "I don't suppose you'd start your staggered shutdown with a three-hour delay?"

"Not a chance."

"I had to try," she replied.

The general picked up a phone. "Pull out number one. Wait on numbers two, three, and four until I give the order."

He put the phone down and sat in a plastic chair like a father outside the delivery room. She had to admit he did not look like he enjoyed beating her in their final battle, which took some of the sting out.

A hand-held radio warbled before a man spoke.

"Sir, box one has been moved. The beam is gone!"

"Yes!" the general crowed. "I knew it!"

A rumble like distant thunder shook the control room.

General Smith's smile wiped off his face. "What was that?"

She looked at a nearby control panel. The energy level inside the collider was active again, which was an impossibility, given that the feeder lines were shut down.

"We have an energy spike inside the ring," she told him. "It's nominal, but growing at an incredible rate."

"What? How?" he asked. "We need to shut down the others!" It was a giant leap of cause and effect she did not agree with in the least.

"No, sir. We have to see what's going on before we make things worse."

He picked up the phone and dialed. With the phone at his ear, he looked right at Faith.

"General, you have to trust me. Please. This is exactly what Bob said was going to happen. If you destroy the other links, you're going to make this worse."

The rumble in the earth increased like the storm was moving closer. Someone's coffee cup fell to the tiled floor and shattered.

We are so fucked.

Faith was scared for her life and wanted to run out of the room to save herself, but she held her position to try until the end to dissuade the general from blowing up the world.

He spoke into the phone.

This is it. She nearly closed her eyes.

"Standby on container number two. Do not, I repeat, *do not*, pull them away until I give the order."

The shaking was now sustained and rough.

"Power is far beyond the hundred-tera-electron-volt threshold," she said to the control room. The power inside the supercollider was measured at the subatomic level, so the scale of energy spinning around the loop was still tiny. However, she had a sneaking suspicion that it was much greater than she would have thought possible before today.

"Is this what happened to CERN?" the general asked with a forlorn stare.

Faith spoke over the noise of the earthquake. "The energy is building up. I think I know what's going to happen next."

She motioned for him to follow her.

"Come with me." She turned and walked out without waiting.

TWENTY-SEVEN

West Wendover, NV

As they crossed the remaining half of Nevada, the sunny afternoon gradually gave way to a more subdued evening. Buck was finding it necessary to actively fight his exhaustion. He'd been tired by lunchtime because of the chase with the bikers, and the blizzard had taken the rest out of him. Now, in normal weather, he was lulled into nodding off.

When Connie spoke to him, he nearly sprang out of his seat.

"Buck? You okay over there?"

He pretended it was no big deal. "Yeah, I was just thinking about... We need to carry some food and drinks with us. A bag of chips and a caffeinated soda would hit the spot."

"Tired, huh? Your eyelids look like they could use toothpicks to hold them open."

Buck smiled at her. "Is it that obvious?"

"I'm sure you truckers have a superhuman ability to

keep awake, but I've been in this chair for the last ten hours, and I'm running on empty. I don't know how you do it."

"Oh, I assure you, we get tired like everyone else." He didn't want to whine in front of her. "But I'm fine."

She gave him a sideways look, then went back to watching the road. A few minutes later, she pointed out a sign on the side of the desolate highway.

"West Wendover, five miles. It shows hotel and food. Why don't we stop there for the night?" Connie also pointed to the atlas on her lap, which she'd kept there most of the afternoon, to Mac's chagrin. "It's the last town before the Utah state line."

"Uh huh," Buck absently replied.

"Or you could let me drive for a while," she said matter-of-factly. "Looks like it's about a hundred miles to Salt Lake City from here."

Hell, no! was his initial reaction.

But then he thought about it. If she was able to drive his truck, they wouldn't have to stop at all. They could travel night and day, taking turns sleeping and driving, and could be back to Garth in half the time.

He'd never considered letting anyone else drive his rig, even back when he was married. It wasn't a male chauvinist thing, either. Buck didn't trust *anyone* to drive while he sat in the passenger seat or slept. It took away his control of the situation, and on the road, anything could happen at any given second.

Connie seemed to realize she'd said something he didn't like. "I didn't mean anything by it. I know we just met."

"Don't worry, you're fine," he replied. "I do appreciate your offer, and if we stick together for a while, I think I could show you how to drive this baby."

"But?" she asked.

"But I think our priority right now is keeping this convoy together. We're faced with a military dilemma here. We can get home fast, or we can get home safe. If you and I tag-team and cannonball run across the whole country, we'll soon lose the four trucks behind us because they'll need to sleep. We have no idea what to expect ahead—"

She picked up on his thought. "So, if we stop here tonight, we can all get a fresh start tomorrow and travel in safety."

"I can make it to SLC," he insisted. "We don't have to stop."

"You are a terrible liar," she taunted, "but I like that." Her next words were more serious. "You aren't fit to drive much farther. Even I can see it."

"I just need a little caffeine." He always scoffed at the federal guidelines that mandated how many hours a truck driver was allowed per day. It was a pain in the ass to keep the records in his logbook, but he admitted that once in a while he appreciated being forced to stop. Now, he wasn't following Uncle Sam's recommendation, but instead listening to his partner.

"Pull over, mister," she insisted with a twinkle in her ocean-blue eyes.

He was worn out, and she knew it.

Buck picked up the CB mic. "Ladies and gents. I've been informed that I have to take an unscheduled overnight here in West Wendover."

"You and the little lady getting a room?" Sparky asked with a laugh.

His face went nuclear red. "No," he replied instantly, sounding like a teenager lying through his teeth. He kept talking. "Can I get you guys to stop with us so we can continue east in the morning? I'd like us to stick together."

Buck went with the soft touch despite wanting them to remain as a convoy. They'd talked about it on and off ever since Monsignor and Eve had discussed dropping their trailers. He'd been able to defer the decision for a while, and he figured he could get them to at least make it to Salt Lake City, but the decision had to be made now.

"Why don't we all get dinner in West Wendover and plan what comes next?" Buck suggested.

Ten minutes later, they were all parked at the town's McDonald's because it had a massive parking lot designed for tractor-trailers. Buck and Connie let Mac out for a much-needed potty break and were pleased to find the restaurant was pet-friendly. The Golden Retriever fit right in with the four other drivers.

After a few minutes of levity and dog petting, he got them on topic.

"I propose we sleep here tonight, then get up early in the morning," Buck explained. "Tonight, let's forget the talk about dropping cargo. We'll see what things are like in the morning."

The McDonald's appeared perfectly normal, as did the town around them. People went about their business, and nothing seemed amiss.

"We heard a lot of radio chatter about jacked-up things in other cities and countries, but nothing appears wrong here. If the chaotic problems aren't everywhere, then we still have a good shot of making it where we need to go. If things are normal here, we can top off our tanks, too. You never know when you won't be able to get fuel."

"If we stick with you," the Monsignor suggested.

"Look, I'm no one special. I'm simply a guy hauling chili across America. I've mentioned my son several times during the last few hours. He's the reason I'm pushing east no matter what, so I won't lie to you and say I'm dedicated to my cargo. However, I plan on carrying this freight as long as I'm able because..."

He had a premonition that the chili would be useful no matter where he ended up. There was enough food back there for ten lifetimes. He'd either get it to the depot where it belonged or hold onto it if things got dicey. Dumping it was not even in his wheelhouse.

Of more immediate interest, he was pleased to see a normal town again.

"I believe us truckers are the ones who will ultimately decide if life breaks down on the highway. As long as we continue to haul our freight, life goes on as normal. People eat their chili. Consumers buy televisions." He looked at Eve and the Monsignor. "And welders get their acetylene to keep on building things."

"I'm with you," Connie said, chucking him warmly on his shoulder.

The others joined in with nods and hands slapping the table as they devoured too many calories of everything on the Mickey D's menu.

The convoy was his.

Somewhere in New Jersey

A crack of lightning spurred Garth into action.

"We have to hurry! What do you need me to do?"

Lydia was now as drenched as he was, but she somehow didn't seem bothered by it. "I don't understand how this machine works," she stated dryly. "What pulls it out? With a wagon, we would push the wheels and put logs and sticks underneath to give it support."

"That's it!" he shouted over the next clap of thunder.

He almost felt stupid for not seeing it earlier, but he'd been focused on getting someone to push. "We can throw sticks and junk underneath the back tires. Those are the ones that drive it."

The muddy evidence of the spinning was all over the side of the car, although much had been washed off in the downpour.

"Spin? But how?" Lydia studied the tires, but he tugged at her sleeve to get her to come with him.

"We have to hurry!" he yelled. "This way!"

He ran into the woods and immediately found some fallen branches that looked suitable. When he had them in his arms, he showed them to her. "Will these work?"

She shrugged at first with a look that said, "how the hell would I know?" but then she nodded. "I think so. Anything to get them to grip."

The storm's intensity built with each passing minute. The wind kicked up too, but it blew in multiple directions as if it couldn't make up its mind. He figured it was because they were between the two storms.

He ran back into the woods after dumping some branches. Lydia passed him with a load of five or six big rocks in her arms.

We've got this.

When he got back with the next load of sticks, it seemed like they had enough piled up. He looked inside the cab for anything that might add gripping power and ended up pulling out the two floormats from the front. He laid them on top of everything else since they seemed to provide a ramp for his extraction.

"All right! Let's try it."

Lightning danced just to the south in the sky above them, and the wind began to drive steadily in that direction.

He jumped into the car, but then hung his head out the broken window. He was going to tell Lydia to stand clear, but she'd taken up a position near the rear of the car like a supervisor.

"I still don't see—" she started to say.

"Just watch!" he cried out.

Once the car started, he gave it a little gas. He prayed it would pop right out, but he wasn't that lucky. The tires whirred in the soupy mud and shot thick brown sludge inside the windshield again.

Come on, he willed the taxi.

He let off, then jammed the gas pedal again, hoping something would happen.

Rain came in through the broken window in buckets, but it only made Garth more anxious to succeed. However, no matter how much gas he gave it, the tires kept slipping in the mud.

"Rock it back and forth," Lydia advised. "That sometimes helps the horses pull it up and out of the mud pit."

Garth accelerated until the tires rose a little on the front part of the pit, then let off the gas so the wheel would roll back into the ditch. When it reached the farthest point in the rear, he hit the pedal again. At first, he had no luck, but after a few tries, he realized there was a rhythm to it.

"That's doing it!" Lydia shouted over pounding of the rain.

He rocked it back and forth many times, and finally he felt the car rise up onto the top of his rock and branch pile. With that, he gave it more gas, and the car jumped out of the slop.

Garth pulled it onto the shoulder of the roadway, then stopped and got out.

Thunder rolled across the landscape with hardly a

break. He ran up to Lydia and shouted, but he couldn't even hear himself. She stood there with a confused look on her face, so he got right up to her ear to talk to her.

At first, she recoiled at his touch, but then seemed to recognize his action.

"I have to get something in the woods," he announced. "You can get into the taxi and wait for me. We're leaving!"

She nodded, and he ran off.

It seemed to take an eternity to find the bushes where he'd put the rifle cases. The rain was now an overbearing downpour, but it was the gale-force winds that made the trees and underbrush appear different. Sometimes they bent nearly sideways.

Once he found them, he took off at a fast walk. He came out of the woods to find Lydia exactly where she was.

"Oh, shit!" He ran over to her, surprised to find her sobbing. "I'm here!" he shouted.

She seemed surprised and relieved at the same time.

The thunder didn't allow conversation, so he set one of the cases down and took her hand so he could guide her toward the car.

"Come on," he said, although she couldn't possibly hear him.

Her face responded, however, and she seemed to recover as they walked the thirty or forty feet to the taxi.

First, he opened the passenger-side back door and tossed the gun case inside. Then he opened the front door and gently pushed her in.

She was reluctant, he could see, but she finally sat down on the soaked front seat.

The lightning was like nothing he'd ever seen before. It branched out in long tendrils too close over his head. He looked at the case sitting by itself on the highway behind the taxi and wondered if it was worth the risk to grab it.

What would Dad do?

Search for Nuclear, Astrophysical, and Kronometric Extremes (SNAKE). Red Mesa, Colorado

Faith and the general ran up the steps of the emergency exit.

"Where are you taking me? I can't be away from the control room." The general huffed up the steps a few risers behind her.

"We're almost there," she shouted.

A tremor forced her to stop and hold on to the banister, and her stomach churned from the fear coursing through her insides. All she could think about was how CERN had blown up and SNAKE was next. That rumbling was the buildup to her death.

"It's getting worse," General Smith lamented.

"I know, but we have to get up here. Trust me."

She started running again as soon as the shaking stopped.

"Hurry!"

Faith was proud to have beat the military man to the top flight, but she hesitated before going through the door. Her heart rode high in her throat as if it too was anxious to see what she was doing.

"Dr. Sinclair, I hope you have a damned good explanation for this."

"Sir, you can call me Faith now. I think first names are appropriate for two people who have basically fucked up the world."

He shook his head in dismay. "I'm trying to save it."

"Uh huh," she said in an agreeable voice. "Then I hope I'm wrong about this."

Faith opened the door and walked out onto the concrete platform and metal shack called "the treehouse" that served as the top landing for the emergency exit. She continued outside.

"Almost there!" she shouted to him.

The pair ran through the woods a short way until they came to an overlook above the SNAKE parking lot. The location gave her a good view of the sky, the Hogback, and the city of Denver to the northeast.

Faith held her breath in anticipation as General Smith trotted up behind her.

"What are we here to see?" he asked.

Nothing, I hope.

Moments went by before she saw anything unusual, then the breath wheezed out of her lungs and amplified her horror at being right.

"There!" she cried.

Red bands of lightning seemingly clawed out of the earth in a line behind the Hogback. The energy flared up, then fell back on itself like spouts of magma in a volcano. As she and the general watched, the number and intensity of the branches of red lightning increased by several orders of magnitude. It became a frothy wave of tangled lightning bolts a hundred feet tall and sixty-two miles around.

From her position, she could only see a portion of the collider ring, but the red energy traced the infrastructure below the ground perfectly.

Before the general could respond, the ground shook under their feet, nearly knocking them over.

The red energy shot upward in a single wave and took

off across the plains. In mere seconds, it was almost too far away to see.

"It came from all the way around the collider ring," she said wonderingly. "But it wasn't inside it. We ARE safe in here."

The red light disappeared over the horizon.

"Did we fix things?" the general said with hope.

"Not in the least, General. You think the blue wave was bad? That bastard there is going to make the blue wave look like a walk in the park."

TWENTY-EIGHT

Somewhere in New Jersey

Garth longingly gazed at the second gun case, trying to decide if it was worth going to grab it. It was only forty feet away, but the lightning swirled overhead like angry sharks looking for a quick bite. One of them could zap him in an instant.

The darkness of the radiation-saturated storm was upon them. The wind gusted hard from the north, and he imagined they were already getting burned by it. When the blustery rain kicked up another notch, it nearly knocked him over, but it also gave him his answer.

"Screw it!"

He kept to his feet and ran around the back of the car. The wind slammed him into the back quarter panel, but he kept low to the ground and slipped into the open door. The driver's seat was saturated from hours of rain, and the last few minutes had put a couple of inches of water on the front floorboard.

"I don't understand how this is going to work," Lydia complained.

He didn't have time to answer; he was deep in his own thoughts while he raced to get the car in gear.

Will I feel the radiation burn me? Did I get Lydia out of the rain in time?

Garth mashed the gas pedal, but let off when he felt the muddy tires spin. The last thing he wanted was to drive off the road again because he was in a careless rush.

"Hold on," he advised.

He set the wipers to full speed, but they couldn't keep up with the deluge. Between the thunder, the roar of rain, and the wind blowing and howling through his window, he couldn't even hear himself think.

"There are more of them!" Lydia pointed as they merged onto the Garden State Parkway. Other cars flew by at speeds he judged to be insane given the road conditions.

"Hang on," he replied. A knot formed in his stomach as the opportunity to merge approached.

One lesson he'd learned from his short time driving was that he couldn't get on a highway unless he matched the speeds of the other cars. He crushed the gas pedal and felt the vibration of the motor, although it barely registered over the nightmare of other noises.

Garth had the taxi up to sixty when he ran out of onramp. He merged into traffic just ahead of a pair of head-lights. The driver flashed them in anger, but there was nothing Garth could do but hold up his hand and wave.

"Sorry!" he shouted to the wind.

"How are we moving?" Lydia asked.

Garth was still afraid he'd been touched by the radiation, so he wasn't in the mood to explain things. The only thing that mattered was getting her away from the nuclear storm. He didn't want her introduction to 2020 to include radiation sickness.

Not that he fully believed her story, but she looked as terrified as he felt. He stopped glancing at her and focused on the road. It was the only thing that mattered at that very moment in his life. They could think about things later when they were safe. If they'd been affected, there was nothing he could do about it. It was already done. If they hadn't been? Then driving at that moment was even more important.

Control what is in your control, he could hear Dad say.

Hurricane Audrey bore down on them, although it was like no hurricane he'd ever heard about. The clouds ahead were almost pitch-black, with lightning continuing like fireworks all around them. The wind now blew from directly behind as if it wanted to push his car into the mouth of the billowing storm.

They drove past a tractor-trailer that had been blown off the roadway. The trailer was bent around a giant tree, the cab wrenched sideways and high-centered on a root bundle. It illustrated the power of the storms ahead and behind, but his concern after seeing the wreck was for another truck driver.

Dad, I hope you're okay out there.

West Wendover, NV

"Do you really want to get two rooms?" Connie asked as they stood at the motel desk.

"I don't want to presume. I mean, you know..."

She laughed. "You're right to not presume. Maybe it's for the best."

If things were getting back to normal, as Buck hoped, then he didn't want to ruin it. He could argue it would be safer to stay in the same room, and she could counter that it was equally as safe in adjacent rooms. All the while, it would hide the truth that after spending the entire day with her, he didn't want to let her go. Or he could spend the entire night overthinking it.

Maybe she'll try to go back home.

He put the thought aside and tried, as always, to appear calm and collected. If the town was peaceful and things were going back to normal, it was a good thing.

"I'll pay for them," he remarked to the proprietor. To her, he added, "It's the least I can do for smashing your car to pieces."

She hesitated, considering if that was fair, but in the end, she accepted his offer. "I'll get the next one."

"Done," he replied immediately.

They walked back to the Peterbilt to collect his gear as well as his dog.

"Hey, when we're settled, we can walk over to the convenience store to get you some of the stuff you'll need. New clothes. Toothbrush. Whatever."

She looked across the street. "Yeah, that sounds—"

Buck was already on high alert, so he whipped his head to look at Connie when she stopped talking. She was facing the convenience store, her eyes focused on the sky.

From West Wendover, you could see a hundred miles into Utah. The pure-white Bonneville Salt Flats spread out before them, and the Great Salt Lake was far beyond. It was a lot like looking out over a flat, dry ocean.

Connie's focus was on the lone band of red energy streaking across the sky like an endless wave.

"Fuck," he blurted. "That's just like the blue light I saw yesterday."

"Uh huh," she replied without emotion.

She turned to him and stood close. He pulled her to him and hugged her tightly as they both watched the sky.

"Buck, am I going to disappear?"

"What? *No!*" After he said it, he admitted there was no way to know.

Connie glanced at the approaching wave for a second, then seemed to gain strength so she could look right into his eyes.

"Thank you for sticking with me," she began, "and for saving my life. Twice." A lone tear trickled down her cheek.

"Connie, I don't know—" He stole a look at the red wave. It had crossed most of the desert and was seconds away from passing above them. He wiped away the tear with one finger.

What do I say?

"I would have liked to have known you better," he got out as the wave passed overhead, and leaned down to kiss her.

"Me—" was all she got out.

A wave of dizziness washed over them. Buck could no longer feel her in his arms.

Somewhere in New Jersey

The endless lightning was the only thing bright enough to light up the road for Garth. Delicate strands crackled overhead in monstrous streaks, often sparking all the way down to the trees. Metal signs next to the highway looked like they were on fire; the lightning practically danced on top of them.

More and more cars went into the ditches next to the road.

"I can't stop," he advised himself.

Lydia sat on the front edge of her seat as if thinking about diving all the way to the floorboard to hide. To her credit—or out of ignorance of the danger—she continued to watch out the front window with him. He wouldn't have blamed her for taking cover.

"Is this normal?" she screamed.

"Hell, no!" he yelled back. The rain pounded in through the window, forcing him to keep wiping it from his face.

Garth couldn't talk; he needed to keep every ounce of his focus on the road. He stuck to the right lane where things moved a little slower, but he couldn't afford to let off the gas. At least twice, cars raced by on the shoulder of the highway, only to crash into parked or abandoned cars on the side of the road.

It was almost as dangerous in the lane to his left, especially since passing cars sent rooster tails of water across his car and into his window.

He stuck to the back of the vehicle ahead of him and rode two car-lengths behind it at sixty-five miles per hour. Garth believed it might have been a tractor-trailer because of its taillight configuration, but the spray coming off their wheels made it hard to say for sure. His driving was mostly about watching the burning red lights.

If he stops, we stop. If he crashes, we crash.

There was no other way.

It was as light as the dead of a cloudy night in the middle of the storm, accented almost continuously by strobes like those in an Eighties disco. It took all of Garth's concentration to stay on the road. His body strained with the effort, even though his mind was telling him that he was sitting in a soft chair and watching the world go by.

Should I pull over and wait it out?

261

That would definitely be a Dad move.

He considered it, but after seeing cars get smashed into on the shoulder, he didn't think it was such a good idea. They were deep in the woods, too, so there were no offramps or pull-offs to use.

But it seemed crazy to ride the bumper of the person in front of him.

Garth was still thinking about it when a car passed him, veered into his lane, and sideswiped the vehicle in front of his taxi.

The knot in his stomach kicked him in the heart. "Oh, shit!"

The brake lights came on in front of him, and he tapped his in reply. The original car careened to the left, crossed into the median, and rolled over. His guide swayed from side to side like he was about to lose control, but eventually got back between the painted lines and drove arrow-straight.

The person ahead hit the gas and got back up to speed. After a few seconds, Garth matched the pace of the tail lights, and he held his breath, hoping they would make it through.

"I think we're in trouble," he told Lydia.

If his hands hadn't already been soaked by the rain, his palms would be sweat-drenched messes. He shuddered, scared by almost wrecking the taxi. His heart hammered and his vision narrowed. He slowed to three and then four car-lengths behind the vehicle ahead. Garth chanced a look at Lydia, knowing she'd be disappointed.

Strangely, she smiled at him. "You're a great carriage driver!"

The knot in his stomach went away. At that moment, he felt like he could take on the world.

For the next hour, he did just that.

West Wendover, NV

The red wave was gone, but to his great relief, Connie was still in his arms.

He tried to help her stand on her own, being a gentleman about it, but she seemed to take longer to recover than him, so she remained against the front of his Hawaiian shirt. Her silver bangles fell to her elbow as she held her arms up on his chest.

"I'm still here," she said sadly. "I'm not sure how I feel about that."

"I wanted you to get back home too, but I'm also kind of glad, you know, that you're still with me."

He supported her for a long minute, until he realized she was the one holding him.

"Thank you, Buck, for what you said. I would like to know you better, too."

"Let's get to our rooms and see what comes next. The red light could be something worse than the blue." He nudged her to stand upright, but she stayed where she was.

"Or maybe it fixed everything," she said, "except for those of us already in the wrong time."

"We don't know what happened," he said sympathetically.

"I do have one request," she said hesitantly. "Will you let me stay in your room? I don't want to be alone while I'm here. I trust you, but if you try anything, I'll sic Mac on you."

"Sure. I'd be honored."

Garth's ringtone burst from his phone, scaring them both out of the moment.

He gently adjusted her so he could pull out his phone.

"Garth!" he shouted the second he pressed Answer. "Where are you? Are you okay? Did you get out of the path of the—"

"Dad, I'm fine. Seriously. We got the taxi out of the mud and made it to the ferry to get out of New Jersey. They even had a Geiger counter to check all the cars coming in, and none of them had any. They told us the radiation cloud had stayed close to Three Mile Island, although they had to shut the reactor down."

Buck sighed like he'd just been told he'd won the lottery and the rest of his life would be easy.

"I know. It's been a wicked ride out of Staten Island. Cars were in ditches. People were standing on the side of every road, looking for rides. You were right, Dad. Taking the taxi was a bad idea. At least I can take it back home. The danger is gone."

Buck felt a tickle in the back of his mind. Something Garth had said wasn't sitting right with him. It wasn't the survival part of his brain; more like the Dad section.

He's hiding something.

"Garth, are you sure you're okay? You sound, uh, I don't know... Different."

"Dad, you have no idea how close we came to dying. The lightning in the storm never shut off. And the wind! It was like riding a tornado inside a hurricane."

I have some idea. He thought back to how close he had come to going inside the giant storm near Sacramento. It was a testament to Garth that he could survive such a situation.

But something still bothered him. Once he was sure his son was safe, he allowed himself to be his father again. That was when it struck.

"Who is this 'we' you keep talking about? Is Sam with you?"

Connie leaned in to hear Garth's response.

Buck held her tight.

"Not Sam..."

Ferry out of New Jersey

"Dad, you don't have to worry about 'we,'" Garth replied, looking at Lydia. They'd both been given warm blankets to dry off, and Lydia kept hers around her as she watched from the railing of the big ferry. "It's just some girl I met."

He cupped his hands so Lydia wouldn't hear. "She thinks she's from 1849. It's really weird, but she's kind of cute." After he said it, he realized how it probably sounded to his father. "Not in that way," he added.

"Son, it's all right. This blue light phenomenon has time all messed up. She probably is legitimately from 1849." Dad hesitated for a few seconds. "In fact, I have my own time traveler. She's from 2003."

Garth had never really talked about girls with his dad, and Dad had never spoken about women with him, but he tapped into a connection through the phone line. "You dirty dog," he said with a laugh.

"Don't make me get the belt, young man," his dad joked.

Garth heard a woman speak on the line with his dad like she had been listening in. "You wouldn't!"

"No," Dad said to the woman. "It's our little joke."

"Dad, should I go back home now? I have all your stuff out. I think I did a pretty good job getting things ready, but I didn't have time to board the windows or much of anything else. I wanted to get it ready for the hurricane, but I ran out of the house when they said the radiation was coming. I'm sorry I did that. I know you sent the text for me to stay."

"It's okay. Listen, can you spend the night somewhere? I want to see what's going to happen with this red light. Maybe things will get better. If that's the case, then yeah, I'd say start making your way back home."

"What red light are you talking about? The light was blue yesterday. Me and Sam saw it."

Buck turned serious. "I know. A red light just went above our heads here in Nevada. You didn't see it?"

Garth looked at the sky. "No, I don't—"

He hesitated when something sparkled on the horizon to the west. The clouds of the hurricane still hung heavy to the north and another batch of clouds was building down south, but to the west, it was sunny and clear.

"I do see it, Dad. What is it?"

"I don't know. It passed over us and didn't do anything that we could see right away, but the same thing happened with the blue light. It went over and was gone. It was hours before I noticed anything different.

Garth watched in awe as the band of light raced across the sky miles above.

"Here it comes," he said into the phone.

"You'll get a little dizzy, son. Hold onto something."

Garth held the railing as it went overhead. People on the ferry cheered and screamed at the light display. As promised, he felt a little dizzy, but it passed almost as fast as the light.

"It's gone!" he said into the phone.

"Has anything changed?"

Garth looked up and down the rail of the ship. People were curious to see the light come and go, but there was nothing otherwise unusual.

"No, I think we're... Wait a minute."

"What? What is it? What's wrong?" His dad was all over him for an answer.

Garth felt the loss more than he would have expected.

"Dad, Lydia is gone."

West Wendover, Nevada

Buck heard the pain in his son's voice. His new friend must have meant a lot to him.

"What did he say?" Connie whispered. "She disappeared?"

"Garth, I'm so sorry. That didn't happen here. No one went away." He held Connie a bit tighter to be sure she didn't try to fade from his reality.

He didn't know what to say. There wasn't a Hallmark card for time-travel anomalies. Garth might have only known her for a day, but he could sympathize. A day was long enough.

"You did the best you could, son. You were up against a lot of challenges, and these red and blue lights are beyond anyone's understanding. You couldn't have predicted what was going to happen there."

"I know," Garth replied distantly.

Buck was searching for more words of comfort when his boy shouted. At first, it was a chaotic yelling which sounded more like noise coming through the phone, but it morphed into words he could understand.

"She's here! I see her!"

"I heard that," Connie said, relieved.

"She came back?" Buck asked with surprise.

"Yes! Dad, I'm sorry for freaking out like that. She

didn't disappear. She dropped her blanket and moved down the rail. Now I see her. Hey, I have to let you go."

Buck's emotions had been ground into fine powder today, but he retained enough of his Dad persona to reply with something intelligent.

"Look, son. I'm glad she's there. Stay the night somewhere. See what the morning brings, okay? That's what I'm doing out here." He paused. "Oh, and Garth?"

"Yeah, Dad?"

"There's money in the bug-out bag. Please tell me you have it?"

"I do."

"Good. You can use that to pay for a motel, but this is important, so listen up."

"Yeah?" he replied with the gravity it deserved.

"I'm happy your friend didn't disappear, but make sure you get a room with two beds, okay?"

Garth went giddy with laughter. "Aw, Dad, that's a good one! She's about my age, but she's from a hundred and fifty years ago. We have NOTHING in common. You've got nothing to worry about."

Buck laughed to himself.

You have a lot to learn about life, son.

Connie looked him in the eyes as he thought about the right reply.

"Well, just do what I would do, okay? You'll be fine."

"Talk to you tomorrow, Dad. I'm glad we're both okay, and I'm glad the phones are working again."

"Me too," Buck said in a more relaxed voice. "I can't wait to meet your new friend."

"Ditto!"

He hung up to find Connie smirking at him. "The

whole world is on edge, and you are worried about your son's honor?"

Buck smiled back. "It's the little things that will keep civilization wheels-down. I like to practice what I preach."

"I've noticed." She finally stepped back from him, but grabbed his hand and pulled him toward the motel room. "Now, let's get you to bed so you'll be fresh for more miles tomorrow. Garth said he wants to meet me. Let's make that happen."

To Be Continued in End Days, Book 3

If you like this book, please leave a review. This is a new series, so the only way I can decide whether to commit more time to it is by getting feedback from you, the readers. Your opinion matters to me. Continue or not? I have only so much time to craft new stories. Help me invest that time wisely. Plus, reviews buoy my spirits and stoke the fires of creativity.

Don't stop now! Keep turning the pages as there's a little more insight and such from the authors.

COPYRIGHT

This book is a work of fiction.
All of the characters, organizations, and events portrayed in this novel are either products of the author's imagination or are used fictitiously. Sometimes both.

End Days (and what happens within / characters / situations / worlds)
are Copyright (c) 2019 by E.E. Isherwood & Craig Martelle

Version 1.0
Cover by Heather Senter
Editing by Lynne Stiegler
Formatting by James Osiris Baldwin – jamesosiris.com

AUTHOR NOTES – E.E. ISHERWOOD

Written February 14, 2019

End Days is doing wonderful because of your support. Please keep the great reviews coming as they are the life-blood of independent authors. We can't thank you enough for them.

While writing about the weird weather in this book, we experienced a similarly weird weather pattern here in Missouri. One day would be a high of 5 degrees F, and a few days later we'd have a high of 60. A foot of snow one day. Shorts weather the next. It makes me wonder if the weather patterns being ruined by the *Blue Apocalypse* really weren't that bad after all? Maybe the next book has to be a lot worse.

I have truckers in a few of my books now. I'm not sure what it is that fascinates me about the profession, but I think

I would have thrived as a long-haul driver. I love seeing the country, and I've been to 43 states, so far. Most of that has been behind the wheel of a car. In fact, during a business trip to New York City, I rented a car and drove through Connecticut, Rhode Island, Massachusetts, Vermont, New Hampshire, and Maine because I wanted to see what was there.

I also love all things military. I visit Civil War battle-fields and military museums any chance I get. It makes for a nice mixture of travel and history. The National Museum of the Marine Corps is probably the finest historical museum I've been to, but I once drove ten hours round trip to spend fifteen minutes on the deck of the battleship *USS Wisconsin*. Totally worth it.

To wrap this all up, one of my dreams is to take a road trip to Alaska on the Alaska-Canadian highway. From a historical perspective, it was built during World War II, but for the personal side it would help me bag one of the states I still need to visit. And, if he's home, I can write off the trip as a business expense when I visit my co-writer Craig for that one week of Alaskan summer. Win-win!

Thank you again for reading *End Days*. We've got more adventure coming.

EE

Amazon – amazon.com/author/eeisherwood
Facebook – www.facebook.com/sincethesirens
My web page – www.sincethesirens.com

Once you've signed up for Craig's newsletter, I would be thrilled to have you also join mine.

That's all the time I have. The next book calls to me!

E.E. ISHERWOOD'S OTHER BOOKS

End Days (co-written with E.E. Craig Martelle) – a post-apocalyptic adventure

Sirens of the Zombie Apocalypse – What if the only people immune are those over 100? A teen boy must keep his great-grandma alive to find the cure to the zombie plague.

Eternal Apocalypse – Set 70 years after the zombies came, a group of survivors manipulates aging to endure their time in survival bunkers, but it all falls apart when a young girl feels sunlight for the first time.

AUTHOR NOTES - CRAIG MARTELLE

Written February 14, 2019

You are still reading! Thank you so much. It doesn't get much better than that.

Storytelling is natural to all humans. Some are better at it than others, but we all tell stories starting at the earliest age. Taking those stories and making them work in written form is a different talent, still storytelling but with a twist. Words have to flow and we lose the ability to emphasize words by raising our voice or slowing the pace.

We have to do it all with words without being repetitive in a way that works across a vast landscape of readers, each with their own voice.

It's a challenge we gladly accept and it's great to see that

End Days has been so well-received. I hope book two lived up to your expectations to set the stage for books three and four. I'm not sure I said before that this wasn't a trilogy, but a four-book set. Which is cool, because when a story is good and the characters vibrant, you can't get enough of them. You want to know more. I hope that we give you more in a new and exciting way with each book.

It snowed a fair bit up here in the sub-arctic, not as much as Seattle or places in the midwest, but we have no hope that it will melt anytime soon. We have not had one minute above 32F since early November. That's nearly four-months straight of below freezing temperatures. But it hasn't been ridiculously cold. We hit -30F a couple times, but that's it. -20F maybe 10 or 15 days is all. Mostly, it's been 0 to 20F. Not bad at all.

Phyllis' favorite temperature is 20F. When it gets to 50 outside, she starts to pant and if it hits 70, she thinks it's the end of days.

End Days. But not like that at all. She just wants to stay in her place in the back closet under a table where it is cool year round. That's her place and where she sleeps during the day. She'll be twelve this year. She knows what she likes and that's lots of sleep and play time outside when temps are between 20 and 50.

As you can see, I'm writing this on Valentine's Day. Phyllis is the only one who made out. She went to the doggy spa to get her nails taken care of. I worked. My wife worked. We ate leftovers.

That's it, now. I'm off to keep writing and working with my co-authors to bring these incredible stories to you.

Peace, fellow humans.

If you liked the story, please write a short review for me on Amazon. I greatly appreciate any kind words, even one or two sentences go a long way. The number of reviews an ebook receives greatly improves how well an ebook does on Amazon.

If you liked this story, you might like some of my other books. You can join my mailing list by dropping by my website **www.craigmartelle.com** where you'll always be the first to hear when I put my books on sale. Or if you have any comments, shoot me a note at craig@craigmartelle.com. I am always happy to hear from people who've read my work. I try to answer every email I receive.

Amazon – www.amazon.com/author/craigmartelle
BookBub – www.bookbub.com/authors/craig-martelle
Facebook – www.facebook.com/authorcraigmartelle
My web page – www.craigmartelle.com

CRAIG MARTELLE'S OTHER BOOKS (LISTED BY SERIES) (# - AVAILABLE IN AUDIO, TOO)

Terry Henry Walton Chronicles (# co-written with Michael Anderle) – a post-apocalyptic paranormal adventure

Gateway to the Universe (# co-written with Justin Sloan & Michael Anderle) – this book transitions the characters from the Terry Henry Walton Chronicles to The Bad Company

The Bad Company (# co-written with Michael Anderle) – a military science fiction space opera

End Times Alaska (#) – a Permuted Press publication – a post-apocalyptic survivalist adventure

The Free Trader – a Young Adult Science Fiction Action Adventure

Cygnus Space Opera – # A Young Adult Space Opera (set in the Free Trader universe)

Darklanding (co-written with Scott Moon) – a Space Western

Judge, Jury, & Executioner – # a space opera adventure legal thriller

Rick Banik – # Spy & Terrorism Action Adventure

Become a Successful Indie Author – a non-fiction work

Metamorphosis Alpha – stories from the world's first science fiction RPG

The Expanding Universe – science fiction anthologies

Shadow Vanguard – a Tom Dublin series

Enemy of my Enemy (co-written with Tim Marquitz) – A galactic alien military space opera

Superdreadnought (co-written with Tim Marquitz) – an AI military space opera

Metal Legion (co-written with Caleb Wachter) – a galactic military sci-fi with mechs

End Days (co-written with E.E. Isherwood) – a post-apocalyptic adventure

Mystically Engineered (co-written with Valerie Emerson) – dragons in space (coming Jan 2019)

Monster Case Files (co-written with Kathryn Hearst) – a young-adult cozy mystery series (coming Mar 2019)

Made in United States
Troutdale, OR
04/30/2024